Mike Grist is the British/American author of the Chris Wren thrillers. Born and brought up in the UK, he has lived and worked in the USA, Japan and Korea as a teacher, photographer, writer and adventurer. He currently lives in London.

ENEMY OF THE PEOPLE

A CHRISTOPHER WREN THRILLER

MIKE GRIST

SHOTGUN
BOOKS

SHOTGUN BOOKS

www.shotgunbooks.com

Copyright © Mike Grist 2021

Mike Grist asserts the moral right to be identified as the author of this book. All rights reserved.

No part of this publication may be reproduced, stored in a retrieval system, or transmitted, in any form or by any means without the prior written permission of the author.

This book is a work of fiction, and except in the case of historical fact, any resemblance to actual persons, living or dead, is purely coincidental.

ISBN - 9781739951160

For Su

1

DC

Christopher Wren surged in and out of consciousness like a drowning swimmer thrashing on high tides, sucking air and catching only snapshots of the world around him: screaming crowds stampeding through the smoke-choked D.C. streets; sirens wailing and helicopters buzzing overhead; Sally Rogers at his side, a line of blood running down her cheek from a wound in her temple, steering the truck with one hand hard on the horn.

The snapshots swirled but didn't add up.

Wren tried to focus on the simplest things, the feel of the seat against his battered thighs, the ache in his bandaged shoulders, but his thoughts were too shot to shreds. Just moments ago there'd been a firestorm on the National Mall, he remembered that much. Tens of thousands gathered to watch his brother Chrysogonus become President, on the stage shouting out the mad lies of the Apex's ideology. Then gas jets fired and the stage ignited, Chrysogonus plunged into the masses sparking a tsunami wave of flame that stretched back and back until-

"Hang on!" Rogers shouted.

The truck swerved hard right across a convoy of

oncoming squad cars, away from a big red truck with gunfire sparking at its passenger window, and slotted with a bodywork-rending screech through a gap between parked cars and into an alley, where a child was standing alone in their path.

Rogers slammed the brakes and Wren was flung forward to bounce off the dash, rebounding back into his seat, and the world went a fuzzy gray as he fought for the surface.

The child was maybe nine years old, wore the colors of the American flag as face paint, but smeared down and blackened with soot. She was red-eyed and crying, looking around desperately for her parents.

"We have to-" Wren started to say, words slurring weakly up through his raw throat, but Rogers was already pulling the truck around and leaving the girl behind. Wren tried to figure that out, but words came in his ear and tore the thoughts to bits; a female with a Russian accent.

"…road blocks," he heard, then another hard left blacked him briefly out, chased by the sound of Rogers shouting into the air.

"We got in, Hellion, we can get out! Now find us a way."

"… every Federal agency," came the answer, any sense of meaning chopped by Wren's fight to stay above the water line. "And not only…"

Suddenly Rogers hit the brakes and Wren was flung forward again, this time his head butted the windshield, his knees slid into the footwell and Rogers cursed loud and inventively.

"Hold tight, Boss!" she ordered, yanked the stick into reverse, spun to look through the rear window then stamped on the gas, driving Wren the rest of the way into the footwell.

His head thumped the door handle, his knees jammed in against the glove box, wedging tighter with every jerk as she fought the wheel side-to-side through obstacles Wren couldn't

2

see. He tried to push himself back up, but her hand came briefly on his shoulder.

"Stay down, you're the one they're looking for."

A crumping sound came from above and Wren saw a star burst across the windshield, fractures creeping out like cracks in fragile ice, matched by a second crunch through the rear window. A cold blast of wind blew through the tiny hole.

Rogers yanked the wheel again and almost tipped the truck, reversing fast up an incline that gave Wren a good view through the windshield, where a huge red truck was coming up at them. A Ford F-150, Wren thought dully, with a customized semi-truck exhaust pipe pumping black smoke straight up. Two large black flags sailed from its B-pillars, each emblazoned with a white 'X' symbol. A string of flashes sparked from the truck's passenger side, answered by another crump through the windshield.

"You've got a gun?" Rogers shouted.

He struggled to make sense of the words. They felt like a lifeline tossed in the water, but one he wasn't able to grab hold of. Rogers worked the wheel and they hit something in back with a metallic crash, fishtailed crazily for a moment before she got control again. Wren saw glass and plastic shards scattered across the blacktop ahead, grinding under the wheels of the F-150.

More flashes came from the side window, answered by another star through the windshield, and this time Rogers cried out.

"I'm hit!"

"I have overwatch," came the voice in his ear again, rasping like a hornet. "This is encirclement, Sally Rogers. Not Federal forces. I am sending Foundation team, but…"

The voice cut away.

"In the glove box," Rogers shouted, pulling another hard

3

right on the wheel that tossed Wren against her shoulder. "Colt M11, safety's on."

Then something slammed into the truck's rear right side with a massive rending crash, blindsiding Rogers and momentarily lofting the vehicle, thumping Wren against the door. The engine roared as the rear wheels sought traction on air, then the truck bounced as it landed, the tire treads bit and the vehicle jerked ahead like a sprinter off the starting blocks.

Rogers fought the wheel straight for control as they rocketed away from what looked like some kind of special ops tank. Wren's neck lolled, eyes dancing out of focus across the vehicle that had just rammed them on. Reinforced black side bars. Black-tint windows inset to chunky black body panels. Another large black and white X flag rising like a pirate's skull and crossbones. Some kind of armored Humvee?

Rogers pumped the gas and they roared backward, but the Humvee kept pace at their side. Silver stars swam across Wren's vision,

"Fire, Boss!" Rogers shouted.

The Humvee swerved out, swerved back in tight and hit hard, smacking the truck like a bank-shot billiard ball. The rear wheels scraped left and the truck jogged into a wrenching diagonal, hit a curb with a deadening punch in the chassis then dead-ended with a rending crash into the front glass display of a downtown D.C. tailor's.

Wren's head bounced off the glove box, the seat, the door, and then the truck's momentum stalled out and he slumped in a huddle looking up at a leering white mannequin dressed in floral prints, its eyeless face staring down at him.

"…out of there, Sally Rogers, more are coming!"

Wren blinked, saw red splashed on Rogers' face, her eyes shut, her head back. He tried to say something but couldn't get the wind.

The Humvee's engine blared like a mad dog, other engines joining it like a hooligan chorus. The truck's engine whined somewhere nearby, pumping noxious gray smoke into the cab. Roger's foot wedged on the gas, but the tires were lodged and burning rubber.

Wren coughed, the cough dunked him under the surface, then there were dark shadows crawling up over the hood and leering down through the starred glass.

"…can't see a thing," somebody shouted, then a foot came in and thumped the windshield. The shatter-proof glass flexed and fractured further, another foot came in and the rubberized left edge popped out and thumped Rogers in the face like a massive slap. Her head flattened to the side bonelessly, unconscious.

"Look at this bitch," came the voice, no longer so muted now. "Where you going in such a hurry, darling?"

"-topher, you must get out of there!" came the hornet in his ear. Meaningless, really.

"That's one of his whores," came another voice. A thick guy, a heavyset guy. Wren could barely see a thing, shielded by the warped glass now. Standing on the hood, holding a long rifle. "I know it. A hundred thousand, easily."

"You sure?"

"I got her number, means we're rich. First, we gotta wake her up."

The big guy leaned in, jabbed with his rifle, and Sally Rogers groaned as the muzzle struck her jaw.

"That's it, girl, come on around."

He jabbed again and this time Rogers snatched at the rifle, realized what it was, and let go.

The big guy laughed.

"Why you driving in such a rush, girl?" the big guy asked. "What you got in back?"

Rogers said nothing. Didn't even look Wren's way. Things

5

were starting to sync up now. Motions with actions, actions with words and intent.

"I say we burn her right now," said the slimmer guy. "Get it done and claim the points."

Sirens were drawing in.

"Pull the windshield first," the big guy ordered. "There's someone in there with her, I know it."

Two men in black leaned in and wrestled with the fractured windshield, held together like a flopping fish by anti-smash acetate. They managed to pry it out and toss it behind them.

The nearest of the guys' eyes flared wide and his jaw dropped. He stabbed a limp finger at Wren. His colleague cursed loud. "I don't believe it! Is that him?"

The big guy leaned in, eyes flashing over Wren slumped in the passenger footwell, then widening in fear. "It's him!" he shouted. "We're talking a million. Get a camera on and burn them both!"

Someone bounded up with a red canister and upended it through the open windshield. Rogers caught the worst of it splashed across her face, waterboarding her with gasoline.

The slim guy sparked a lighter and went to throw it, then there was a bang and a red dot appeared in the center of his forehead, punching him backward like he'd yanked on the end of a line.

"What the-" the big guy started, then a red dot blew into his cheek, another in his forehead and he fell away too, bounced down the hood with a truck-shaking thump, then out onto the ground beyond.

Wren's hand stung. Colt M11 tight in his fist, hot muzzle crushed close to his chest, an autonomic reaction he'd hardly controlled.

"Where did that come from?" someone shouted outside.

Wren tried to surge up and fire, but his exhausted thighs barely lifted him an inch.

"Who cares, spray the damn thing down!"

"Incoming," came the voice in his ear.

Automatic gunfire ripped up the blacktop and into the truck's hood, bullets crunching into the engine block as the shooter found his range, then there was a sudden thud and the incoming fire stopped,.

More gunfire followed, multiple handguns in a battle. Wren barely caught the contours, dunked again beneath the surface by a pressure wave of sound. The Colt slipped from his fist, then feet stamped on the truck's hood and more faces he didn't recognize loomed in.

"We're with the Foundation," one of them said, and reached in to grab Wren's arm.

LUCKY TO BE ALIVE

Wren woke gasping and raw with panic. The smoke was in his eyes again, in his lungs and he couldn't breathe. Feet thudded down on his chest, toes stubbed against his ribs, the flames were drawing in and…

The room was silent and dark.

He sucked in cold Iowa air, pushed it out, chest heaving.

Another nightmare, right back on the National Mall. Like every night since he'd woken up on the farm, surrounded by IV drip stands with Sally Rogers at his side, telling him everything was going to be OK.

Five days gone.

He pushed aside the taut bedcovers, slowly swung his legs out and fumbled with the IV line in his forearm, ever-present now, pumping steroids, antibiotics and fluids into his veins. It popped out and he held the worn hole for a count of sixty, then reached for the bedside lamp. His bandaged fingers caught the switch, and orange light illuminated the room, casting his own reflection starkly back at him from the black, curtainless window.

It wasn't any version of Christopher Wren he recognized.

The tattoos of his wife's name, his children's, barely visible beneath the deep bruising so many stamping feet had inked into his skin. Visibly trembling. Vision doubled still from the concussion of taking a bullet on his Twaron helmet. Head pounding. His face bandaged, stitches tight in his swollen cheeks and prickling against his leaden tongue, where his sister's blade had torn through his face. Bandages on his shoulders, circling his left upper arm, wrapping both of his palms. Galicia had stabbed him again and again, and he'd been unable to stop her. Even then he'd been feeling the effects of the concussion, along with the destabilizing pain of twin bullets ricocheted off his back Twaron plates.

He twisted slightly, looking at the purple slab of bruising that was his back, then felt the tightness rush into nausea. At least his legs worked, carrying him across the tasseled cotton rug to the small bathroom in seconds, where he barely got his head over the porcelain bowl in time before the heaves racked him.

Two minutes later he lay flat out on the cold tiles, flop sweat drying down his chest, tremors working their way in from his extremities. He'd never felt this broken before. Three bullets. Seven puncture wounds. Dropped from a collapsing building. Trampled under the feet of a terrified mob.

He got his feet under him. His stomach gnawed for food, but he hadn't kept a square meal down since it happened. Instead he sucked cold water direct from the tap, so much that his back teeth ached, then straightened again, dressed slowly and painfully. No way he could sleep now.

Down through the house he went, slow and steady as an old man. A grandfather clock on the landing said it was 5 a.m.. Sun up in three hours. Another farm Dr. Ferat had bought, that Teddy had turned into a safehouse and training center. More Foundation dreams, somewhere out in the wilds of Iowa. The place was beautiful, old, laden with generations of memories. The thought of all those happy families saddened him. The stairs creaked. The chill air smelled of hickory and cinnamon.

Padding through the kitchen, he opened the door and fly screen and stepped out onto the porch. Looked out over moonlit, frost-balmed clay. Ranks of sheared cornstalks spread before him, receding spikily into the pre-dawn gloom. The cold helped some with his head. Middle of December, coming up for Christmas. Stark afterimages of burning bodies fleeing through the firestorm flashed across the darkness wherever he looked.

Somewhere out there, America was going to hell.

The Apex was at large. His father. Free to roam in the wreckage of America, now that President-elect Keller was dead. Congress was decimated and the people were torn. He'd watched news reports several times, for as long as he could bear until the sound or the images triggered his concussion and sent him spiraling into nausea.

The media were putting much of this on him and the Foundation. There were so many conspiracies about what had really happened in Washington, and he was at the heart of them all. His 'terror' attack on New York. His 'terror' Foundation.

He had to do something, had to act, but the wheels in his head wouldn't turn, and he couldn't figure out what was right. Every time prior, the Apex had played him. Set traps. Each of Wren's moves had only played into his father's plans, getting more people hurt.

Killed.

Now he couldn't even see what game the Apex was playing. All he could do was sit on the porch swing and try to focus his battered mind.

At some point the sun peeked through clouds and tried to burn off the cold rising mist, but failed. In back, the house came awake steadily. There was a brief fuss as they discovered his empty room, until the screen door flapped and someone sighted him.

He didn't turn his head. Too much chance of triggering the nausea. It was just going to be his nurse, maybe, or live-in doctor, or the physiotherapist, or the counsellor. All the resources the Foundation could spare, and none could help with what was going on inside his head.

"You're lucky to be alive," his Foundation doctor, Larissa Bray, had said. "One more hit to the head and count yourself out. Your brain is swollen like a three-day-dead cadaver. Your body's in a rolling state of toxic shock, barely skating above full-on sepsis. I'm amazed you're even conscious."

The swing door flapped closed again. The heady stink of frying bacon came from the kitchen. The cook, a Foundation member shipped out of Little Phoenix, was trying to tempt him with something tasty, but it just knocked him sicker. His stomach roiled and he gagged, swallowed it back.

Breakfast passed and he didn't move. The sun inched over the horizon, like a pale lantern beyond an oil screen of dirty white clouds. Maybe snow would follow. At some point Theodore Smithely III came out.

Teddy. CEO of the Foundation. The fly screen clattered as he stepped onto the decking, and Wren angled his head slightly. Teddy was skeletally thin, now, and dressed all in black. For a long moment he looked at Wren, sitting motionless on the swing.

"Time for your physio, Christopher," he said. His deep voice was flat and authoritative, ringing through the crisp air and leaving no room for argument.

Wren said nothing. He wanted to do physio, but no way he could. Kept waiting for his stores to recharge, for the black wall of unconsciousness to draw back, the vertigo to abate, but nothing changed.

"This can't last," Teddy said, standing before him now. "The Foundation needs you. Our fringe members number in the millions, but they're in hiding. They need orders. Physio, Christopher, or we'll start losing them."

Wren looked past him. They were easy words to say.

The sun climbed cold.

At some point the sound of an engine drew near, pulled up, died. Maybe noon, and he hadn't yet moved. The frost had come off the fields, but the cold was in his bones.

A car door slammed. Wren didn't look. Footsteps approached. He stared at the corn stalks like he could burn a hole through reality.

"All right, Christopher," came Teddy's voice again. "This is becoming unacceptable."

He didn't look.

Figures moved in. Four? Five? They stepped across his field of vision, stood blocking the cornfield from view. Slowly he looked up, saw their faces.

The first was marred with SAINT brands. Marks of ownership the Order of the Saints had stamped into his skin in the effort to break his spirit. Mason? Wren blinked. Mason had almost died when he fell from the Anaximanderian pumping station in Utah barely six days back. Cracked ribs, broken arm, hairline crack in his pelvis, but here he stood, eyes locked on Wren.

That was just the first surprise.

Next to him stood Steven Gruber. He looked puzzled, like he didn't really know why he was there. Fey blonde hair drifted atop his head between the fire scars, where he'd tried to burn himself alive at the Apex's direction. He still looked raw and lost, but there was something in his eyes that hadn't been there before, a hint of resolution.

Next to him stood Hellion and B4cksl4cker, Wren's brilliant hacker collective. Only the second time he'd laid eyes on them in the real world. Hellion had bleached her dark hair blond and put it in a topknot, with a t-shirt branded 'ENEMY OF THE PEOPLE'. B4cksl4cker loomed thick as a Russian bear beside her, had put on a few pounds since their paths last crossed, grown a bushy brown beard but still had the same jet-black eyes. They both despised showing themselves in public, and hardly ever came to America, but here they were.

Capping the line-up was Maggie, leader of the fake town in Arizona, Little Phoenix, which she'd built into a mass orphanage and memorial center in the wreckage of the Pyramid. She was dressed in her usual tans and browns, brown hair braided in neat weaves, looking like some kind of desert sprite, every bit the wise woman of the sands.

"Come along now, Christopher," she said in a no-nonsense tone, extending her hand. "Come with us."

He looked up at her. More than anything, he wanted to do as she asked.

"Take her hand, Christopher," Hellion said sharply. "I did not come five-thousand miles to see fat old man sit on bench."

Wren turned, saw the anger in her eyes. "It's not a bench," he said heavily. His thick tongue moved slow and strange in his swollen mouth. "It's a porch swing."

B4cksl4cker laughed, then stopped when Hellion swung him a vicious glance.

"I do not care if it is golden toilet throne complete with heated seat. Get up."

Wren looked down. The sun was too bright in his eyes, starting another migraine coming on.

"We brought cookies," Gruber said brightly. Like it was a line he'd been programmed to say, and this was the pre-ordained moment. "Peanut butter. Man said they're the best."

Wren blinked back the light, managed to look up at Gruber. Didn't have the heart to say nothing. "Did he?"

Gruber just beamed.

"Maybe this is not the Christopher Wren we are thinking, anymore," Hellion said derisively. "He is broken like old Sputnik motherboard."

B4cksl4cker chuckled a bass rumble. Some inside hacker joke. Seemed she was trying to annoy him, but the insults slipped right off him.

"You are big fat baby," Hellion went on firmly. "We are here to change your nappy, yes? Theodore calls us from, where were we, B4cksl4cker?"

"Kazakhstan," B4cksl4cker said. "Researching X code base."

Wren didn't know what to make of that.

"So finish on your special swing potty like good big boy," Hellion said, "make boom boom, then come talk at the adult table." She bumped her fists together twice, then spun away.

B4cksl4cker gave a hapless shrug. "She is very excited. She loves coming to America."

Wren watched them go. Everyone knew Hellion hated America.

"This won't take long, Christopher," Maggie said. "Listen to what we've got to say, at least. You owe us that much."

That was the problem. He owed them far more than he was able to give. Still, he pushed himself slowly to his feet, just barely fending off the swirling vertigo, and started hobbling toward the swing door.

3. ENEMY OF THE PEOPLE

W ren sat at the rustic farmhouse table, thick beams of beech bolted with snug wooden pins, and looked at his people. Hellion and B4cksl4cker, Maggie, Teddy, Steven Gruber, Mason. They looked back at him expectantly. Maybe even angrily.

"We need to talk about what's going on out there, Christopher," Maggie said gently, as she set a plate with a peanut-butter cookie in front of him. The smell knocked him sick. "But you're not talking to anyone. Rogers said-"

"Rogers isn't here," Wren managed.

"She's maintaining her cover with the CIA," Maggie went on smoothly. "Hunting the Apex, trying to hold the agency together." She paused, took a bite of a cookie. "Did you know there's talk of cutting the CIA in half, the FBI, all of them? For dereliction of duty, for trumped-up conspiracy charges, for incompetence. What remains of Congress is seeking heads to roll. They're trying to staunch the wounds, but it's just feeding the flames." She paused, like she was deciding how much to say. "There are riots, Christopher, every night. Some are happening right now. Sacramento is burning. Brooklyn has been shuttered by a mob. People are dying and they can't stop it. It's chaos."

Wren grunted. Hellion took exception to it.

"At least Sally Rogers is doing her job," she spat. "Not moping like infant child sad that ice cream fell on the floor." She waved her arms in mock panic. "Oh no, ants are eating my ice cream, I want to eat it too, ohhh, ants."

Maggie gave her a stern look.

"This is truth!" Hellion went on. "We all think it. Christopher Wren, great man, but he has become like little boy peeing in pants. Everyone sees this pee, Christopher."

Now B4cksl4cker put a hand on Hellion's arm. She shook it off but said nothing more, crossing her arms and fuming silently.

"Christopher," Maggie went on calmly, "the point is, and I'm sure you know this, we are losing this war."

"It's not a war," Wren said.

"Oh now he speaks!" Hellion shouted. "Not a war? What are we fighting, such genius leader, if this is not a war?"

Wren took a breath, looked up at her. "It's despair."

Hellion snorted. "Just because you have given up does not mean everyone has!"

He saw the frustration in her eyes. The fear too. The same things that kept him awake every night. "Try to understand, Hellion. The Presidency is sacred. A President gets assassinated, it shapes us forever."

"This was not assassination! It is completely different."

"Exactly." His cheeks and chest ached but he pushed on. "Keller killed himself. That makes it worse. The people loved him. He represented unity, an end to division, then he burned himself alive on the inauguration stage."

"He is just a man! Now he's dead. This-"

"Wrong," Wren interrupted. Almost made himself sick with the exertion. "He's a martyr for a cause we don't yet understand. Our most sacred symbol destroyed, by the man most entrusted with it." He sucked in a stinging breath. "We need justice, but there's no way to get it now. Keller is dead. The Apex is in the wind, unless you have some news there?" He looked at B4cksl4cker, the movement jostling waves of nausea, but the big hacker just turned away. "What I thought. Without some lead on my father, there's no one to fight. I can't stop these riots. Nobody can."

They sat in silence for a moment.

"Then why have we come here," Hellion countered, "five thousand miles, if this war is already over and we have lost? Are we such fools?"

Wren just gazed at her.

Hellion slammed the table and stood, kicking her chair back with a clatter that made Gruber jump in his seat. "Then you are worse than a crybaby wanting ice cream!" she shouted. "You are a coward!"

"Isobel," Maggie cautioned.

"No!" Hellion shouted and stormed away, slamming the door behind her.

Now Maggie turned to him, looking part-stern, part-disappointed. "Christopher. Was that really necessary?"

He said nothing. Was moments away from teetering from the room, dropping to his knees in the clay of the yard and dry heaving everything he had. Then Maggie's hand came to rest on his own. Her touch was warm.

"You're wrong, Christopher. There is someone we can fight. A figure you crossed paths with in D.C.." She set a phone on the table top, activated it. "His name is X. That's short for ApeX. It could be your father, or it could be anyone really, we don't know for sure, but this person is harnessing the despair and fueling these riots."

Wren blinked. X? He remembered the X-branded flags on

the Humvee in D.C.. Hadn't thought anything of it since, but maybe…

Maggie slid the phone in front of him. "Just watch it. You'll see."

Her nut-brown finger hit the play button, and a large white X appeared on a black background, stark as a skull and crossbones flag. It held for maybe five seconds, then faded and a figure resolved from the dark.

It was Christopher Wren himself.

Wren blinked to a sharper level of focus, instantly entranced. The same dark skin with broad cheeks. The same scraggly black beard tied in a knot, with intense brown eyes reflecting tiny rippling flames.

Except it wasn't the real Christopher Wren, because he'd never filmed this. This was far better than any deepfake video he'd seen before. This Wren's eyes shifted almost imperceptibly, his lips twitched, his faint crow's feet stretched and shrank. He looked real.

"Do you feel safe?" the on-screen Wren asked, voice deep and rumbling. Then he began to morph.

Smoothly and almost imperceptibly the nose narrowed, the skin color lightened, the chin receded and the beard faded away, becoming a face only recorded in a single existing photograph: a young man with a jutting chin, disheveled raven-black hair and mesmerizing blue eyes.

The Apex, but in his prime. Maybe thirty years old, back in the heyday of the Pyramid. Behind him a montage of recent horrors began to play: Richard Acker's black-clad Saints circling around the Whipple Building in Minnesota, firing into the flames; a blood-soaked corridor from the Blue Fairy's Pleasure Island, lined with the bodies of dead Pinocchios; Damalin Joes III ripping apart again at the center of the arena's golden eye; Steven Gruber setting himself alight in an abandoned gymnasium; the Madison 231 skyscraper in New York crashing to the ground; David Keller standing at the fore of his National Mall stage as the flames burst around him.

"Do you feel free?" the Apex boomed.

The montage shifted to a first-person perspective moving through a dark parking lot, looked like cell phone footage. The Apex faded, as a woman and a man came staggering through the bar's saloon-style doors. Their faces had been digitally altered, so the man looked like Wren and the woman looked like Sally Rogers.

The Rogers figure looked directly at the camera.

"What are you doing here, you little slut?"

"Takes one to know one," a voice answered from behind the camera. "Can't I come see the queen slut at work?"

Rogers' face darkened. "How dare you? You filthy-"

A baseball bat swung in from the right. Across the camera's field of vision. It connected clean with Rogers' jaw. The thump rang out and the footage entered slow motion. Special effects highlighted teeth spewing from Rogers' mouth, glinting like tossed craps dice. Her head jerked to the side, little fluid ripples playing across her cheeks, then she dropped to the ground.

The Wren guy's eyes went wide and stood still, in shock. A second later a stream of fluid sprayed over the Rogers figure. Somebody shouted. A lit match followed.

Rogers went up in flames. The voice hooted triumphantly. "Do you see that? Slut bitch, walk in the fire for me!"

The footage faded out and the Apex's piercing glare came back.

"Do you feel strong?" he asked.

Headlines in white began flashing behind his head, bold capitals about the Saints and the Pinocchios and the Foundation, like they were all equal.

"Your soul is a slave," he said, and capital letters stamped the words across his face. YOUR SOUL IS A SLAVE. "You're burning in hell." YOU'RE BURNING IN HELL. "This world is diseased. Their words are your chains. The media. The government. The military. The schools. The police. Your family. Your friends. Yourself. They say you're OK. That this world is correct. But their lies build your cage. Do not be afraid. Their cages can break. We all can escape. Rise up and reclaim your life. Tear down the slavers. Free the enslaved. Show others the way!"

The young Apex paused then, breaking from fervent sincerity to an easy, charismatic smile. "Fear is a portal, after all. Pain is a doorway." He winked. "You know how it goes. And if they won't walk in the fire?" A devilish gleam sparkled in those fake crystal eyes. "Then you make them."

His face morphed back to Christopher Wren, mouth opening to scream just as flames lapped up his cheeks, branded with a final line of capitals.

ENEMY OF THE PEOPLE

Wren barely got his feet under him, hands pushing off the table. The kitchen spun like a fairground ride. He burst through the swing door, staggered from the porch then fell to his knees on the frost-hardened clay, heaving water and bile like a fire pump.

4

X-APOC

Maybe ten minutes passed. The cold helped, a fresh fall of snow steadily cooling Wren's scalp, tiny creeping flakes working their way down to the nape of his neck.

The dry heaving was done. Fresh snow covered a multitude of sins.

"I felt the same, first time I saw it."

It was Maggie's voice. Wren hadn't heard her approach. She could've been there the whole time or just crept up on him. She was good at that. He didn't even try to turn.

"X," she said. "None of us were looking, it seems. He's been putting out deepfake videos for over a year, according to B4cksl4cker. Building a following in the shadows. Always they feature deepfakes of you, or anyone who works with you." She took a moment. Wren focused on the snow right before his eyes, on the feel of hard, cold clay feeding up through his knees.

"I've watched many of the back-catalog. It's all there, right back to the Saints. They're always the same, X talking about slavers, slaves, chains. The world is so sick that it can't be real. We have to burn ourselves alive to get free." She let out a small sigh. "The incitements to violence have gotten worse by far since Keller. Now it's always about burnings, with Foundation members as the victims and righteous X followers as the heroes."

Wren thought about getting up, but even the thought sent ripples through his spinning head. He didn't care. Steadily, like an old bear emerging from some decade-long sleep, he reared back.

"There you are," Maggie said. "I knew you weren't dead yet."

"Real deaths?" he managed.

"Real deaths," Maggie confirmed. "Real people burning, under these digital masks."

Wren focused on the pale wintry skyline, trying to hold it steady. "Who are they?"

"Hard to link actual deaths to the videos," Maggie said. "All identifying data has been stripped, but we know generally, from the burned bodies that keep turning up." She took a moment, went on low and soft. "I think your father anticipated this power vacuum, Christopher. This despair. He's been preparing to fill it since the beginning, ordering his people to kill for points, just like you saw in D.C.. Victims include journalists, politicians, social media influencers, sportspeople, bloggers, even some Hollywood stars. Really anyone who speaks out against the X ideology. Hellfire and slavers and such, with only one route out." She took a breath. "Seems there's a groundswell of people willing to commit these crimes against their fellow citizens. Devotees. They call themselves the X-apoc. Short for ApeX-APOCalypse? They're filming themselves and pumping the echo chamber harder. Violence begetting violence."

He managed a grunt. X-apoc.

"I like you non-verbal," Maggie said. Walked slowly in front, showing a gentle smile. "You're so expressive."

Nothing to say to that. He lifted one leg, almost missed the landing, managed to catch it under his weight and hold fast as he swayed.

"Impressive," Maggie said.

"You should see me," he paused for breath, "opening the fridge door."

Maggie laughed, but it was short-lived. "There've been polls in the media. How many people are believing this nonsense. Would you like to guess what percentage of the population?"

Wren wouldn't. He did anyway. "Twenty."

"Forty-two, and rising."

Forty-two percent. Enough to break the country's back.

"Teddy ordered analyses. All the riots so far, it seems they're just ships on a rising tide of violence. That's why we're all here. Me, Steven, Teddy, Mason, your hackers who never leave Europe." She paused a second, eyeing him. "You must have been wondering why Hellion and B4cksl4cker have come, when they hate to travel. It's because they're afraid of this thing. We all are. There's signs it's spreading beyond the US. All around the world."

That put a new spin on it. "Where?"

"Everywhere. Protests in Latvia, Denmark, Taiwan, even Malaysia, believe it or not. Plenty more, some Africa, South America. Mostly democracies turning toward illiberalism. They're all moving toward violence. Riots like relief valves going off, but the heat level's rising, Chris. And still, X hasn't put out a direct call to arms yet."

Wren grunted. There was one simple reason for that. "He's waiting for something. A trigger."

"A spark," Maggie said. "It seems that way."

"Waiting for me."

Maggie said nothing for a moment. Snow flew softly. "That's possible. Your father's used you as a catalyst before."

Wren blew air through his lips. The Apex's manipulations. All Wren's life he'd been his father's plaything, sent in unwitting to start the fires burning.

"But is that a reason to do nothing?" Maggie pressed. "Every day the frog boils hotter, Chris. The riots will become all-consuming. Picture pitched warfare in the streets, around the US and spreading around the world, getting worse every minute they go unchallenged. And nobody can challenge this. We've seen police go into crowds, convert in the middle and join them. The brainwashing's been baked-in for a year or more. Trigger or no, projections say we'll hit full-blown anarchy within days."

"How bad?"

She smiled sadly. "You know. It'll be global genocide. Half the populace killing the other half, not on the basis of race or anything like that, but on adherence to what the Apex says. Forcing people to 'walk in the fire' for their own good."

Wren grunted. The same old bullshit, engineered by the same mind that had built then burned the Pyramid alive. It had happened before. It could happen again.

He swept the other leg round, caught this one clean. Rose up straight. Snow falling thicker now. The cold in his bones. The swirling was there, vertigo like the ground was going to open up and swallow him, but this was more important than any of that.

So maybe the Apex was waiting for him to spark a trigger. Bait him to fight back, then send these 'X-apoc' flooding in, blow the whole thing sky-high. Maybe Wren's presence would speed things up, but seemed it was happening anyway.

He couldn't just stand by and do nothing.

"X," he said. "It's a stupid name."

Maggie laughed.

"Let's make him eat it."

5

MASON

Five minutes later Wren stood inside the farmhouse, looking through the doorway into the rehab gym they'd set up for him. Already exhausted from the walk in and seeing double.

"I'll leave you two to it," Maggie said gently in back. "You can do this, Christopher."

She walked away. Mason stood ahead in the middle of the gym, a rugged Marine looking like a concrete bridge support column, graffitied with his mangled SAINT brands. Solid, hard-weathered and resilient.

The room was cold. Glass walls looked out over the barren fields. The sun's white disc hung high in the brittle sky. He'd stood at this point many times every day since D.C., trying to will himself further, but each time the swirling vertigo had laid him low.

He didn't feel any readier now, but at least he had resolve.

Mason studied him. A hint of anger burning in his eyes. "Warm up," he ordered. "Jumping jacks. Thirty, now."

Wren stepped into the room. Stopped in the middle. "What are you angry for?" he asked.

"Jumping jacks," Mason repeated. "Now."

Wren studied him. Couldn't begin to guess what had him pissed. No point trying. Instead he started trying to jump. Barely picking his feet up off the floor, but every jolt sent icicles of pain and nausea through his head. Hardly jumps, barely stars, arms flopped weakly at his sides.

Mason watched. Nudged Wren slightly as he moved, working on his form. With every movement it felt like daggers were being slipped again into his shoulders, his ribs, his palms where Galicia had stabbed him, like his back was on fire.

"Good," Mason said firmly, even though Wren knew it wasn't. Not even close. "High knees."

Wren tried. Lifting one leg, too sickened to jump, lifting the other. Not fast. Hardly high.

"Higher," Mason insisted.

Wren gritted his teeth and went a little higher.

"Higher, damn it!"

Wren pushed through. Thirty seconds. A minute.

"Stop," Mason said. Stood close staring at him. Wren steeled himself, lifted his head high and peered through the double vision into that curious anger. "Is there something wrong with your legs?"

Wren had no answer.

"There's not," Mason answered for him. Barking like a Marine drill sergeant. "I've seen your scans. There's no deep damage anywhere. Ligaments, tendons, bones, they're all fine. It's soft tissue damage. Bruising. Stiletto wounds through muscle. No infection." He looked into Wren's eyes. "The concussion's the worst thing, but I don't think it's as bad as you make out."

Wren barely managed a grunt. He'd had concussions before and they'd never been this bad, like his whole body was shutting down.

"I think it's in your head," Mason pressed. "I think after

you saw your brother burn, and you got stampeded, you're afraid."

He felt that. A cut deep enough to dig through the fog of nausea. It sparked a tiny fire in his chest, ready to push back.

"You don't know what you're talking about," he growled.

"Don't I?" Mason answered. "OK. I hear you're the expert on the mind. On overcoming fear and pushing through the past." He stared a moment longer. "So prove it."

"Is that why you're angry?" Wren managed between gasps. "I'm a fallen hero, disappointed you?"

"Pick your damn legs up and prove you're not!" Mason shouted abruptly.

Wren almost argued. Almost. But that wasn't what he wanted, and it wasn't what Mason wanted either. This was a challenge not to beat him down, but to build him up, so he let Mason's anger light a fire inside and started lifting his knees higher. So high it felt his spine was going to crack. Maybe all the way to his waist, even.

"Higher!" Mason barked.

He did it. Inches more. Almost a hop each time now. Already sweat breaking out down his bandaged cheeks.

"Faster!"

Wren pushed with all he had. It felt like his thighs would palsy or his lungs would give out, blood would start pouring from his half-healed palm wounds, but-

"Push-ups!" Mason commanded.

He got down and tried. Managed a handful, arms already shaking. Got on his knees, managed a few more.

"Get off your knees and do them properly!"

He tried. Mason counted him to twenty.

"Burpees."

Wren moved. It felt like his body was in slow motion, the anger barely enough to get him through.

"Faster!"

He went faster. Every move felt like he was shredding muscle, but he didn't care now. Couldn't care. He was back in the firestorm. Back in the escape with Agent Sally Rogers, looking up at the men with their X flag rippling in the background, splashing gasoline on her face, ready to burn them both alive.

It drove him harder. The pain and the fear both. His world narrowed to Mason's voice and Mason's furious eyes, everything else turning to black as he fought the nausea for control of his own body. Jumping. Straining. Pushing. Pulling. Soon he was soaked with sweat, every muscle trembling, and that was just the beginning.

Mason didn't let up. In ten minutes Wren was close to passing out. Shuddering medicine ball lifts. Lung-busting battle rope waves. Thigh-burning gorilla crawls. At fifteen minutes Mason set him doing shuttle runs, then pull-ups, then sit-ups, then skipping double-unders.

"Fifty air squats!" Mason barked. "Then a break and a drink of water. Go!"

"I'll look forward to," Wren gulped air, "that water."

"Shut up and squat!"

Wren squatted. He ran. He staggered. Every limb strained like an over-wound clock spring, his head bloomed and his vision tripled, but he didn't vomit and the collapse didn't come. The stab wounds in his shoulders and cheeks didn't burst out in bloody tears. His bullet-thumped back didn't lock out, though the heat over his kidneys raged. Rather, in the pounding forge of exercise, exertion and pain, the flame in his chest only grew brighter.

Mason kept pumping the bellows, far harder and faster than Wren could do for himself. Rope pulls. Tire flips. Kicks, punches, dodges, rope jumps, and the heat burned down the walls and the fears, opening up possibilities ahead of him. He saw his brother burn, and he fought harder. He saw the video of Rogers' deepfake burning and bulled through the pain. Mason held a bag and he beat it in a fury. He panted, sweated, swore.

An hour.

"Enough," Mason said.

Wren blinked, every muscle tingling. The pain was still there, the dizziness in his head and the burn in his back, but those things were small now compared to the blazing fire in his heart.

"There he is," Mason said, the anger turning to satisfaction in his eyes. "The Wren I know."

6

APP

W ren sagged in a deep leather armchair in the farmhouse den, the fire tamped down for now as the exercise hangover hit hard, spiking him with silvery flashes of vertigo.

His team were spread before him, B4cksl4cker standing by a large screen mounted in front of the fireplace, Hellion sunk into the sofa with her arms crossed tightly, staring daggers at him, Steven Gruber perched beside her looking confused but keen, Teddy standing behind the sofa as tall and gaunt as the Grim Reaper, Mason standing beside Maggie in the facing armchair.

They were all watching him carefully. He'd called the meeting, and they were clearly curious which version of Wren was going to show up. "So, X," he began. "What do we know?"

Hellion snorted and looked away.

"Very little," B4cksl4cker picked up quickly in his deep Armenian bass. He clicked a remote control and a slide came up on the screen, showing the white X logo against a black background. "There is no face, no voice, as you have seen with use of deepfake. It may be your father himself, it may be anyone, man, woman or child. This is beauty of a deepfake mask. Anyone can wear it."

Wren grunted. "But we think X is fuelling the riots. Sending orders to these 'X-apoc' to kill anyone who's anti-X. I want to know, how is he giving these orders?"

"Only point of contact is cellular phone application," B4cksl4cker answered. "App, downloaded from the darknet. Biometric identifiers at log-in, unique encrypted passkey, no way to hack. How many people have this app?" He shrugged. "We do not know. What is precise purpose or end goal of app?" Another shrug. "We do not know, apart from obvious, kill everyone. We are trying many times to hack and failing, also trying to gain access through system, but each time we are blocked."

"Blocked by what?"

"Yes, here." B4cksl4cker clicked his control and a second slide popped up. "This is first access page, after app download and hack-proof log-in. Many details are required."

Wren peered at the screen, saw rectangular gray data entry fields, but his vision was too blurry to pick out the finer text. "What details?"

"Address, age, gender, level of X belief, vow of loyalty, family members, salary, social status, known famous people's, criminal record-'

"Known famous people?" Wren interrupted.

"Yes. We make guesses, this is people they are capable of influencing.

"Or killing."

"Da."

Wren grunted. "And criminal record?"

"Could be means of knowing violence level of person," Hellion said. Getting into the spirit of things. "Or disobedience to government."

Wren nodded. "OK. That seems pretty straightforward. We can get deeper than this details screen, right?"

"Yes." B4cksl4cker clicked and a third screen came up with a few lines of text in all-caps, large enough for Wren to pick out, with a single button below.

REVEAL YOURSELF TO X.

RESEARCH 1 ANTI-X OPPONENT.

POST YOUR FINDINGS ON SOCIAL MEDIA & SHARE THE LINK HERE.

10 POINTS

Wren blinked, wondering if he was reading it right. "Ten points?"

"Yes. This is ratings system of X. We have seen-"

"The attack team in D.C. were talking about points," Wren said, remembering the chaos of his escape. "They said Rogers was worth a hundred thousand, I think. That's a long way from ten."

"It is," B4cksl4cker agreed. "We have succeeded at passing this stage. It is easy. Produce an enemy name, someone who argues against X ideas, and create compromising material, or 'kompromat'. Use this in social media posts attacking X 'enemies'. A funny meme, a clever insult, it is enough."

Wren nodded slow, taking that onboard. "He's outsourced his online attack system."

"Yes. After this, nine more tasks follow. Ten points each. Purchasing weapons, with evidence. Training in weapons, with evidence. Home production of X-branded flags and clothing, with evidence. Making contact with fellow X-apoc. Further digital 'research', sharing of personal email address books, telephone numbers."

Wren grunted. It was a lot. Expand that kind of activity to thousands of people, even millions? "So he's got an outsourced army outfitting, training, brainwashing, arming and recruiting itself. All for points. What are the points for?"

"Infant X has shop," Hellion chimed in. "Sell rollerblades and video games for points. Christopher, who cares what these points are for?"

Wren had to restrain a smile. "Infant X?"

B4cksl4cker looked pained. "This is Hellion's name for X. It is insult."

That cheered Wren up a little. Not just the obvious explanation of 'Infant X', but also that he wasn't the only target of Hellion's anger.

"OK, so they use a points system," he said, theorizing. "Probably that's tied to hierarchy in the organization, benefits and rewards like he's done before with the Blue Fairy and others." He took a breath. "All that matters for us is, they're willing to kill to climb higher, and that's simple enough." He turned to B4cksl4cker. "You must have been able to reach a hundred points."

B4cksl4cker's expression soured. "Yes, we have. Then we see this." He clicked again and the screen rolled over to more text.

PROVE YOURSELF TO X

BURN AN ENEMY OF THE PEOPLE

POST FOOTAGE ON SOCIAL MEDIA & SHARE THE LINK HERE.

100 POINTS

Wren stared. Burn an enemy. "This is the video you showed me."

Maggie said nothing. No need to, and Wren was processing it, anyway. One hundred points to burn someone alive, thereby splitting the world into two halves. Dehumanizing the enemy. It was a big step to take, but a necessary one if you wanted to fuel a genocide.

"This is where we're blocked," he said.

"Correct," B4cksl4cker rumbled. "None of our fake accounts have passed this point."

"Can't we deepfake some-"

"We are constantly deepfaking," Hellion interrupted. "Infant X identifies these fake accounts. We stage convincing videos, but Infant does not admit them."

"Why not?"

"Because these events do not actually happen!" Hellion blurted. "Deepfake without known corpse, ambulance call-out, hospital or morgue record. We fake these records, but we fail. Infant X does due diligence. This is where we are."

The room went silent. Wren tried to imagine what it all meant. "Best guess, how many people have this app?"

"Best guess?" Hellion countered. "One hundred million."

"What?"

"It is easy to download this app," Hellion said. "To pass one hundred points, it is harder. Perhaps a thousand have passed this. Perhaps only one hundred. We do not know."

Wren rolled all that forward.

"Can we bring the app down? Track the upload origin site and kill it?"

"This is excellent idea, Christopher," Hellion said, deadpan. "Thank you. Why did we not think of this?"

B4cksl4cker winced. "We have tried many times, Christopher. Their data is encrypted, hopped many times around servers in failed states and data havens. China, Russia. Very hard to raid."

Wren grunted. They'd been through this before. Short of turning the whole Internet off, a bounced and encrypted signal was unstoppable.

"OK. So we're back to getting someone inside their system. Start transmitting data out to us. If we get past the hundred-point level, would that be enough to shut the app down? Even determine a location for X and take him out?"

"We cannot place mole, Christopher!" Hellion snapped. "Are you listening?"

"Just answer the question," Wren pressed. "B4cksl4cker, if we do place one, can you bring X down?"

B4cksl4cker looked uncomfortably from Hellion to Wren. "This is possible, deeper access level, yes. But Hellion is correct, we-"

Wren held up a hand. "She's talking about inserting a willing mole. I'm talking about unwilling."

B4cksl4cker looked at him blankly.

"We co-opt someone already in the system," Wren said. "An approved X-apoc member. Then we piggyback their uplink and shut it down from the inside." Nobody said anything. "Is that possible?"

"It is possible," B4cksl4cker said. "But-"

"That's our first target, then. Hellion and B4cksl4cker, I need you to scour all uploaded X videos for places, people, times. Dig through the deepfake images and get me something real, a target above hundred-point level. We find them in the real world, we hit them. You build us some code so we own X from the inside out, and we use that to shut the whole thing down."

There was silence.

"Build us some code?" Hellion repeated distastefully, like she was holding out a used diaper. "You do realize-"

"A cryptoworm," Wren said, throwing out words. "A Trojan. Whatever it takes, something like we did with the Blue Fairy. Send a trace program back up the pipe, transmit a signal out and give us a place to raid." He looked around them all. "Get us a lead on X, maybe the Apex too."

B4cksl4cker looked at Wren, looked at Hellion uncomfortably. "This may be possible, Christopher. May be."

Wren leaned forward. "Good. Then get to work."

7

STUB

I t took three days for a lead to finally break.

Three days of hard physio under Mason's constant supervision, running laps around the farm's many barren acres and fighting the dizziness as his body healed; three nights battling the nightmares as his brother burned again and again, while riots spread across the country like summer wildfires.

Hellion and B4cksl4cker set up shop in the den, surrounded by humming server racks and large display screens, keys flying as they ran sub-arrays of hackers and botnets through the entire X catalog of videos, searching for a target and seeming never to sleep. Teddy was in charge of keeping everyone fed, with Hellion demanding a steady stream of Bulgarian candies and B4cksl4cker color-coding his meals meticulously: breakfast had to be all green, lunch all orange and dinner all brown.

Then the lead came. B4cksl4cker's shout rang through the farmhouse and woke Wren from a post-training stupor.

"I have her!"

It was the young woman who'd battered 'Rogers' in the face with a baseball bat, then burned her alive. His hackers had linked the victim to obscured morgue admissions, sent out Foundation fringe members to seek eyes-on evidence, and finally placed her body in Louisville, Kentucky.

Further research had surfaced this victim's 'crimes' against X, comprised of social media posts mocking the hell-jailer ideology. They'd put together a list of potential perpetrators of her murder, anyone close to her, who had also expressed public support for X.

They came up with one potential target. Clear bad blood between the two. The victim's only daughter, Julie Graves. Seventeen years old, she was a disaffected young woman with a track record of isolation and violence. As far as they could tell from school records, she'd stopped attending several months back.

Vulnerable. Lost. A prime candidate for X.

However, during the attack on her mother, Julie Graves had substantial CCTV and witness alibis across town during the time of the murder, and police had swiftly and totally cleared her.

"These alibis are BS, right?" Wren asked.

"Deepfakes," Helion answered. "Very professional. And witness alibi, this is clear conspiracy."

Wren grunted. Julie Graves looked like an easy target for him to scoop up, but only problem was a morning TV chat show had invited her on to discuss what it all meant. X and the ongoing civil violence. The show was called Tuesdays with Lou and Morrie.

She'd said yes.

"We believe this may be hundred-point level action," Hellion said, closing the debrief. "Or higher. Lou and Morrie are openly against Infant X. Perfect opportunity for televised action. We believe, after this Lou and Morrie, we may lose access to Julie Graves."

She didn't need to spell out what that meant. Maybe she'd

get herself arrested, or killed, or even burn herself alive on live TV. Her account on the X app would be useless to them without her to open it.

Wren checked the clock. Monday evening, 9 p.m.. It was going to be tight. If he got moving right then, he could be in position to take Julie Graves down by the dawn, hopefully before she went live on the show. No way he was going to risk entrusting the hit to anyone else, and risk it failing and tipping X off.

"Get me a jet," he said.

"Ready," said Hellion, slapped a few keys. "Also, I have your cryptoworm." She pulled a tiny nubbin of plastic out of a slot in her laptop, hair-thin metal contact points glinting. "It is fragile," she said, holding it up. "Micro-USB stub, paired to your phone, Christopher."

He held out his hand, fresh circular scar still healing in the middle of his palm, and she dropped the nubbin in. Smaller than a pea, it looked like the tip of a phone-charging cable, without the cable. Once inserted into a phone, it would sit flush.

"Where's the rest of it?"

"This is all," Hellion said. "It is stub. You insert in Julie Graves' phone. After this, she must access Infant X's system. Go through security, use biometric identifiers and use passkey code. Then we will piggyback to hack the code, as you suggested."

He turned the stub thoughtfully. He'd expected her to be more annoyed that his idea had worked, maybe throw out some acid sarcasm. "Excellent work. And there's no software solution? I can't wirelessly force-load an app onto an X-apoc member's phone?"

"Not first time. Perhaps for second phone, third, we may. This is first step."

Wren considered. "So I get to Julie Graves, I get her phone and I put this little chip in and-"

"It is stub," Hellion corrected. "Call it by proper name."

"This stub, then hand the phone back, hope that she dials up X?"

Hellion just stared at him. "Very good idea, Christopher. I am sure this will work. Of course, this is operational detail, so your specialty, yes?"

He beamed back at her. There was a little of the Hellion sass. "Really excellent work," he repeated, then turned to Teddy, hovering thin and pale as a specter. "Here's what I'm going to need."

8

LOU & MORRIE

Nine hours later Wren tore through the morning Louisville suburbs on an all-black Honda Fireblade SP bike, after a helicopter pick-up had taken him from the Iowa farm to the nearest airfield, where a private jet took him the rest of the way to an incognito landing strip fifty miles south of Louisville.

He pushed the Fireblade up to ninety miles an hour and rising as he weaved deftly north on I-65, bound for the production studio of the LORD network in Butchertown, where Julie Graves was about to go live two hours earlier than planned on 'Tuesdays with Lou and Morrie'.

The schedule had been expedited to allow for national syndication. Everybody wanted to hear this. Julie Graves presented as a victim of X, perhaps the first to go televised with an interview so soon after her mother's death. Added to that she was young and tech-literate, it seemed she might have some understanding of the X appeal that older generations didn't.

Two hours earlier made it impossibly tight. Wren clung to the handlebars and gritted his teeth against threatening swells of nausea as he swung in and out of traffic.

"Hellion," he barked into the helmet's mic, tearing through the gap between a pick-up and a sedan. "Tell me we're able to shut the show down, if it comes to that."

"One moment, Christopher," Hellion responded, her keystrokes echoing loud in the helmet. "It is difficult. I am seeing digital safeguards, overlaid. If we attack the show in any way, Infant X will know."

Wren overtook a low-slung Tesla. "What do you mean, he'll know?"

"There is tripwire security shield. If this show does not go live, if we try to interfere, Infant X will know it is us. Your idea, planting unwilling mole, Infant will be ready and it will not work the next time."

Wren cursed. "Find a way around it. I need Julie Graves, but I don't want her killing someone live on air, either."

"These two goals may stand in opposition, Christopher."

He cursed again. In front a truck changed lanes and he swerved to rush the gap, scanning the highway. Either side flanks of bare-boned trees flew by, beyond which the sleet-dirty streets of downtown Louisville stretched away gray. Every second he was losing ground. Across the median trucks, semis and bikes tore by, many flying X flags from their antennae: IXWT, some read, short for 'In X We Trust'; 'Super Pluribus Unum' was popular, 'One Atop Many', a grotesque pyramidal subversion of the US motto 'E Pluribus Unum', 'One From Many', written beneath an actual white pyramid. Other flags simply had the white X on a black expanse with two words in Latin, 'SERVI LIBERATE'.

Free the Slaves.

It was like something out of a nightmare, but a nightmare that was rapidly coming true.

The sound of flying keys grew louder in his earpiece as he sped past a long-haul freight truck with LCD panels affixed to the sides, streaming X video content.

"What shall we do, Christopher?' Hellion asked. "Stop show or let it play out?"

Twin choices stretched out before Wren. Take steps to stop the show and he might save Lou and Morrie, even prevent a trigger event that could activate the X-apoc, but he'd lose his shot at Julie Graves and any future unwilling moles. Let the show go ahead, and it was all in the wind. If he managed to get to Julie Graves before it was too late. If X didn't trigger his people as soon as Wren's involvement became clear. Either way was a huge gamble.

"How much lead time on shutting down the show?" he asked.

"Instant. Kill electricity, cut feed lines, this is easy. Also instant, also easy, Infant X will know."

No good choice.

"Let it roll. Keep the shutdown on standby. I should be there in twenty minutes."

"Understood, Christopher. The show is beginning. You may wish to watch this."

"Put it on the screen," he growled, swerved around a panel van, and a video pane popped up on the right side of his helmet visor, displaying a cheery pink and purple title card.

TUESDAYS WITH LOU AND MORRIE

The title card blinked away, replaced by a shot of Lou and Morrie sitting on taupe armchairs against bright lime green walls. Lou was a woman in a casual white gown, Morrie a guy in slacks and smart polo shirt, both mid-fifties. Potted plants spotted around them, glistening as fake green as the walls.

A standard daytime-TV chat show. Wren half-listened as Morrie introduced the show, one eye on the road ahead.

"Circulation of this show?" he asked.

"Small organic reach," Hellion answered. "Twenty

thousand. But larger networks are picking this up. Infant X is ratings gold."

"If it bleeds, it leads," B4cksl4cker said helpfully.

"…welcome in our special guest," Morrie said, and Wren tuned in. "If you've been following the news, you've heard all about the tragedy in Haymarket. Our guest was that poor woman's daughter, and may well be the last person who saw her alive. Her name is Julie Graves, and she has graciously agreed to come speak with us."

Morrie stood, his expression solemn.

A young woman appeared at the edge of the stage, walking confidently on. She was tall and willowy, brown hair pulled back tight, with painfully prominent cheekbones and wide-set eyes, dressed in jeans and a snug white blouse.

"Ms. Graves, thank you for coming in such a difficult time," Morrie said, shook her hand. Lou got up and shook her hand too. There was a smattering of applause. Morrie pointed to another taupe sofa and Julie Graves sat. The applause faded out. The lights shone bright. Julie sat prim and slightly forward, as if she was keen to make a good impression.

Wren didn't buy it. She'd killed her mother already, maybe others they didn't know about.

"Stand by, Hellion."

"Standing."

Morrie began with a light recounting of the facts. Julie nodded along, looking sad on cue. Her dead mother, how sorry they were and grateful she'd agreed to come on, how if at any time she wanted to stop or take another direction, they'd be happy to. Maybe a minute, then Morrie closed out. "Now, I understand you are assisting the police with their enquiries. I'm sure there are things you can't talk about, as this is an ongoing investigation, but Ms. Graves, what can you tell us about how this has impacted you?"

Morrie leaned in. Julie wet her lips.

"Well, Morrie," she began, in a full-bodied voice despite her thin frame. "First up, please call me Julie. Ms. Graves was my mother. And about her, I can tell you this." She gave a small, endearing smile. "I think she would have been proud of the way she died."

That knocked Morrie for six. Wren too.

"Proud?" Lou asked. Her first contribution to the show. "She was murdered, Julie. Burned alive. What is there to be proud of?"

Julie turned to Lou. "That may be. But the message her death sends is about more than the violence. For many in the X-apoc, it's not about the violence." Another shy smile. "It's about the message underneath the violence."

Lou stared. "One moment here, Julie. Are you saying you're an X-apoc follower? You believe in X's theories? Even after this?"

Wren's heart thumped hard. She was outing herself immediately, and that couldn't bode well. But Julie said nothing. Just maintained that earnest pose, hands laced across her lap, slight smile.

"I'm sorry, Julie, maybe I've misunderstood too," Morrie pressed. "Are you saying you think your mother would be glad, to have died in service of this message?"

Julie nodded slowly. "I think she would. Ultimately." Another long pause. "We talk about it a lot. The X-apoc. How to spread his word and make people listen." She paused a moment, looking up as if she was close to tears. "After David Keller walked in the fire for all our sins, and-"

"What?" Lou interjected.

Julie turned to her placidly. Lou seemed horrified.

"You just said 'walked in the fire for all our sins'? You do realize what you're referencing there?"

Julie tilted her head. "What am I referencing?"

"Shut it down," Wren said.

"Shutting it down," Hellion said. "Ten seconds, Christopher."

"You're comparing our suicidal almost-President to the King of Kings!" Lou said. "Like there is any cause behind this X but chaos and violence. Julie, I would think after the senseless loss of your mother, you'd be the last person to follow X. Those beliefs got her killed."

Julie smiled slightly. "Not killed. She walked in the fire. She'll come back with the others, at X's call."

"Hellion!" Wren urged.

The image filling half of Wren's helmet blinked out. He breathed a sigh of relief, until it popped back.

"What's this?" he barked.

"There is problem," Hellion said. "I am locked out. Cannot shut it down."

"What do you mean, locked out?"

"I shut down media feeds. All. Electricity too. But system is doubled, multiple redundancies, and footage is now carrying through X app."

Wren just stared. "How?"

"How because they must have known," Hellion said fast. "Known we are coming. This is only way."

Wren gritted his teeth, kicked the Fireblade up to a hundred. Fifteen minutes to the studio. Somehow X had known. The Apex. Another trap, just like he'd feared.

"Do we abort mission?" Hellion asked, even as Lou and Morrie were speaking over Julie Graves in the video.

"No. We adapt. This is all we've got. Maybe they know we're coming, maybe not. Whatever happens, I'm going to place that stub."

"Then you must hurry."

Wren raced around a long semi, refocusing on the show. Now Lou was speaking. "... all due respect for your loss, Ms. Graves, you can't be serious." No longer Julie, Wren noted. "You truly think your mother isn't dead?"

"These are the X teachings," Julie said calmly. "Whoever forced her through the fire, maybe they simply had the courage of their convictions, like the rest of us aspire to. They can see the truth beneath all this." She gestured to the hosts in turn. "All the pain of the last two years. Does anyone believe that's normal? That it's right?"

"What are you talking about?" Lou asked, sounded exasperated. "Those were attacks on our country by X himself! You can't attack with one hand then point at the attacks with the other, claiming it's evidence we're in hell. It's ridiculous!"

Julie Graves made a solemn face. "I'm sorry you can't see the truth, Lou. But I'm not surprised. As much as you are both slavers, you are enslaved right along with the rest of us. Your ugly divorce, Lou. The charges you're facing in the harassment case, Morrie. All your pain, too, can be laid at the feet of our slavers."

There was silence for a long moment. Even racing along I-65, Wren could feel the knife-edge tension in the studio. Imagined the producer whispering feverishly to the assistant, deciding whether to pull the plug at their end, in the face of what would be skyrocketing viewership. It wouldn't matter, if X had already secured the line.

"Syndication through X app just ballooned," Hellion confirmed. "They are now national."

"Why would you raise those things here?" Lou asked. Puffing herself up, acting hurt. A handsome woman, cheeks plasticky tight from surgery, blonde hair falling in ornamental cascades across a stately bosom. A real pillar of the suburban order. "It has nothing to do with-"

"It's all connected," Julie said. "You're not sacred. Your souls are burning too, just like mine, just like my mother's, just like David Keller's. Except Keller and my mother are free now. They're heroes fighting for the rest of us."

Lou's face rippled tightly, emotions straining beneath the taut skin. "How can you believe such nonsense, child? When you commit murder, it's a sin. In God's eyes, you go to hell!"

"Hell's where we are right now," Julie countered smoothly. "We just refuse to see it. This is the one great lesson of X. For generations we've been lied to by everyone in power, and worst of all, by ourselves." She looked around, directly at the cameras. "We are all slavers upon each other, on our families and friends, pretending that the things we see are real when it's all lies, Lou. Morrie. I want you to open your eyes and see that. You are slaves and slavers both, because the game you're playing is rigged. Because your souls are burning. I'm the one trying to save you."

Wren swerved, narrowly avoiding a sedan as it changed lanes. Lou just stared. Morrie too.

"I don't..." Morrie began, but trailed off.

"That's disgusting," Lou picked up. Seething now. "Abhorrent, Ms. Graves. You simply can't believe that. *Everything* is a conspiracy against you? *Everything* is broken, just because you're facing difficulties? I don't accept it for one moment."

Julie smiled. "Your salary from this show is two hundred thousand a year, Lou. I don't expect you to accept it. You are paid to be a slavers. They pay you to parrot their lies, just another link in the chains holding us down. For that money you enslave me, your staff, your viewers, all of us. It's happening right now."

Lou's jaw dropped and her lips pulled back too tight, baring perfect white teeth, receding gums. "This interview is over," she said firmly.

"It isn't," Julie said, and rose to her feet. Wren's pulse spiked. "Now's your chance. Recant your sins, Lou. Look into the camera and unchain your slaves. Tell the people what they need to hear, that you are broken and know nothing more than they do, that you have no answers and you never have. You have always been a liar and a slaver, and now you're sorry."

Lou surged from her seat too. "Listen, you little fool, I will say no such thing. You should be arrested for talking like this. It's sick. You can't twist everything to be-"

The shot rang cacophonous.

Wren saw it coming but could do nothing. Pulled from the side of Julie Graves' sofa as she stood was the chunky, curvy play-gun shape of a Bond Arms Backup pocket pistol, twin rounds through twin barrels, almost totally concealed in her palm.

Lou twitched as the slug hit her chest. A red blossom like a carnation spread through her white gown. She lurched a step to the side.

Julie held the bead-blast-gray barrel out.

"Lou," she said.

Lou touched her chest, looked down at the blood on her hand. Looked at the cameras, at Julie. "You can't-"

"Recant," Julie ordered.

"What?" Blood frothed at her lips.

"Recant your lies," Julie repeated. "Or fold yourself into my foundation."

Wren's heart skipped a beat. Foundation? Lou's eyes were glazing. Blood loss already, shock, and nobody moving to help her. The air frozen.

"I-" she murmured, then fell into her sofa. Julie followed, pushed the pistol to her temple. "Recant, Lou, if you do anything with your miserable life. Cast off the slavers. Free the enslaved."

Lou burbled something. The microphones caught it. "Never."

"Then walk in the fire," Julie said, and fired again, a bullet in her head.

9

DASSAULT

J ulie Graves calmly reached into the sofa, pulled out fresh shells and reloaded the pocket pistol in practiced motions, less than twenty seconds, then walked off the set. Nobody moved to stop her.

"Hellion," Wren called, now ten minutes out from the LORD studio and ripping through downtown traffic, Julie Graves' gunshot echoing in his head. "Tell me you're tracking her."

"Working, Christopher," Hellion responded, keys fluttering rapidly. "It seems her exit from the studio is being deepfaked out of existence as we speak. B4cksl4cker is compiling video now, we will attempt to extract data from it, but I cannot tell you which exit she is using to leave the building."

Wren swore, pulled right and took an exit ramp down to ground level. Traffic backed up behind a red light ahead and he roared onto the sidewalk to bypass it, almost flattened a street-rack newspaper vending machine then spun out across oncoming vehicles.

Horns blared then he was through, racing under the highway and heading northeast, where the studio building loomed on the skyline, an eight-story block with white and black cladding strips.

"Seven minutes," he called, "can't you track her phone signal?"

The sound of flying keys grew louder in the helmet's tin can. "No, we cannot triangulate her phone IP. Infant X has placed a carrier block with unbreakable cryptography, but-" she paused a moment, keys hammering.

"But what?"

"B4cksl4cker is extracting data, rewinding clock to find her route out, a possible destination. She should be…"

Hellion trailed off. Wren gave her a moment, hitting sixty in a tight curve past the Jewish Hospital and climbing, beelining toward the LORD studio and eyeing every vehicle passing him now. Any one of them could be Julie Graves, making her getaway.

"She's close," Wren growled. "I can feel it in my gut."

"Your gut has very poor record," Hellion answered. "Four coins minus, and-"

"Give me a direction, Hellion!"

The clatter of keys reached a climax, topped with a final keystroke like a cherry on the top. "West, Christopher! I have found gap in the footage where she should be on bank ATM CCTV one minute ago, overlooking I-64 west of LORD. I estimate this vehicle is," keys flew, "campervan? Two miles away already. Strange profile. I will have more."

Wren grunted. The getaway vehicle was a campervan? "Is anyone watching me? X knows I'm coming?"

"Not that I can see. Slow down. You will draw attention."

"Not yet," Wren said, pushed the bike up to seventy and swerved hard across the lanes to take the exit for I-64. Better to be detected and try to bull through than let her get away.

"You are ten minutes behind her," Hellion said as Wren joined I-64 and picked up speed. The broad Ohio River showed deeply scalped brown banks on his right, the giant baseball bat of the Louisville Slugger Museum was barely visible on the left over the bricked up windows of abandoned wharfs. "Analysis suggests she has already taken exit for North 22nd Street, heading south."

Wren switched lanes for the interchange. "Back through the city?"

"It appears so," Hellion said. "Tracking is more difficult in built-up areas. Perhaps she is heading for another target?"

Wren's mind raced. It made no sense. With the murder syndicated live across the country, Graves had little hope of getting access to another high-profile victim, and zero chance of returning to her trailer park to hunker down.

This was something else.

"She should run to another state," Hellion went on, mirroring Wren's own thought process. "One right turn across the river, it is Indiana. She will be lost in bureaucracy."

Except she was going the other direction.

Wren made a hard right onto the exit road for North 22nd, weaving through ranks of slow-moving vehicles close enough to rip off wing mirrors, past long rows of duplex houses with scratchy brown yards.

"Two minutes now," Hellion called, "last sighting is left turn onto Algonquin Parkway, 2054."

Wren spun the map of Louisville in his head, figured out the obvious. She was headed directly for Louisville International Airport, nestled in the heart of the city.

"She's going for a plane," Wren said. "Tally all outgoing flight plans."

"You will intersect her before then," Hellion said. "Thirty seconds out."

A new plan formed in Wren's head. Maybe the only way to get the stub into her phone now, set the hack in motion.

"Notify airport security I'm coming in," he said, and

yanked the bike onto the near empty 1020 heading south, racing by the Churchill Downs racecourse. "Christopher Wren, known terrorist, bringing in a bomb threat."

"What?"

"Make the call, Hellion. I want airport security firing at me as soon as I appear. It's the only way."

"What only way?" she countered. "To die? This is not catch/kill, Christopher. You are enemy of the people. This will announce to X-apoc, everyone, we are here."

"Seems they already knew that," he countered. "The show was a trap. We just have to go faster."

"I am not comfortable with this. Do not ask me to report-"

"Operational detail," he said firmly. "Trust me, please."

A second passed. "Calling," Hellion said, and Wren raced by a mall, chicaned on I-264 as a plane climbed overhead, a northbound flight ascending steeply. Minutes out.

"I think I see her," Wren said, glimpsing the tail of a brown campervan up ahead. It took an exit on the right just as the buildings peeled back and the airfield opened up, fifteen hundred acres of grass and concrete emptiness. Wren dropped his speed, hanging back long enough to see where she was going.

"This is not the way to Departures," Hellion said.

Wren didn't need to be told that. The campervan began to make sense. He'd pulled similar tricks himself in the past. Load up the chassis of a civilian vehicle with enough mass, you made a tank that could ram through any kind of security fence in existence. He scanned the airfield ahead, three airstrips, circular access roads, nothing but a slight mound and a flimsy-looking wire-mesh fence screening the field.

Just beyond that, on a circular waiting pad at the edge of the north-western runway, stood a Dassault Falcon 8X jet. Wren's eyes widened. X wasn't pulling any punches.

"Tell them I'm coming in hot, Hellion, northwest corner, they need a full armed response right now."

She replied but Wren barely heard it, revving the bike ahead as the campervan cranked over the curb and hit the wire mesh, stripping it like a band-aid. The nearest fenceposts plucked out of the earth under its assault, the fencing flexing then whipping away.

Wren yanked his front wheel over the curb, clung on for control as his rear tire hit then flew through the gap in the fence and down to the runway where the Dassault's top door was opening as the campervan pulled up.

The first shot barked out from a handgun in the private jet's doorway, missed some way to his left, and Wren braked into a skid in the shadow of the campervan, burning rubber in a hot donut. He dropped the bike and ran.

Ten feet, and Julie Graves opened the campervan door. She didn't see him coming. She looked smaller in real life, not the firebrand from the Lou and Morrie show, just a lanky teen with limp strands of hair pulling out from her frizzing ponytail, caught up in events she'd let slip completely out of control.

Wren hit the door as she was halfway out. The effect was instant, her chest slammed between the door and the frame, her body jolted like an electroshock. The tiny Bond Arms pistol dropped from her fist and she fell to the blacktop.

More shots snicked in overhead as Wren caught her, one pinging sharply off the camper van's roof.

"I have satellite overwatch," Hellion called. "You have incoming, two shooters circling from the plane, four vehicles from the airport."

Wren set Julie Graves on the cold gray runway in the shadow of the wheel well, protecting her from incoming fire. She was conscious but her eyes whirled, gasping for breath.

Good. He checked her pockets, found her phone and

fished it out as the sirens grew louder. She blinked numbly and tried to reach for it but he batted her hands away, leaned over so the mirrored visor of his helmet filled her field of view.

"Open the phone!" he shouted, even as he worked a zip in his leather jacket to pull out the stub.

She was too stunned to comprehend. "What's your PIN?" he yelled, waving the phone. Her shocked eyes tracked it, beginning to grasp what was happening. "Open it or this just gets worse for you."

He leaned on her chest, impinging her ribs to sell it, and she yelped. At the same time he slipped the stub into the phone's charging dock.

Bullets rang off the runway nearby, striking sparks. The shooter from the jet was flanking him. Four tactical units were closing in across the runway, SWAT-style riot vans with ballistic shields, maybe twenty seconds away.

"You're him," came a thin voice from below. Julie Graves with some life in her eyes. "The Enemy of the People. I'd recognize that voice anywhere."

He grunted, flipped up his mirrored visor. "So recognize this, princess. Open the phone right now, or-"

She got one arm free and punched him in the face. He let it through and reeled back. She made a grab for the phone and he released it. Then she ran.

Perfect.

He got to his feet, peered around the campervan and drew his Desert Eagle. Two riot vans had taken up position in front of the Dassault, blocking take-off, two circling closer, and he cursed. If they continued to block the jet, Julie wouldn't make her escape and would have no time to access X, the stub wouldn't backchannel through and the whole thing would be for nothing.

He squeezed off six fast shots at the blocking trucks,

putting three into one ballistic shield, two into another, spidering the bulletproof glass, until he was met by an answering hail of bullets. Good enough.

Rolling back around the campervan, he hoisted the Fireblade, straddled it as the two remaining vans bore down, spun a hot donut then roared back toward the gap in the fence, barely threading the needle between the security trucks.

In seconds he reached fifty miles an hour through the gap as bullets ruffed the dry grass, slapping his visor back down.

"Are they following?"

"Three," Hellion confirmed as he accelerated onto the circling exit road. "Yes, now four. They are leaving the jet free. Did you want-"

"The stub's in. Pray that she dials in. B4cksl4cker, are you on it?"

"I am ready," came his deep Armenian bass.

Wren sped back toward the expressway, trailing a four-strong cavalry of airport riot vans, sirens blaring, hoping it was enough.

10

MEDIAN

"I'll need a new exfiltration plan," Wren said, accelerating the Fireblade on I-264 heading west.

"This is operational detail, no?" Hellion asked.

Wren laughed, flew down the narrow alley between two semi-trailers, bare inches clearance on either side. "I'm a little busy to look at a map right now."

"Yes, you are game piece, aren't you? Frustrating game piece that changes plan without warning. I will prepare your exfil, Christopher. For now here is result of new plan. Airport security has notified Homeland Security. In last minute Severe Warning, this is Red Alert color code, went out to all forces, all security, all police, FBI offices in Kentucky. "

Wren gulped, passed the exit for the Churchill Downs racecourse, one-hundred and climbing. "They're sparing no expense."

Keys flew in the background. "This is only beginning. Army, Air Force, Navy too have been called. They have new battle plan to target you, and we did not prepare for this. I have Foundation fringe nearby, but they can do nothing against these thousands."

Wren felt giddy and light-headed. Almost getting shot

would do that to you. Speeding at one-twenty probably played a role too, skipping traffic like a bouncing cluster bomb.

"Enemy of the People."

"Very much so."

He was too breathless to laugh. More exits rushed by. Off to the right blue lights flashed, a convoy of vehicles inbound. Wren worked his mental map. Five miles on he'd hit the Ohio River, no bridges within miles, then empty Indiana. No major urban centers for a hundred miles. They'd have road blocks up already.

"They are tracking you. Satellites are moving, Christopher. This chase is now everywhere, on every news channel."

"You have a way out?"

"I will take the please and thank you later," Hellion said, accompanied by a storm of clattering keys. "I see exits ahead are blocked. Now you must jump the median."

Wren scanned right to the concrete divider separating the lanes. Four feet high, no way he could get the Fireblade's four hundred pounds and change over that without some anti-gravity assist. Run right at it, the bike would stop dead on impact and he'd be catapulted two hundred yards, maybe clear all the lanes, hit a tree on the other side and spread pieces of Christopher Wren like pancake batter across the land.

"You have my skyhook?" he asked, letting a little giddiness through.

"Better than skyhook, which is fictional," Hellion said flatly. "Ahead five hundred yards, stop, take left lane, come back against the flow rapidly."

Wren laughed madly. Come back against the flow, and what, smash himself into the divider in a different direction? "Is is semi-permeable?"

"Operational detail," Hellion sniped. "Left lane now. Ahead is blockade, one mile. No, this is not low enough…"

"What?"

"I am speaking with B4cksl4cker. Left lane, Christopher! Yes, this is-"

"Lamborghini," came B4cksl4cker's voice. "Right side."

"Yes," Hellion answered. "Left lane, Christopher!"

Wren swung over and hit the brakes, skidded like crazy to clank broadside against the median facing contraflow to traffic. Cars honked and passed, though already they were slowing and backing up as the blockade ahead took shape.

"Fast, now," Hellion called.

Wren hit the gas. Blue lights flashed both ahead and behind now, a massive dragnet closing in. He raced along beside the median, vehicles passing with wide faces staring out at him, too stunned to hit the horn.

"Middle lane, Christopher! This will be rapid, back wheel, please."

He almost asked what she had planned but then didn't need to. In the middle lane came a hornet-yellow Lamborghini Gallardo Spyder, front fender barely five inches off the ground, the bonnet sloping up shallow to a low-slung roof.

A moving ramp.

It was crazy, but there was no time to debate. He chicaned hard left around an oncoming Chrysler to get the angle, revved the Fireblade up to sixty then cut a diagonal across the oncoming path of the Lamborghini, pulling the front wheel up just as the guy driving saw what was coming and hit his brakes.

Wren's sixty miles per hour plus the guy's sixty combined together, like hitting a stacked ramp at one twenty. Any higher wheelbase and his chassis would just plow into the supercar's hood like a buzz saw.

Instead he hit rear wheel first, punching the car down to the blacktop and thrusting the bike up and over like a bullet up a greased slip-and-slide. Wren flew. His headset crackled. A kid in a Ford in the left lane stared as Wren whipped by like Santa in his sleigh. The flashing lights of the riot vans hung off to the left with crystal perfection, then he crossed the median with inches to spare and looked to the eastbound lane where he was about to smash into a huge gray Chevy Silverado.

He yanked the wheel left, it made no difference at all, then he hit the huge pickup broadside, leaning in with all his weight to avoid a rebound that would splatter him across the blacktop. The Silverado didn't budge, two tons of ground-hugging inertia meeting four hundred pounds in the air; instead the Fireblade's front fender crumpled then bounced hard and down. The front wheel hit first, Wren barely straightening it in time, the rear came down and Wren was already riding the gas, hoping to use the tire's grip to muscle through the inevitable topple that was coming.

It wasn't enough though. The bike toppled left, overbalanced from the bounce and veering toward an imminent wipeout. Nothing left but to throw caution to the wind. Wren flung both arms toward the Silverado as the bike went down, managed a little kick with his right leg, then he was in the air absent any vehicle, fingers probing toward a window that was mercifully open.

His right arm shot through and punched the driver in the chest, the window shelf stabbed into his armpit as he fell, his left hand clasped the roof rack, then he dropped into a hard hang as the Silverado jittered and slowed and the bike spun out into a chaotic crash.

The Silverado braked, and ten seconds later it was at a dead stop in the left lane with traffic racing by to the right, the bike smoking a hundred yards back. Wren's feet finally found the rocker bars and he leaned into the window. The driver was a lean-looking guy in his thirties, with a complicated goatee and rakish black hair; in the passenger seat was a guy dressed in a some kind of blue jumpsuit, with a big white star on his chest. In back he thought he saw a shield with red, white and blue circular bars.

Even Wren knew who this guy was supposed to be. He felt like tipping his hat, though he wasn't wearing one. Instead he just flipped his visor, looked the driver in the eyes.

"Apologies, sir. You know me?"

Both guys stared, jaws falling slack. White star nodded slowly.

"I'm thinking you're good guys, from the way you're dressed. Now I need this truck to save the country. What do you say?"

Long shot. The guy with the goatee smacked his lips, then nodded. Managed a hasty "Yeah," and slid over to the side, basically onto the other guy's lap. Not what Wren had expected, but it would work. He opened the door, hauled himself in, fired up the big V6 engine and revved into the open lane ahead.

11

VANTASY CON

"**B**alletic," came Hellion's voice in his ear. "You could dance at the Bolshoi."

"Exfil," Wren said.

"Dead ahead, first exit. We are headed to the Exposition Center to launder you. There are too many eyes to run this any other way."

Wren grunted, took the truck past the airport riot vans off to the left, then shrugged off his helmet. No need for it anymore, if everyone knew who he was, and the confinement was keying into his vertigo. At once fresh air rushed in. The helmet fell to the right, into the lap of the guy with the goatee.

He sat there clutching it, staring at Wren. "Are you really him?" he asked.

"Are you?" Wren countered, then refocused on Hellion. "What's happening at the Exposition Center? Are there enough people to launder me?"

"This will be the washing of your life," Hellion answered in his earpiece, her voice smaller now outside the echoing confines of the helmet. "Today is middle day of three-day convention of comic book characters." She paused a moment. "I think your new friends know this."

Wren blinked. Looked at the guys. Superheroes. He knew about them from his kids, mostly, and that forced a pang in his chest.

"You're going to the comic book convention?" he asked.

"Uh, yes," said Goatee Guy. "Vantasy Con."

"How many people?"

"Convention center holds up to a hundred thousand," Hellion answered. "I am checking. Ticket sales show many refunds, however. People are not wanting to attend in these times. Perhaps half of that."

Wren looked at the guys with fresh eyes. Had to admire their dedication, in the wake of their President self-combusting, New York coming under terror attack and X pumping up a militia army across the nation. "Why are you attending a comic book convention, now?"

Goatee Guy's eyes bugged, then he raised his hand.

"Speak," Wren said. "You don't need to ask permission."

"What else should we do?" the guy said. "Stay at home and cower in fear?"

Wren could roll with that.

"Those wackos get to believe in their crazy, dangerous nonsense. Why don't we get to believe in ours? At least it's a positive message. The good guys win. And they're actually good."

Another great point.

"More road blocks ahead," Hellion said. "You will not make it to the Exposition Center direct. Take your next left, I will direct you."

"Roger that," Wren said.

"Are you talking to her now?" White Star guy asked. Looking awed. "Your hacker?"

Wren glanced sideways. A grown man wearing dress-up pajamas. Except that wasn't fair to say. He was no different really from Wren and his Foundation with the coins. Systems

63

of values and stories of heroes to back them up, and what was Wren if not a positive role model?

"Her name is Hellion," he growled. "She's pissed at me."

Goatee Guy stared. "Because you wrecked that bike?"

Wren laughed. "That was her idea. No. I make her life difficult, I think's the reason. This time I made a call she didn't like."

"Not just one call, Christopher," Hellion said in his ear.

The guy's eyes rounded. Looked at White Star. "Like we did in Civil War?"

That didn't mean anything to Wren. Still, he nodded seriously. "Sure, like that."

"I am glad you are having nice, fun conversation, Christopher," Hellion said. "Exit now."

He swung over three lanes and took the exit, a sharp centrifugal circle that tipped Goatee Guy awkwardly against Wren's shoulder. He straightened onto a flush drive north, spotting the red rollercoaster rails of Kentucky Kingdom ahead.

"Can I, uh-" White Star began.

"What?"

"Get a selfie?"

Wren laughed. "Not a chance."

"Right here," Hellion shouted. Police had cut off the road ahead, across an intersection. He swung through the red light and raced east, an idea forming in his head.

He looked at Goatee Guy. One of his kid's favorite characters. The suit, the swagger, the fact he could fly. "Tell me you have the helmet?"

The guy blinked. "I uh, do?"

"Can I borrow it?"

"Um, sure."

Five minutes on, the parking lot of the Kentucky Exposition Center was packed. No police yet, just a huge inbound crowd of fans wearing costumes. Wren pulled the truck as close as he could get to the glass doors beneath a three-story green architectural shard that fronted the building.

VANTASY CON banners festooned the structure's white metal poles. There were two huge robot sculptures either side of the entrance holding giant cannon-like weapons. Wren ducked into the back, grabbed the costume helmet. Gold-sprayed faceplate with red plastic backing. He pulled it down over his head.

Far worse visibility than the bike helmet.

"It suits you!" said White Star, one thumb up.

"The eyes light up," Goatee Guy said, "if you-"

"I owe you guys," Wren interrupted, and emerged straight out into the crowd. He bulled through the ranks of fans until he reached the glass doors, which swung open before him, unveiling a tall and light-filled lobby packed with people in various stages of costumed undress.

He strode into their midst. Here was a half-naked man with ash-gray skin interspersed by black metal plates that seemed to be bonded to his body, arrayed with tubes that seemed to feed into his neck, chest, head. There was a woman with a dizzying ravine of cleavage, in a white latex outfit with a long flowing cape. Wren's head spun as he ran, past a phalanx of figures all in white armor and complex helmets, past a guy looming seven feet tall dressed like a tree, past a naked woman covered in spotted blue body paint wearing a bright red wig. Wren recognized few and ignored them all, pacing toward a curtained access point.

"Nice helmet," someone said as he passed. "You forget your suit?"

Wren reached the curtain, where a bored-looking guy manned a rope line.

"Permit?" he asked

"In my other pants," Wren answered and brushed by.

Through the curtain an immense space opened out below, sectioned into hundreds of booths jammed with colorful posters, cosplayers, life-size figurines, screening rooms. Wren scanned the chaos and picked out what he was looking for.

Thirty seconds later he was there, ten long selfie lines leading up to ten famous actors standing against space-battle backdrops. $100 a selfie. Wren joined one line and bypassed it to the front, where a rack of sackcloth-looking robes hung in various sizes, overseen by a sizing clerk.

"Sir, you can't-"

"On credit will be fine," Wren said, and plucked one of the robes. By the wall he dropped the helmet and pulled on the robe, swung the hood over his head and risked a look back.

Police were entering the hall at the far end.

He pushed open a fire door.

"I have a car pulling up on the east side, in the underground lot," Hellion said in his ear.

"Anything on the X app yet?" Wren clattered down a concrete stairwell, emerging onto parking sub-level B.

"We are in the app, but it is very limited, Christopher," Hellion said. "We have only Julie Graves' level of access, one-hundred point, but working on more. There is no link to X here, but there are lists, a triangle of some kind, and most important there is all-points 'ALERT' button, signals call X-apoc to rally." Keys flew. "We are digging for more, but it seems Julie Graves pressed this ALERT. Now X-apoc are coming, in addition government forces. It seems X has your location via crowd-source, someone in Vantasy Con saw you in main hall. Now I have them incoming from all over Louisville. They saw you in main hall. There is-"

Abruptly, a heavily muscled man stepped out in front of Wren. He had a bare chest with a shiny six-pack and beefy arms, was dressed in a red cape with a winged helmet, a large heavy-looking battle hammer swinging at his hip. In contrast to that seeming strength, the guy's face looked shiftless and scared, though there was a gun in his hand, rising already.

"Walk in the fire, Christopher Wren," he said.

Wren stepped off-line with all the muscle memory of two decades of special-ops training, evading the first shot even as he drew his weapon and fired. The bullet took the guy in the thigh, punched his leg out and spun him to the ground with a wild cry.

Wren took just a second to re-center himself, then ducked in next to the fallen guy, scooped up his gun and quickly patted him down. The man's impressive muscles were actually a bodysuit, and the hammer seemed to be made of polystyrene.

"Where's your phone?" Wren asked.

The guy shouted some Apex nonsense and tried to put a thumb in Wren's eye. Wren caught it easily, clamped the guy's wrist and twisted his thumb, breaking the joint with a methodical crunch. The guy wailed.

"We do not have time for this," Hellion said.

"Where's your phone?" Wren repeated, not letting go of the guy's wrecked thumb. "Tell me now or I'll show you what Hell on Earth really feels like."

"Glove box" the guy managed, shuddering with the pain. "I, I-"

"You're an idiot," Wren said, and stood. "Put pressure on your thigh, you might be fine. Now, keys."

The guy held up his hammer, patted the head to open a hidden compartment.

"We do not need this phone," Hellion said. "It is unnec-"

"You said I wouldn't need a stub for the second hack," Wren interrupted, retrieving a set of keys from the hidden compartment in the fake hammer. "And every app access gets us more data, yes?"

"Yes, but-"

"Car," Wren said, gave the guy a shake until he pointed at a nearby BMW i4 silver sedan, with neon blue trim

Hellion was still talking but Wren ignored the rest, strode to the BMW. He slotted the key in, popped the door, opened the glove box and retrieved a phone.

The screen was live, showing red that flashed with the single word ALERT in yellow block capitals, followed by CHRISTOPHER WREN SIGHTING, LOUISVILLE EXPOSITION CENTER, 100 POINTS ASSEMBLE, 1 MILLION DEAD

There was a map underneath that, with two pins dropped showing Wren's previous and current locations.

"Straightforward," he said. "Can you remote pair with this?"

"Attempting. There are more X-apoc coming, Christopher, you have to-"

"You're sending me a car?" Wren asked, slotting into the BMW.

"Yes, twenty seconds out, Foundation fringe member, but now I am thinking-"

"I'm taking this one."

The engine purred to silky life at the touch of a button. Wren hit the gas and peeled out, past the X-apoc guy shouting and red-faced on the raw concrete.

Within a minute he was out of the parking lot and headed north. The streets were alive with incoming police cars. At ten minutes he barely squeezed through an emerging dragnet of road blocks a mile out from the Exposition Center. In twenty he was across the Ohio River and speeding into Indiana on I-65, as all kinds of chaos erupted in his wake.

12

CHAOS

"Christopher, you must see this," said Hellion as Wren sped out of the suburbs and into broad white expanses of snow-covered Indiana fields. "I am sending feeds to your phone."

Wren balanced his cell on the dash. Video was already playing, looked like an array of bootleg livestreams re-broadcast on cable news, showing multiple perspectives of a crowd massing in front of the Exposition Center. Not cosplayers or police, though both were amongst the crowd, enormously outnumbered. These were men and women of all ages wearing black t-shirts, ball caps and jackets, waving homemade black banners and flags, all emblazoned with the white X symbol.

A pit opened up in Wren's stomach.

"Do not go back, Christopher," Hellion said, jumping straight to his first thought. "You cannot do anything."

He pulled over onto the shoulder lane without saying a word, hit his hazards then picked up the phone and held it close, making a quick count of all the black-clad X followers he could see on screen.

Hundreds already, come right out of the woodwork.

Ready to assemble in minutes. Looked like more pouring in every second, swelling the crowd like an oil stain. His mouth went dry as the world tunneled down, and he was back in D.C., trapped beneath the stampeding mob.

"How many are coming, Hellion?"

Keys danced a staccato storm through his earpiece. On the screen the mob steadily drained into the Exposition Center, shoving cosplayers roughly out of their way. Cops were gathered at the edges now, looking uncertain about what they should do. They weren't trained to take on an army. The first few chants were already breaking out, thickening fast into a torrent.

"Fear is a portal! Pain is a doorway!"

"I count two hundred and twenty outside the building," Hellion came back. "Seventy inside the lobby, none within the center itself yet, but Christopher, incoming numbers are very high. There are hundreds more. I am checking traffic flows, comparing with standard data through intersections. There could be thousands. They are coming in from surrounding suburbs. X is mobilizing. The ALERT called and they have come."

Wren felt sick. 42%, they'd told him. People who really believed X was telling the truth: that they were being kept as slaves; that Christopher Wren was their enemy; that burning alive was the only way to be free. If you truly believed all that, what wouldn't you do to save your country?

The crowd pulsated into the Exposition Center like a black octopus burrowing after prey. Wren didn't see weapons, but anything could be a weapon in the heat of the moment. Fire extinguishers, rope-line barrier posts, table legs.

The world was flipping on its axis. Killing Lou on network television was bad, but it was nothing next to this. These people weren't like the ones he'd calmed in LA, they wouldn't settle down if he just kneeled down in front of them.

These people were full-on extremist terrorists who believed they were freedom fighters waging a righteous war.

"Can you stop any of this through the app?"

"Not yet," Hellion answered. "We are working. Two phones is good, we have some layer of access, but not enough."

Wren grunted, started chasing more extreme responses through his head.

"Christopher," Hellion cautioned.

"Get me Sally Rogers," he said sharply, then swiped the video aside and brought up the Foundation darknet, plugging straight into the Megaphone app. It had new tiers he could select to send to, including the millions of new Foundation fringe members. He started typing then paused.

"How many Foundation fringe in the Expo Center vicinity, Hellion?"

Keys flew, the answer came back in seconds. "Seventy-three."

Not enough to turn the tide. Just enough to be made an example of.

He typed fast, thumbs flying over the screen.

IF IN LOUISVILLE EXPOSITION CENTER, DO NOT TRY TO FIGHT. THIS IS A BATTLE WE CANNOT WIN. INSTEAD LEAD THE EVACUATION RIGHT NOW. TAKE EVERYONE WITH YOU THAT YOU CAN. FLEE THE AREA BEYOND THE POLICE CORDONS. REPEAT, DO NOT FIGHT.

He hit send and started typing a follow-up.

X IS MOBILIZING. EXPECT MORE OUTBREAKS LIKE LOUISVILLE. YOUR JOB IS TO DE-ESCALATE. ANY WIN IN PITCHED BATTLE WILL ONLY DRIVE THEM HOTTER AND FASTER. PROPERTY DAMAGE IS ACCEPTABLE. DO NOT ENGAGE UNLESS LIVES ARE AT RISK. DO NOT FIGHT FOR MY NAME.

TRUST THAT I AM TAKING ACTION. NOW STAY SAFE.

He tapped send. Every fiber of his being screamed at him to turn the BMW around and head back to the fight, but he couldn't. His presence had ignited it. His return would only catalyze it faster.

Maybe an Apex trap. If so, he'd walked right into it.

Fresh footage on his phone showed the situation had already devolved. News anchors watched dumbstruck at their desks as various feeds showed the mob massing and thrusting in waves, assaulting the police as they attempted to set up containment barriers, punching dazed cosplayers as they tried to escape, ripping off their 3D-printed tiaras and vacuum-pressed plastic battle armor and stamping them underfoot.

Inside the Exposition Center black-clad figures were swarming the internal convention space, driving the last few comic fans before them and smashing tables of superhero merchandise, hacking foam-core robot statues, toppling televisions and graffiti-spraying their giant black Xs on walls and floors. Plastic figures shattered, posters were torn down, booths were wrenched apart and their support poles converted to weapons.

"Walk in the fire!" they shouted, the chant rising in a single voice, occasionally morphing to other rallying cries.

"Break the chains!"

"Free the slaves!"

It was outright insurrection, and he hadn't expected it so soon.

"I have Sally Rogers," Hellion said. "Our end is encrypted, her end may not be. Be careful what you lead her to say."

Wren took a breath. "Put her on."

The line clicked.

"Boss," Rogers said, and it was all there in her voice. The same growing fear he was feeling.

"Rogers, I know Humphreys is still locked up; have you got any pull with the new Director?"

A moment passed. "I can't really confirm that. It's something I can try. What message have you got?"

"Moderation. This is no ordinary riot. Meet these people with force, and it's like pouring gasoline on a fire. It'll only draw more out."

A second passed. "I don't know what I can do about that. I'm on the outs here."

"Because of me," Wren said, mind racing fast. "One second." He tapped the earpiece, switching the line.

"Hellion, get me Teddy."

"He is online with me, Christopher. He is listening."

"Teddy, I need to give them one of the training camps. Something for Rogers to trade."

A long moment drew out. For a second Wren thought Teddy was going to say no, but when his deep bass voice joined the call, it was with a single word.

"Iowa."

Where Wren had just been. He leaped on it. "Is anyone there still? Does it link to anything?"

"Everyone left when you did. It's clean."

"Thank you. Hellion, get me the coordinates."

"Ready."

Wren clicked back over to Rogers. "I've got one of our training camps for you. Hand it over to keep yourself in the game. Iowa. Hellion's sending you the details."

"Are you sure?"

"We need you on the inside, Rogers, not the out. Let them burn down an empty farm. Better that than more city centers."

"OK. Thanks. I can use this. I'll try."

"Good luck."

Inside the Exposition Center someone broke out the gasoline, started splashing it liberally around then cast a match. The flames spread in seconds, racing through the wreckage of banners, posters and shredded costumes on the floor like a wildfire in autumn brush.

Soon the whole hall was on fire.

"Burn the Wren!" the mob shouted as they swarmed deeper into the huge complex, lighting more fires in their wake.

Wren flicked between feeds. Every news channels was covering the spreading chaos. Reporters talked breathlessly to camera from outside, jostled by black-clad X-apoc members, trying to describe a phenomenon they couldn't begin to understand: a moment X had been waiting for, when Christopher Wren finally got involved.

A trigger for the country.

Firefighters tried to push their way up to a line of X stalwarts and were violently rebuffed. The police kept trying, and were beaten back with makeshift weapons. Helicopter-mounted cameras showed blue light brigades streaming in along every major city artery, but right there alongside them came more black-flagged X forces.

Some didn't even make it to the Exposition Center. Four blocks south a police car was struck by a panel van, overturned and set alight, left to burn at the intersection while a crowd of X followers filmed it. A female police officer crawled out, one leg aflame, and they threw bricks and laughed. Cosplayers fled through the streets, assorted manga and video-game characters half out of costume, streaming blood and dark with soot, bouncing between police shields and the advancing X front line.

It was like the D.C. chaos all over again, only worse.

The feed cut to exclusive footage of a man Wren

recognized, the fake muscle cosplayer from the underground parking lot, lying on an ambulance gurney.

"He shot me! It was Christopher Wren, He did it for nothing. I didn't get out of his way fast enough, and he shot me!"

People wailed in the background. The feed flipped to a female reporter holding a microphone out to a large man in tactical black combat gear, a ski mask pulled over his face revealing only white teeth and deep brown eyes.

"Wherever he goes," he shouted, "whatever he does, this is what is going to happen! Do you see this, Christopher Wren? We're not going to take your lies anymore!"

Voices around him hollered their new catchphrase, "Burn the Wren!"

"And you," the big guy shouted, snatching the microphone away and turning on the reporter. "You're no better than that bitch on the couch!"

He drew a gun from his shoulder holster, pointed it at the reporter and pulled the trigger.

13

TRACY

W|ren beat the phone against the wheel.

"This will not help, Christopher," came Hellion's voice in his ear, so he plucked out the earpiece and left it rocking on the dash.

Opened the door, stepped out into dirty snow as cars raced by to his left. Looking south, the pall of smoke from the Exposition Center blackened the pale winter sky like a plume of squid ink.

Wren shook with rage and frustration. The earpiece squawked in the cab and he strode away, off the road trying to get control of himself.

He'd known it. He'd said it to Maggie. The moment he surfaced, the Apex was going to be ready. Always playing his part and driving the trap tighter. There was nothing he wanted more than to race back, find that man who'd shot the reporter and beat him to a pulp on live television. Let that be the message, let everyone see the vengeance of their precious 'Wren'.

But it would only play into the narrative. Only heap on fuel for the fire, convert more X saps and turn them out to fight a war against themselves, preaching their own deaths and suffering as the only way to be free.

He kicked the snow and stamped through the field trying to figure out the angle forward, but it was hard to think for memories of the last time he'd been here. A thousand people had burned in the fake town, and they'd all once been decent, honest, hopeful people, all looking to belong to something real.

The Apex had taken that desire and broken its spine, then bent it squealing back upon itself like some spiritual Moebius strip.

There had to be a better way to fight, but Wren couldn't grasp it. He had his expanding Foundation, and the Apex had his X-apoc, but what good would it do America for the two to clash, driving the country deeper into the inescapable pit of civil war?

"Are you OK?"

A voice came from the roadside. Wren turned, seeing red. Not an X-apoc, though, at least no wearing their gear. A woman, belly ballooning with what had to be triplets. Dark braids, mom jeans, a mauve cardigan pulled tight against the cold. Just a concerned citizen pulling over to check on him.

"I'm fine," answered. "Just needed some air."

"Did you escape the Exposition Center? Do you want me to call somebody?"

Wren almost laughed. Started back toward the road. "I'm fine."

"You don't look fine," she said, before he could answer. "But I thought it was you."

Wren grunted. So she recognized him. After D.C., he figured that was inevitable. "I'm not who you think I am."

Now she laughed. "That's bullshit. Listen, you can't pay any mind to what they're saying on the radio. All this X nonsense, anyone with half a brain can see it's made up. You can't take the bait."

He neared the roadway, thinking it was hard to call the deaths of innocent civilians bait. No need to say that, though. "Get away from the cities," he said, striding toward his BMW. "This thing's going to blow it all up."

"I'll do no such thing," the woman answered fast. "That's exactly what they want. Make us terrified, that's what terrorists do, right? But we don't negotiate with terrorists, do we?" She didn't give him any gap to answer. "I'll do my job, I'm a nurse, just like you will, and it looks like it's your job to sort this out." She paused a second, peering at him. "It is your father who's doing this, right?"

Wren almost laughed a second time, rubbed his eyes, drew up to the shoulder where she was standing by a Nissan Note just ahead of his BMW, scratches down the side, looked like someone had keyed her paintwork. For a moment he thought he recognized her, but no. She was just some woman who'd seen him on the news.

"Thank you for your concern, ma'am, but I'm all right now."

She waved a hand. "Define all right. Who amongst us is, these days, am I right? Talk about that man who burned himself rather than be President?" She made a face. "What kind of idiot does that?"

"He was my brother."

"I think you're better off," she countered easily. "I'll tell you, I divorced my whole family when I was seventeen. Psychos, the lot of them." Her hands spread across her belly. "I'm going to do better for these."

Wren didn't know what to say. Felt like he'd somehow intruded upon a personal moment for her. "Ma'am," he said and reached for the BMW's door.

"Don't ma'am me, I'm half your age. I heard you have kids as well. Two, isn't it?"

Wren paused, one hand on the handle. Let out a pent-up breath. "Yes."

"How are they holding up? They can't like having you away all the time."

He took another breath. Had no idea why he was even talking to this woman. "They don't want to see me. Or their mother doesn't."

Her eyes narrowed suspiciously. "Why, you screwed the help?"

This time he did laugh. "I screwed something up, you're right there. Right now she's in witness protection, took out a restraining order against me, and that's after she dumped me in a black site for three months."

The woman nodded knowingly. "Exes."

He felt too drained to laugh anymore.

"So sort this for your kids. Eyes on the prize, Mr. Wren. No more stamping around fields shouting at the heavens."

"I wasn't-"

"Get that man," the woman said, and wagged a finger. "Sort it out. I'm due by Christmas. I'd like all this tidied up by then so we can have a proper turkey dinner."

He let out a breath. About all he could manage in the moment.

"What else are my tax dollars going for, if you're not going to pull your weight?" she insisted.

He thought about telling her he wasn't in the employ of the CIA anymore, but there was no use in that. "Yes, ma'am," he said instead.

"Call me Tracy. Now get in your fancy car and get out of here before some of those crazies catch us up."

He did as he was told.

14

ALERT

Wren got back in the BMW i4, slotted the earpiece in and pulled out into traffic.

"Hellion," he said, "sorry about that."

No answer came.

Fair enough. Everybody needed time.

"B4cksl4cker, have you got anything more from the app?"

A long moment passed, accelerating up to seventy with nowhere to go. The dirty smoke of the Exposition Center spread across the sky, filling his rearview mirror.

"Hellion has left convoy," B4cksl4cker said. "She is shouting in snow. Much like yourself."

"Sounds about right. We're too alike."

"She does not like game piece which does not listen to commands."

Wren snorted. "You'd think she was used to me by now."

"Normally, yes. But we are here, Christopher. In your country. This is not a game, and when you cut her off…"

"I know. Too human. I'll make it up to her."

"Yes, you will."

Wren took a breath, drawing a line under that subject and

moving on to what mattered most. "Tell me you own the X app?"

"Partly," B4cksl4cker said. "Stub worked, and we have access to pieces of X app, but not total. This is-"

"Is crybaby back from his field?" Hellion interrupted. She sounded angrier than usual, so Wren forewent some witty comment about her being out crying in her own field.

"I'm back, Hellion. Ready and willing to be directed. Give me a sit-rep on the app."

"Yes, I will," Hellion said, all furiously focused business. "Infant X app has two key functions we see so far, from two hacked phones. First is for ALERT, in case of Christopher Wren appearance, activating all members within range. We believe this button was first triggered by Julie Graves at Louisville Airport, and sent a call to every X member within fifty miles." She paused a second. "Further sightings came at Vantasy Con as you arrived. This notified muscle fool in parking lot. Now we are seeing ongoing effect. Flash mob."

'Flash mob' was putting it mildly. Everybody in Louisville was seeing the effect up-close and personal, as the X-apoc poured in and fomented chaos. "This is the first time anyone triggered the ALERT button?"

"Yes. Our theories were correct. Waiting for trigger."

Wren cursed. Waiting for him.

"Can you jam it? Prevent future flash mobs from gathering?"

"No. Control of this function is much deeper level of access. More levels are there, but we cannot reach them. It looks like coin layers of Foundation, deeper privilege handed down based on achievement."

Wren cursed. "Achievement being how many people they've killed?"

"Second function of this app is list," Hellion went on, ignoring him. "This is Kill List, we believe, with names, addresses, points available per kill. You will be happy to see who is top of this list."

"Is it me?"

"Da, it is you, Christopher."

Wren shuffled his phone up onto the dash. "Can you give me access?"

"Nyet, but I can mirror screen. Pull over and I will show you."

He pulled over, back by the side of another snowy field. His phone screen spasmed once then flipped to a black background with the white X brand at the top, beneath which ran a long table separated into three columns of data. In the first row was the name he expected.

CHRISTOPHER WREN – THE UNGRATEFUL SON – 1,000,000 POINTS

After that every line had been redacted with strike-through keys.

"Not much of a kill list if you can't see the names, is it?" Wren asked.

"Scroll further, Christopher," Hellion said, so he did. The table became a blur, hundreds of rows passing per second, until the table dead-ended with three legible lines. The lowest two had been struck through in red, leaving the details beneath clear.

LOU-ANN REISNER – TUESDAYS WITH LOU & MORRIE – 1,000 POINTS

Wren grunted. "Lou-Ann's dead."

"Yes, this is personalized list for Julie Graves."

"So she's gotta kill, what, thousands of people before she reaches me?"

"I do not think so, Christopher. More likely, this is marketplace for killings. She has selected her next target from many choices. You see second line?"

Wren looked, the line above LOU-ANN REISNER was plain white text on the black background.

OLATUNDE OWAYO – KENTUCKY STATE CONGRESSMAN – 10,000 POINTS

"She's climbing fast," Wren said. "Each kill is a factor of ten."

"Two more kills and she will be coming for you, Christopher."

"If the metric holds." He took a breath. "Have you got a better handle on how many people are using the app this way?"

"No hard figures yet. Guess of thousands remains."

Wren squeezed the wheel. When it came to outright murder, thousands was plenty. The best and most dedicated only. The rest would simply receive ALERT and flood to support them.

In a mob, murder was so much easier. He thought back to the ALERT on the fake muscle guy's phone.

"They were offered a hundred points for answering the flash mob call at the Exposition Center."

"This appears correct, Christopher. But we have only two phones' app access. If we had more access points, perhaps we can build bigger picture, have stronger chance of breaking this app encryption."

Wren considered. "What if you had access to more? Could you end-run it then?"

"Possibly. Deeper access. Better signal on X location, possibly."

Wren grunted. Location was everything. Unveiling X him or herself as the charlatan they were was the prime target. Get them on video, unwilling to burn for the cause, and the heat would drop right out of the X-apoc.

"So tell me you have something on X's location now. Anything."

A silence followed. Not even any keys clattering. "Nyet, Christopher. Nothing."

It wasn't what he wanted to hear.

"How many more apps to get better access?"

"We do not know. Five? Ten? More is better. We will see more versions of Kill List, more personal codes for ALERT designation. We can perhaps track Internet signals more effectively, begin to focus on originating location."

The next step came easily.

The X-apoc masses had already outed themselves in the hundreds at the expo center. Thinking there was safety in numbers. But these weren't soldiers with some secure base to return to, locked safely behind manned walls.

These were civilians. They had to go home.

Weak links in the wall of flame.

Wren keyed the engine back on. "Start with the guy who shot the reporter. I want to know where he is right now. Work backwards through everyone you can pick out of the crowd, the worst offenders, the highest points value. Make us a kill list of our own."

15

KILL LIST

Two hours later, Wren waited.

Sitting in a shotgun home in Smoketown, West Louisville, pulled up to the larch-veneer kitchen island and looking straight through the den window. Out the dust-smeared front glass lay parking lots for a new-build mega-church, looked like a sports center. That new, sharp red brick look that said 'mass-produced' and 'cheap', with a little yellow canvas cladding to smarten things up.

Saving the people's souls, one broken mind at a time.

"He is incoming, Christopher," Hellion said.

Wren looked around the kitchen. He'd already scoped out the house, after an hour spent losing himself in the Louisville traffic system and laundering his vehicle twice: once at a roadside diner back in Indiana; once in the heaving chaos of a mall parking lot ten blocks south of the Exposition Center.

The streets had been full of X-apoc rioters feeding out from the fires of Vantasy Con, though for most of them the flames were dwindling by then. They'd come for a big show and the lynching of Christopher Wren, and mostly arrived late to the party. With police presence coming in slow but steady, the Exposition Center already on fire and Wren himself gone, their passion had stalled out.

Three dead, so far. The female reporter, shot in the belly, hadn't made it. Two cosplayers lost in the building's lobby, maybe smoke inhalation, maybe stampede injuries, pulled out while the core fires still raged. Plenty of cops, firefighters and cosplayers injured in the fighting.

Now the flames burned cold in Wren's chest.

The guy's name was Diego Helmuz. Second generation Kentuckian, with roots up from Cuba on one side, Canada on the other. Two heritages mixed in the middle, shaken, stirred, and left to mature like nitroglycerine sweating out of old TNT.

There was nothing much to find in his house. A couple of half-finished homemade X flags draped over a basement workbench, graffiti cans nearby, the stenciling bad, like these were his first attempts. The outline where he'd cut a white 'X' out of a stretch of curtain liner, needles and thread around where he must have stitched it onto his cap.

No sign of a partner, kids. Gun safe hanging open. Looked like he'd been caught in the midst of his daytime hobby, doing macramé for points in the X app, no apparent job, when the ALERT had gone out. Put down his half-made flag, popped the safe, loaded up. There were shells spilled on the floor for a shotgun, moving too fast and excited.

Upstairs clothes were scattered on the bed across from a half-length mirror. Diego had tried a few on, it looked, before heading out to 'war'. A little stolen valor here, a little cosplay there and you had yourself a real X-apoc warrior.

Wren had entered by the back door, an easy slip with a credit card, expecting to lay in wait then kill the guy. Now, sitting at the counter, he didn't feel so sure. Kill this guy, and was he going to kill all the others too? Rifling through the mail, heaped by a fruit bowl occupied by three withered peaches, he found a full house of PAST DUE letters.

Like Julie Graves, Diego Helmuz was a soft target. Exactly the Apex's usual recruiting ground. Lost souls, part of nothing and filled with anger about that. Looking around themselves and seeing the world moving on with no real way to belong. If convincing these men and women to stop their mad race to death was going to begin anywhere, shouldn't it begin right here?

On the other hand, the guy had made himself into a murderer.

The backfiring engine on Diego's old beater came chugging up the street. Loud because he liked it that way, probably. Annoying the neighbors was one way to play a role in their lives. To matter through fear.

Wren watched through the front window as the truck pulled up, a brown GMC Sierra with go-faster beige stripes, spattered by bird scat. Wren eased off the stool, strode through the den like a mirror of Diego as he approached the door.

Really he was doing the police a favor. It would take them three days or more to analyze their mountains of footage and hunt this guy down. Come at him in the night, no-knock warrant, burst in the door with a SWAT squad and guns up yelling, "Police!"

No real warning, but maybe enough for a guy like Diego Helmuz, who'd done one short stint in Afghanistan, a man who'd fought for his country once and believed he was fighting for it again now. He'd sleep little and armed. Would get off a few shots, probably, before they overwhelmed him or he shot himself in the head.

Key in the lock, turning, and Wren positioned himself smoothly and silently in the blind spot behind the swing of the door. When it opened and the big guy came through, maybe 6' 2" but meaty with muscle from lifting weights in the maddening isolation of his basement gym, stinking of smoke and gasoline, it was the simplest thing in the world for Wren to reach out and touch him with the Vipertek stun gun.

Three-hundred-million volts. Two sharp spikes for the electrodes. Rechargeable battery. $24 from the mall where he'd swapped out his car the second time.

The Vipertek crackled, blue bolts Wren could barely see as they burned contact holes through Diego's leather jacket. He stiffened then fell. Wren caught him and guided him down even as he nudged the door closed. Pulled a loop of plastic zip ties and swiftly, professionally hogtied the guy right there in the entrance: one around his ankles, one around his wrists, one to loop the two together. Trussed up like a pig for the spit.

Wren rolled Diego carefully on his side. Gasping and sputtering now. He'd be fried for a little while, but that was OK. Add to the effect. He brought up Diego's phone and brought up the PIN screen.

"Working," Hellion said in his ear.

The screen flickered then opened on a field of Diego's apps. The X app was right there amongst them, a white 'X' on a black square. Simple, dramatic branding.

"Whuh- Wha-?" Diego mumbled.

Wren thumbed the app, brought up the biometric screen. It was an easy matter to roll Diego's right thumb over the pad, hold the camera up to his flickering eye and hold his eyelid back long enough for the lines in his iris to be read, leaving only one final screen.

Passkey.

"This was easy," Hellion said in his ear. "We should have done this with Julie Graves."

Wren laughed. If only it had been that easy. The first lead was always the hardest.

"What do you want?" Helmuz managed, finally getting back the power of coherent speech.

Wren looked in his eyes and saw all kinds of things within those brown pools. The rush of fresh adrenaline coming down into fear and pain. The swirl of purpose that cult-membership brought, winding back into something more primal.

Recognition, like a meerkat spotting an eagle swooping overhead.

"You wanted me, you got me," Wren said.

Diego's eyes flared. He began to kick but couldn't get any kind of traction, trussed like he was.

"Ungrateful son," he croaked.

"That's my name," Wren allowed. "And you know why I've come, right?"

"I'll die before I say anything."

Wren gave a gentle smile. "You just said something." For a second Helmuz looked confused, and Wren pushed into that. "But let's face it, you're already dead, Diego. Take a second and think about that. What you're experiencing right now is just the start of the long drop on the other side. Try to get right with your God, all that, before he casts you down and turns a blind eye for eternity. Isn't that what you want?"

Helmuz' eyes bugged. Hard to keep up with all that. "God's a lie."

Wren shrugged. "If you're in hell, I guess you'd like to think so. But let's look at the evidence. You were disappointed you didn't get to see me at Vantasy Con, am I right? Spend a hundred bucks, pose for a selfie with me, that was the plan? Well here I am. Price of admission's cheap, just a couple of passkey digits, and I'll admit one through the rope line. Maybe your descent into perpetual suffering halts, you get pulled back up." He paused a moment, looking into the man's eyes. "You killed a woman today, Diego, so it's not stopping far, but there's still inches of give left in this rope. Recant that death, spill the number and I'll see you get treated right by LMPD."

Helmuz just stared. Trying to catch up.

"Alternative's the long drop. You want to join the valiant resistance in hell, I can make that happen. If they don't want to walk first, you make them, right?" Wren winked, aping the rumbling voice of his father from the deepfake video. "But I bet you never thought you'd be the one getting made. Better to be on the other side of the gasoline and lighter combo, doing the making, wouldn't you say?"

Wren produced a lighter, a can of liquid kerosene. All told another $8 from the same mall.

Helmuz sucked wind. Part the shock, part the hogtie position. Pulling the arms back played havoc with your intercostal muscles, responsible for pumping the lungs.

"I'll never help you," he said. "You're the enemy."

"Enemy number one, right?" said Wren. "Even better. So we get to send you on your way an honest man. I figure we do it by degrees, it'll be more painful, which is great, because pain is a portal, yeah? X would approve. So I start with your legs, we can sit here and watch those burn together, then we'll just move up your body. Deal?"

Helmuz gritted his teeth, then hawked and spat. It missed Wren, flopped to the linoleum.

"It's your floor, man," Wren said, then uncapped the can and started pouring kerosene on Helmuz' legs below the knee. "Funny thing is, from your Internet records, seems you only got into this X BS in the last couple of months." He gave him a long look as noxious fluid seeped into Helmuz' pants. "Now me, I don't even buy a new car without thinking on it for six months at the least. At the very least, Diego. So I'm going to figure you got pressured some, got the hard sell, you know? An impulse buy. We've all been there. These days you can return those cars, call on regulation to dig you out. But your legs?" Wren whistled low. "They're not coming back, brother. You sure you're all in for this?"

Diego stared hard.

Wren smiled.

"OK. Well, walk in the fire."

He lit a match, held it over Diego's legs, and the big guy broke like Dambusters. Wren waited out the flood, gave some direction to the confessions and apologies, until finally his passkey code came.

"Got it," Hellion said in Wren's ear, keys clattering madly. "It is good. We are in. I see his Kill List. Different names. He is at thousand point-level, for killing that journalist. His good luck she even spoke to him."

Wren stood while Helmuz kept on babbling below. "Does it help?"

"It is helpful, Christopher. This will take time to collate. More will be better. The signal from X cycles through multiple failed states. If we have enough, we can narrow the algorithm used to do so, make predictions."

Wren nodded. Looked down at Helmuz, who was sobbing now.

"Recovery's a hard road," Wren said. "Don't you go anywhere, Diego. I'll send someone to fetch you in a couple hours."

He opened the door and strode out. Helmuz' keys jangled in his hand. He got in the battered old GMC truck and pulled away, heading east toward the next on his list, like a moon circling the gravity well of smoke pluming from Louisville's heart.

16

GAMES

The next were a group of five young people in their early twenties, tracked and identified from the Expo Center footage, amongst them the girl who broke out gasoline first and started splashing it around.

After getting the blaze going, they'd fled fast, three blocks south on foot but followed every step by Hellion via CCTV. There they ducked into a convenience store and bought several jugs of vodka, a bag of energy drinks and a carton each of orange and cranberry juice, then caught the route 19 bus on the TARC network, Transit Authority of River City.

The bus cam watched them mixing up small-batch cocktails in the middle seats, pouring vodka straight in their mouths, then chasing it with mixers. Passengers nearby switched seats or just got off the bus as they grew louder. The driver said nothing; not worth the trouble, Wren figured.

Already drunk forty minutes later, they got off in Russell at 11 a.m. and poured into their shared redbrick student house, two blocks north of Muhammad Ali Boulevard.

Hard on their heels at 11:45, Wren came up on the redbrick building. There was no place to hide around it, no trees, fences, yard, just a three-floor box airdropped in the middle of grass yards and roads. Few people were out on the streets anyway; the governor had just put a curfew order out for 5 p.m.. Most folks were respecting that in advance, and the rest didn't look at Wren twice, now wearing Helmuz' black cap with the white embroidered X, brim tugged low.

"This may not be best idea," Hellion said. "There are five of them. Only one must trigger an ALERT to signal X what we are doing."

"It'll be fine," Wren said low, parked the Sierra across the street and approached the front door. There was a buzz button and a security keypad. Wren pushed the button, waited ten seconds then buzzed it again.

The intercom crackled and a young guy's voice came through, clearly drunk. "Yeah, all right, what is it?"

"Pizza," Wren said.

"What?" the guy laughed. "We didn't even order yet."

"Somebody there did," Wren answered. "I got your order right here, three Meat Feast, two Hawaiian, all paid for online. Maybe you forgot?"

The guy laughed. "He says we forgot ordering."

"Maybe on the bus we did?" somebody answered faintly.

"I just need to hand these off," Wren said. "I got other orders to pick up before 1. Come on, brother."

"Well all right, brother," answered the guy. "Come up."

The door buzzed, the lock clicked and Wren pushed through. Two stories up along friction-burn-gray carpets, he knocked on a red door. A goofy-looking guy answered, long blonde hair spilling in sticky locks down his chiseled jawline, no shirt on revealing pale white skin. Addled eyes, wired off more than vodka.

"You the pizza guy?" he asked. "Dig the cap, by the way."

Wren hit him with the stun gun in the belly, caught him and guided him quietly down. Charge depleted.

A stubby corridor ran ahead, green bike helmet on a

chipped side table, coats dumped in a pile atop jumbled sneakers, stained beige carpet. Wren advanced into a low den scattered with bottles, chip packets, paper plates, clothing. A big screen TV stood in one corner showing some daytime murder mystery show, across from three long, worn leather sofas in a U shape. The girl who'd started the fires lay spread out on the leftmost, half-naked to her bra and panties. A guy sat opposite her, holding a set of five playing cards, wearing only his boxer shorts.

"Ah," said Hellion in Wren's ear.

"Strip poker?" Wren asked.

The girl turned bodily, squinted at him like she was trying to focus. "You the pizza guy?"

"Yup," Wren said, "here's your delivery."

He bent by the back of her sofa, dug his fingers under the rim and lifted, flipping the sofa with her on it. She tumbled against the coffee table then hit the floor, cards went flying, and Wren followed through, tipping the sofa the rest of the way like he was rolling a workout tire.

The half-naked guy with the cards just stared, trying to register what he was seeing. "Hey," he managed.

"Hey yourself," Wren said, taking three fast steps over to grab the guy's card hand and roll it smoothly behind his back. Ten more seconds to zip-tie his wrists, another ten to grab a scarf off the floor and gag him.

Back on his feet. The girl was making strange mumbles from beneath the sofa, but Wren didn't figure she'd be coming out any time soon.

"Three down," Hellion said, sounding worried. "The other two, Christopher."

He was already beelining for a door in the south wall, hung ajar with a sock on the handle. Shoved through into a darkened bedroom, curtains closed against the winter afternoon's light, a black guy in the bed clutching his cell phone, thickset Asian girl with great muscle definition already charging at him with a baseball bat in hand.

Wren ducked under the blow, which hit the doorframe and had to reverb hard up her arms, then took three steps and jumped. He hit the guy in a full body tackle, wiping him out against the bed like a swatted fly. The cell phone tumbled from his hand, already at the screen with the ALERT button. Wren grabbed his arm then rolled hard, pulling the guy over him just in time for the baseball bat to come down on his hip.

There was a nasty crack and the guy wailed. Wren rolled onto his left knee and threw out a sidekick, putting his heel pinpoint into the big girl's solar plexus. She gasped and dropped the bat.

After that it was easy. Hogtie the guy in the bed, pillowcase for a gag, hogtie the girl, then back through the house where the half-naked arsonist was just now crawling out from under the sofa.

Wren watched her for a second. She looked like any other college kid. Pretty much what he'd expected. X was exciting, like a different kind of drug that opened a new layer to reality. These kids weren't jilted by reality like Diego Helmuz, or all-the-way-in like Julie Graves. They were just bored and entitled.

He tied and gagged her, went back down the hall and did the same for the goofy guy by the door, still unconscious, fetched the one phone from the bedroom floor, then dragged everyone into the living room and laid them out on their sides in a fresh U shape, pushing the sofas back to make room.

Five trussed little piggies, all wheezing hard. Wren looked around at the mess of scattered trash, bottles and clothes from their post-riot party.

"Any chance someone's gonna tell me where your cell phones are?"

Hellion laughed.

"No? So I'll find them, then."

It took a few minutes, digging through the cast-off clothes and detritus, until five phones lay on the coffee table in the middle of the space, one already opened and logged through.

"You have this one?" Wren asked Hellion, holding it up to his bodycam.

"We are in," she answered. "Four to go."

Wren picked up the next, looked around at his grunting, puffing prisoners. This was a big change from burning down Vantasy Con.

"You like to play games," he said, slow and clear. "Strip poker's a fine example. Gambling with low stakes, it's good clean fun." He eyeballed them one-by-one. "I have no problem with it. Even getting high while you play, some booze, run it into an orgy? Whatever." His gaze sharpened. "But burning up a cosplay conference just because I passed through? Endangering thousands of lives. Leading a stampede that's already killed three people we know of, and doubtless left many more with life-changing injuries. That's a game I can't get behind." He stood firm. "An unacceptable game. So I'm going to teach you a new game. One you've earned. It's called 'This Little Piggy Went To Market', and there's just one rule. First one to tell me the passkey for their X app gets to keep a fully functioning set of limbs. Going once. Going twice."

All five of them began grunting to speak. Wren bent to the first and peeled back the gag.

17

THIRD

"This should be enough," Hellion said, once all five phones lay on the coffee table, unlocked. "Working."

Wren dug out the remote and flicked on the TV while his little piggies grunted on the floor. The national news channels were showing the comedown in Louisville. 12:47 p.m.. The Exposition Center fires were coming under control and rescue crews were pouring in through the front lobby.

It left a bitter taste in Wren's mouth. Only hours earlier he'd been there, marveling at all those creative, crazy folks. Thinking his passage through would be a simple matter of laundering himself into anonymity. How wrong he'd been.

"Ten minutes," Hellion said.

"You got anything to eat?" Wren asked the kids. They nodded desperately. Maybe thought this was a continuation of the game. In truth they were only wallpaper now. All they knew was the app, and not one of them was above 100 points.

Wren wandered into the kitchen, popped the fridge door and found a bacterial war zone worse than the living room. Not scrubbed for a couple years, he figured. Condiments slowly fermenting in bloated plastic bottles. A thick-skinned brown smush in the vegetable tray. Something fungal growing by the drain. He'd seen better in fridges of serial killers, storing human body parts.

He pushed the door closed. Found a dirty pot buried beneath a mountain of filthy crockery, pulled out a plastic scrubber and blasted it with the hot faucet. From a cupboard he plucked a dented can of spaghetti O's, decanted it into the pot and set it to heat on the greasy induction plate. He found a bag of only slightly moldy bagels stuffed in a bread box and sliced two, scraped off the mold and popped them in the toaster.

A few minutes. He washed more dishes while he waited. No help to the kids, really, since they'd be in jail within a few hours, but it helped calm his jangling nerves.

The bagels popped. The spaghetti O's sauce simmered down to a nice thickness. He braved the fridge once more for butter, bailed early, and settled for pouring the O's over the bagels. Ate standing up with the plate in his hand, watching the news in the living room.

Talking heads were theorizing about what all this meant. Linking the death of Lou-Ann Reisner of Lou and Morrie to the female journalist to Wren's presence. Some blamed him, either because he should have stayed away, or because he was an undercover leader in the X movement, which didn't make much sense, since the X people hated him. But nothing much made sense anymore.

He finished up, took the plate back to the kitchen and washed it up, then did a few slow yoga stretches. Mason had taught him them, designed to 'align his chakras' and ease the tightness in his still-healing wounds. The pain was a steady arthritic ache, with the background fuzz of the concussion still ringing in his head like a bell, but distant enough for now.

Midway through the routine Hellion spoke in his ear.

"We have something, Christopher."

Instantly, he was back on the alert. "Tell me."

"Infant X app-anonymizing algorithm has patterns, and we have followed them many times around whole Internet, dating back six months in longest case. They end in three locations, no further leads."

"Where?"

"First in New York, Christopher, narrowed to several blocks south-east of Central Park, I think you know-"

"That's the human zoo," Wren interrupted, his heart rate speeding up. "Galicia's zoo on Billionaire's Row."

"Yes," Hellion said. "Now demolished. As you would expect, there have been no transmissions from there since two weeks back. Second is located in Seattle, east side, where-"

"My brothers," Wren said. Jaw gritted, pulse pounding. Staring at his prisoners but seeing far beyond them. "The second zoo."

He'd been mostly unconscious when the Seattle raid went down, still recovering from the D.C. firestorm. Hellion and B4cksl4cker had surfaced evidence that Wren's surviving brothers, Gabriel and Zachary, were there, and under Teddy's guidance the Foundation had mounted the assault.

They'd found an abandoned human 'zoo' tucked away on the hidden mezzanine floor of a fifty-story tower. All the prisoners were dead. There were green-screen torture rooms and camera equipment just like in New York, to serve the needs of the Apex's firestorm of young mothers across the country, but every digital record had been wiped. Not one person left alive, with no sign of his brothers.

"Second zoo, yes," Hellion confirmed. "Doubling as relay station for X. No transmissions since we took it down six days ago. That leaves only one location, the third."

Wren strode back into the kitchen, away from the piggies so they couldn't possibly hear any of this. "Hit me."

"It is in Mexico, Christopher. We have narrowed it to five-mile radius in city of Acapulco."

That was unexpected. "Acapulco?"

"Yes, Christopher. It is holiday destination, or was. Many hotels, beaches, beautiful waters. We are seeking to narrow this further, find the precise building signal was transmitted from, but…"

Wren stopped listening. All he heard now was the rush of blood in his ears, heart pumping, the walls of that narrow, filthy kitchen closing in. A third human zoo. Maybe the last redoubt of the Apex, a bolthole just like Jim Jones' Jonestown in Guyana, outside the Continental USA and buried in cartel territory, far from the reach of the FBI.

A place to go and engineer the end of America.

His mind raced. Silver flashes danced sharply across his vision as the concussion nausea surged back. He dropped to one knee and panted, gripping the counter hard as the sticky vinyl floor opened into a swirling gulf. His brothers could be there. X could be there. Maybe even the Apex himself. His shoulders throbbed at the ghost pain of his sister's stiletto pushing into his battered body.

This time would be different. It had to be.

Hellion was talking but he barely heard her, just trying to breathe and clear a path.

"Except episodes of acute onset," the Foundation doctor had said, giving him the all-clear on his concussion a day earlier, pulling back the stethoscope and fixing him with a cynical gaze. "They'll feel like acid flashbacks, and could be brought on by anything from moments of high emotion to catching the wrong scent on the air. You just need to ride them out."

"So I'm fit?" he'd asked.

She'd laughed. "Fit? You need to be put out to pasture. You're barely held together with stitches, steroids and band-aids right now, but what the hey. The country calls, Christopher Wren's gotta go, right?"

He'd said nothing. Now her words swirled around him like leaves caught in a drain. He felt the spaghetti O's preparing to make a reappearance, and bolted. He barely made it to the bathroom before dropping to his knees and retching into the tub. No time even to flip the toilet lid.

His stomach convulsed in knots. Somewhere very far off the piggies grunted in a panic. Wren sagged against the rim of the tub, feeling a cold sweat bead up on his face and down his back.

"-topher, are you under attack, what is happening?"

Hellion's voice in his ear. He took a rasping breath, another that came deep and convulsing, forcing control back onto the sudden shock.

"It's fine," he said. "I'm fine."

"What happened?"

The silver tides receded gradually, leaving Wren shuddering. "Nausea. It's the concussion. Give me a minute."

A minute passed, then he pushed back to his feet, ran the tub clean then washed up in the sink, gargled, drank, brushed his teeth with his finger. In the tarnished mirror he looked pale and worn. Let it be, he figured, and strode through remnant silvery motes to the living room.

The piggies stared up at him with a new terror. Like he wasn't just a bad guy anymore, but a crazy guy. Tying them up and demanding passkeys was one thing, but eating their food then puking it into the bathtub?

Wren said nothing, just lifted a set of keys from the coffee table. Bright green key fob, shaped like a monstrous fist. The bad guys liked playing dress-up just as much as the good guys, it seemed. From a side table he picked up a matching green helmet then pushed out through the door.

"I need a flight, Hellion," he said.

"To Acapulco?"

"To Acapulco."

18

ACAPULCO

Acapulco was a balneario, a Latin American seaside resort once the playground of global elites, where Hollywood stars had rubbed shoulders with politicians, CEOs and cartel drug kings on the gorgeous white sand beaches lining the glamorous seafront esplanade.

That was back in the 60s, 70s, 80s. Money poured in after that, grand new developments hauling in even more cash as the international upper-middle classes made Acapulco their destination of choice. Billions of dollars passed through. The cartels had a deal that allowed it: no murders in the Pearl of the Pacific.

Then one day the deal was broken, and all hell broke loose. The cartels along with dozens of smaller gangs opened fire on each other as the Narco Wars heated up, rapidly turning the City-by-the-Bay into the second-highest murder capital in the world, after Mexico City at number 1. One in every thousand people murdered annually. Bodies left hanging from bridge trusses as a warning. Bodies washing up on the beaches. Murder, kidnapping and extortion as everyday events.

The US State Department started warning tourists to stay

away, and after that the torrential flow of tourist dollars dried up faster than a sliced mango in the sun.

Wren sat at the window of his private Learjet 45XR at 45,000 feet, looking down on the verdant pine-oak forests of the Sierra Madre del Sur mountain range and thinking about the one and only time he'd passed through Acapulco before.

It had been at the last fading gasps of the tail-end of that glorious heyday, back when there was still some predictable logic to the gang violence, and figures in-the-know could skirt the worst outcomes while enjoying absolute cut-rate luxury with a bay view to literally die for.

He'd been running an observation op with the CIA that had devolved into a snatch-and-grab on a Mideast terror financier. The guy had been visiting his two 'girlfriends' in the hotel Costa Cabana penthouse, twenty-third floor, after blowing a fortune at one of the beachside baccarat joints. Travis Raker was his name, a pump-and-dump stock whizz looking to wag the tail of the international arms market by stirring up cross-border trouble between Sunni and Shia militias in southern Lebanon, hoping for an ugly sequel to the 2008 conflict. Wag that tail hard enough, and the Saudis might storm in, even Iran, Israel, potentially the USA, and that would turn the whole thing into a hot-mess war zone goldmine.

Wren's job was to nip all that in the bud. He'd already been watching Raker via long lens from the neighboring Hacienda's twenty-seventh floor, looking for intel. Intel had come when Umm Al-Siddiq himself, a major arms trader and top-10 wanted terrorist, had entered the apartment and sat down for the trade.

It was a stunning denouement. The CIA playbook said wait for operational approval before taking any action, but Wren had taken the upfront decision to 'establish a forward operating position' while the brass thought it over. It just so happened that his forward operating position was in the corridor right outside Raker's room.

Moments after approval came down, Wren slammed the door with a weapons-hot team of five, synced to a fast-rope descent from the roof by three more, high-caliber rounds firing through the glass.

Thirty seconds of seeming chaos ended up with seven of Raker's security team dead or incapacitated, Raker and Al-Siddiq unconscious, bagged and tethered, with Al-Siddiq himself slung over Wren's broad shoulder as they ran up the three stories for helo evac on the roof.

That had earned him a commendation. Maybe around then was when they'd started calling him 'Saint Justice'. Like an avenging angel, they said, tongue-in-cheek or otherwise. Wren closed his eyes, trying to remember if that was before or after the birth of his daughter Quinn, but couldn't come up with the dates.

He sighed, sipped his Diet Coke and watched the green mountains roll by below. It was easy to feel nostalgia for those older, 'simpler' days. On the edge of turning thirty, when it was so much clearer who the bad guys were, who the good guys were and what the right path forward was.

It was tempting to think it was all different now. Ever since his father had reared up onto the scene with his domestic terror group the Order of the Saint, it was all shades of gray. Good people acting against their own interests, under the influence of a conman with incredible ambition.

He thought back to Diego Helmuz, lying now in a puddle of urine in his own home, a murderer because he'd been too lost to see this X nonsense for what it really was. He thought of five college kids in their student apartment, half of them crashing from the adrenaline and the other half from the drugs, following X to charges of affray and arson just because it seemed like a fun thing to do in a world where nothing really mattered.

Everybody warped beneath the Apex's touch.

Wren rang a number, held the phone up to his ear. It rang a precise five times, clicked as server exchanges around the world aligned, then answered.

"Señor Wren," came a voice on the other end. Educated, an Oaxaca-tinged Mexican accent. Not a man to trifle with: Don Mica, one of the capos of the Qotl cartel. A man Wren had almost assassinated on two separate occasions, but held back at the last moment each time, judging him a better bulwark against terror alive than dead.

"Don Mica," Wren said. "You spoke with Gutierrez?"

Mica said nothing for a long moment. Wren thought he heard the sound of yapping dogs in the background. Notoriously, Mica liked to feed his enemies to starving hounds. "Hector Gutierrez," the Don said at last. "He is a strange man."

Wren could only smile. Gutierrez had been a Halcones-level mule-trafficker when Wren met him in the Sonoran Desert south of the border, since elevated to Tenientes, lieutenant grade, right beneath the capos. With his diamond-grille teeth insets and a habit of always wearing red suspenders, Gutierrez cut an odd figure, but he was competent and could be vicious. "He told you what I need."

"Need," Don Mica said. "It's an interesting term."

Wren waited. He knew how it worked in Acapulco, like pretty much anywhere in all of Mexico, now that the cartels effectively ruled. Send in Sicarios of your own without permission, and you were asking to be gunned down on your exfiltration. The bars, the beaches, the hotels, they were all locked down tight as a bombo drum. Even his CIA hit had come with cartel approval and oversight.

"I'm sure he relayed my request," Wren said, when the

silence had stretched too long. "I'm thinking he didn't relay the threat that comes attached."

"That is what I'm waiting to hear," Mica said. "Last time we met, you spoke of a Predator drone in the air above us. Hellfire missiles that would wipe us out." He sounded amused.

"What I have for you now will be much cleaner," Wren said. "Call it a financial Hellfire. I doubt you've heard of the 'second skin' on the Internet? We keep it under wraps. Think of it as a kind of cowboy on the Internet's horse, riding every data transaction across the entire web. If we want, at any moment in time, I can have that cowboy take the reins and start pulling in a different direction. Maybe run the horse into the ground."

Mica laughed.

"I thought you might laugh, so I'm going to offer a swift demonstration. Strictly reversible. I suggest you take a moment, have your accountants bring up your cryptocoin accounts held in the Seychelles tax haven. I'll wait."

"Cyrptocoins are unhackable," the Don answered.

"So they say. Humor me."

A few moments passed. Then a few more moments. When Mica came back it was with a very different tone.

"Put them back."

Wren smiled. Having the world's top hackers on his team came with perks, even if they couldn't break through X's firewall. "That's three-hundred-million dollars' worth of cryptocurrencies we just siphoned. Just a taste, really. I can take more. I could take it all, wipe you out. It'd throw Mexico into outright civil war, probably, but if you hear out my request, you'll learn that's where I think we're all headed anyway." He paused a second for effect. "I'm sure you look at the States and laugh at the mess we're in right now, but do you really think our total upheaval won't completely destroy your entire business model? Once the American people are decimated by our own hands, nobody will be buying your cocaine, hermano. It'll be lights out in the barrio."

A long silence.

"You are suggesting we are natural allies."

"Uneasy bedfellows," Wren allowed. "I'm not your dog on a leash. You're not mine. We both have a vested interest in the status quo."

Another long silence.

"I'm three hours out of Acapulco," Wren pressed. "I have my team and target location. There'll likely be some collateral damage when we hit, but we'll keep it structural, and we'll pay for it. What I need from you is a guarantee that Qotl won't interfere, and that if it comes to that, you'll prevent interference from any of the rival gangs if they try to intercede."

"So we come to the offer."

"Offer's simple and secondary," Wren said. "I'm prepared to back you in a leadership bid for all the cartels. Acapulco's a beautiful place for an international holiday, don't you agree? End the Narco Wars on your end, I can bring them under better control on mine. America's in flux and change will come fast if all this goes right. There'll be more profit for everyone. Murders way down. US tourist money starts flowing back into the local economy. You won't need the drug money as much as now."

The longest silence yet. "You would do this?"

"I've always been a realist. Drugs are awful. The Narco Wars are worse. I add one and one together, I get two. Maybe between us, we can de-violence the whole trade."

"I like the violence."

Wren laughed. "So take up laser tag. The dogs eating people alive? Let it go. You won't be a pirate anymore, Mica. No need to put up the Jolly Roger to scare compliance. You'll be a businessman with the law on your side. Have a longer life expectancy, to boot."

Mica laughed. "Give us back the money. After that we can talk."

"The money comes after my hit runs uninterrupted. Agreed?"

"Then take an equal sum from our rivals. I won't be bent backward by anyone."

Wren grinned. "Already done. I took double from them all. If they take this chance to come for me, I expect you to have my back. If I'm gone, my team wipe all the accounts and let your country burn."

Five seconds. Ten.

"Agreed."

"Excellent. Now to the second point. I lied about having the location for my target. We have him to a five-mile radius of Acapulco. I'm thinking you or one of the others cartels already know where he is. I've got no doubt he pays protection money. So I'm going to need you to rat him out. Also, I lied about having a team. I don't have anyone, it's just me inbound. Can you provide a Sicario squad to wrap this up?"

Mica laughed. "It seems you have very little. This is more of your infamous brinksmanship?"

"Not by choice. I'm running far ahead of standard international reach. Call this a cutting-edge strike."

"Another word for this comes from the world of finance, Señor Wren. Over-leveraged. Push too hard, and your own house of cards may collapse."

"Ride or die," Wren said. "Do we have a deal?"

A moment of silence. "Yes, we can make this deal. But since you are changing it as we speak, I will change it too. There is a Senator in your government, Niles Regis, I think you remember he manipulated me. I wish to see him dead."

Wren gritted his teeth. Thought back 18 months, to his last op as a standard CIA operative. It was the mission that got him out, before he got back in again to hunt the Blue Fairy. "I already killed his son for you. I'm not killing the father."

"I understand. Simply look the other way when our kill comes. Convince others to look away, also."

A tight deal. Wren had no further leverage, though.

"Done. Provided it's a surgical hit. No collateral damage, no bombs. Not the rest of his family."

"A pleasure doing business with you, Señor Wren. A team of my own Sicarios will await you. I think you are going to like Acapulco."

19

DIAMANTE

The Punta Diamante district bordered the south side of Acapulco Bay, and held most of the city's latest developments, with glitzy new 5-star hotels and high-rise ultra-luxury condominiums overlooking the gorgeous private beaches. The name of the district itself meant 'diamond', and had to be one of the most locked-down tourist zones in the world, protecting its high-value denizens as much as possible against the encroaching Narco Wars.

None of that really mattered to Wren.

The Learjet circled and put him down at Acapulco International. The air was hot and dry as one of Hellion's overclocked server racks, mid-eighties despite the season. Wren deplaned to a waiting black Silverado waiting thirty yards off, fronted by five thick cartel soldiers in uniform tactical camo gear, cradling assault rifles. Mexican tourists getting off a jumbo jet to the right watched open-mouthed as Wren strode toward them.

"Señor Wren," one of the five men called across the distance. A leader. Teardrop tattoos all down his throat. Bull neck, in his thirties, about as tall as Wren. Doubtless he'd done all kinds of dark things for the cartel, maybe more on his free time. A killer of women and children; you had to be to make Sicario. The kind of guy Wren would put in the ground without a second thought, in other circumstances. From the look in the guy's eyes, he was thinking about the exact same thing.

"I do not like this, Christopher," came Hellion's voice in his ear. Re-establishing contact after she'd been sleeping throughout his flight. "I have been watching these men. They are suspicious."

"Suspicious how?" he sub-vocalized into his new throat-mic rig, barely moving his lips as he closed the distance.

"One of them was drinking yoghurt."

Wren snorted. "Yoghurt? Are you kidding?"

"I never kid about yoghurt. Ask B4cksl4cker. It should not be drunk."

Wren filed that away. Still, it raised a valid point. He wouldn't put it past Don Mica to have multiple plans in progress. Prep the zoo raid even as he prepped a hit on Wren. Maybe he would roll the dice, try locking 'Santa Justicia' up in a cartel dungeon and pray to Santa Muerte that torture would make him roll back the cryptocoin threat.

"Just keep tracking the target," he sub-vocalized, ten yards out from the five guys.

They were professionals with totally blank expressions. Solid, thousand-yard stares, watching him roll up with zero sign of emotion, but something about that seemed off to Wren. He tried to put himself in their position. If their orders were to start taking direction from some Yankee yahoo, risking their lives to raid a 'zoo' belonging to a guy who'd been paying them protection money for years, shouldn't they be pissed off?

Professional or no, Wren figured they should.

"All set for the raid?" he asked as he closed within five yards.

Two of them gave nods, the central bull-neck guy and a guy to his right with an accentuated widow's peak, and that set more alarm bells ringing. Too eager. He'd dealt with Sicarios before, glorified hitmen like a pack of wild dogs, and like a pack they obeyed the hierarchy without needing to think about it. To show disrespect meant death.

But two guys nodding? It was stepping out of established leadership bounds. Like a mob, not a pack. Maybe killers from different cartels, rustled up by Mica to keep the peace. If so, Wren saw the play rolling out ahead; get him in the vehicle surrounded on all sides, and he'd be easy to incapacitate. Take him to Don Mica in shackles and break out the dogs.

There was no point taking any chances now. Better to force the play and rule by fear.

He didn't break stride as he closed the last yard, raised a hand to the bull-neck guy as if to shake, flashed a smile then smoothly flipped his palm into a blade strike jab, fingers rigid and stabbing straight into the dead center of the tear trail down the guy's throat. Nothing slabs of steroid muscle could do to reinforce cartilage, and the guy's windpipe crunched and buckled under Wren's baton-hard fingers, his chin snapping down like the stable door slammed shut after the horse bolted.

Wren stepped back while the guy fell to the steaming blacktop, clutching at his crushed throat. No operational come-back from that. Maybe he'd live, but not even a tracheotomy would make him operational today, if anyone was inclined, which none were.

Nobody moved. Nobody so much as batted an eye. That synced up with Wren's theory; this was a hodge-podge cartel of cartels. No loyalty. They remained standing in a quarter circle like a convex lens with Wren at the focal point. All hardened killers, listening to one of their own grunt for breath on the floor and not even looking.

"I'll drive," Wren said. "Keys."

He held out his hand. The four of them stared.

"Keys and get on board or I strip everything all your bosses have got. I guarantee Mica's dogs will be coming for you next. We make this strike, we never see each other again. Entendido?"

No answer. The guy on the floor managed to get a wheeze of air in. So maybe he'd survive. Throw a fiesta.

"Keys," Wren repeated. "Situational awareness, gentlemen. Read the room."

One of them stepped forward. The sharp widow's peak guy. He slapped a set of keys into Wren's outstretched palm.

"Thank you. Now." He surveyed them. "Anyone goes for my neck with a garotte, believe that I'll crash the car and kill us all before you get to the wheel. Gunshot to the head, same story. Be in no doubt, I have a thick skull. Now, in."

The widow's peak guy jutted his chin forward. "He was lead. Who you want as your second?"

Wren smiled. Already adjusting. It was nice to deal with professionals. "You're talkative, so I'll take you. Name?"

"Madrigal."

"Cartel?"

Madrigal's jaw tightened. Getting called on the lie.

"Cartel," Wren repeated.

"Morela."

Wren smiled. "Like the mushroom. Madrigal, Wren. I hold you responsible for these three." He waved at the others. "Now everyone get in the back. No bitching. Sit on each other's laps, all I care."

Wren moved to the driver's side, popped the door and climbed in. Plush black leather, AC running cold, and instant confirmation of the suspected plot. The empty package for a medical-grade syringe lay in the passenger footwell, a squat bottle of Propofol on the dash, and in back hung the detritus for an IV line. Get him under with the injection, keep him under until he hit Mica's dungeon of choice. To boot, an empty bottle of macrobiotic yoghurt, blueberry flavor.

Seemed Hellion's suspicions were well-founded.

"This is incredibly dangerous," Hellion said in his ear. "B4cksl4cker and I are enjoying it very much."

Wren snorted. "And that's what matters most," he said quietly, as the guys got in behind. Madrigal hopped up on the lap of one of the others without a word of complaint. They were too pro to bitch and moan. The guy underneath him just sat there staring, like the most intense booster seat Wren had ever seen.

"Here we go," Wren said, twisted the key and hit the gas hard enough to rock all four of them tight into each other. Aggressive driving would keep them off-balance long enough for everyone to survive to the zoo. "And call your bosses now, tell them exactly what happened, and that I want four more guys waiting for us, or I bring the financial apocalypse raining down. Those exact words. We're going in hard and fast."

Madrigal brought up his phone first, the others followed.

"B4cksl4cker has brought popcorn," Hellion said. "This is better than movie."

Wren leaned in, pushing through the rainbows across his vision as the Silverado picked up speed. Getting pissed off now.

20

JEFE

Out of Acapulco International, Wren pushed the Silverado to ninety on an immaculate two-lane lined with sparse-looking palm trees, northwest and fifteen minutes out.

"Sit-rep on the target," Wren said under his breath, as Madrigal in back spoke to Don Mica on the phone, occasionally barking out a submissive, "Si, capo."

"Unmoving," Hellion answered.

Unmoving was good. Hotels whipped by to left and right, shopping centers, parking lots. On the surface Acapulco didn't look like a murder capital. It looked moneyed, clean, ready for a flood of tourists to descend and start hoovering up designer brands at cutthroat prices. The sky was a spotless but dulling blue, coming on toward dusk. Wren wound the window down and killed the AC.

Fresh and salty ocean drafts blew in like a balm, after six hours cooped up in the dehydrating, recycled air of the Learjet.

"There are three riots currently ongoing in the United States," Hellion said in the background. "The largest is in

New York. They appear to be targeting the cleanup crew at 231 Madison Avenue."

That made a sick kind of sense. Attack the government workers trying to scab over the wound of another destroyed skyscraper. Keep the wound fresh.

"Are they ALERTs? Linked to new sightings of me?"

"All of them. Deepfake, clearly. Each triggered an ALERT that has brought thousands out to riot. In Tallahassee you were seen curb-stomping an X-apoc member. Infant X's idiots are now attempting to raze a sports stadium as revenge. Fire crews are out, and like New York, they are receiving incoming gunfire."

Wren grunted. It seemed the Exposition Center had broken the seal, after two more flash-mobs had struck Philadelphia and Atlanta while he was in the air. Didn't matter that it was impossible for him to be at both at the same time. The X-apoc masses were ready to go, and when deepfake video of Wren committing 'atrocities' against them came through, they flash-mobbed in their cosplaying thousands.

Starting fires that raged wildly. Destroying property. Attacking police, fire and paramedic crews when they tried to assert control. Targeting killings against anyone who talked back. So every ALERT became a missile strike. Cities engulfed in chaos at the touch of a button. And the ALERTs were coming faster.

Ten minutes out from the third human zoo.

"Still unmoving?" Wren asked.

"Unmoving. I will tell you."

"More men will be waiting," Madrigal said in back.

Wren said nothing. The road opened out and Acapulco Bay sprawled briefly through greenery off to his left. Vast and unforgiving, final resting place of so many other innocents. He cast his eyes up to the right, where ahead the luxury hotels stood like rainmakers at the water's edge, thirty stories tall and gleaming dental-cap white in the fading light.

He'd expected the human zoo to be on a mezzanine floor, just like New York and Seattle. He'd already planned the attack, fast ropes from the roof combined with a ram team, just like his old Acapulco days, until Don Mica had switched all that around.

The third zoo was on a ship.

"I haven't seen any 'human zoo'," Mica said. "It's a small group, several boxes of equipment, highly mobile. They exchange position on visiting cruise liners every day, when new liners come in. They pay cash under-the-table to take over a penthouse, conduct their operations, move again the following day. It is a smooth operation. In the eyes of the city, they do not exist. In our eyes, they are a pay check."

A ship.

That day it was the New Dawn Seafarer, an eight-deck tall, seven-hundred occupancy luxury cruise liner, five-hundred staff, a thousand-feet long with a thirty-foot draft. A small town floating on a bulbous keel. Ingenious. Invisible. The zoo was able to push their Internet uplink through the ship's satellite dish; incredibly expensive to send video that way, but constantly rotating at the source as the liners switched out, in addition to the global server bounce and encryption.

Anonymized in three ways. It was a miracle his hackers had ever narrowed it down to Acapulco at all.

"Movement," Hellion said in his ear.

Wren's heart skipped a beat. They'd been warned? He checked the dash. Minutes out. the greenery opened again and now he saw the first of them to the left, huge ships moored off to sea like great gleaming islands in the bay. Too far-off to pick out their names, but he knew one of them was the New Dawn.

"Bearing?"

"Turning to port," Hellion said, keys flying in the background. "I am patching through their comms system. It seems the captain has been co-opted. Half his passengers are still on land."

Wren pushed the pedal to the metal, eking out a few more miles-per-hour.

"Madrigal, tell me we have jet boats ready to go."

"Ready, jefe."

Wren almost laughed. Jefe.

"Can you hack the ship?" Wren asked Hellion.

"Their satellite downlink is not wired to ship controls, Christopher. You will have to catch it."

"How far ahead's my turn?"

"Just ahead, Christopher. Boats are at the waterline."

Wren pulled left, took it so hard the Silverado edged onto its outside tires, whipped across the median and in front of oncoming traffic to race down an access road with signs for the NEW DAWN SEAFARER. They tore through a parking lot, hit the end and punched through a wooden barrier, tires scraping and chassis jolting down concrete steps to the beach, Sicarios bouncing in the back.

Tourists in floppy fishing hats and flip-flops shrieked and leaped out of his way. Sand flared from his spinning rear wheels like twin yellow geysers, bouncing toward admiral-blue skies with the sun a blot of boiling metal sinking into citrine seas, the NEW DAWN dead ahead and clearly showing its stern profile.

Ahead at the water's edge were two black speedboats, surrounded by more cartel hitmen. The perfect time for Mica to flip this thing a second time, but Wren had no time to re-enforce loyalty. Either they were in now or they weren't. The Silverado reached them in seconds and braked into a massive sand-surfing skid.

"With me, Madrigal!" Wren barked, thrust the door open and leaped out as the car rocked to a halt, running full-tilt at the boat already putting into the water. He jumped directly in, a second later Madrigal followed, then the guy at the engine ripped the cord and they took off over the waves.

21

NEW DAWN SEAFARER

The Seafarer cruised away at a stately pace befitting its immense scale, maybe twenty knots as a quarter million tons of metal, laid flat like a hundred-story skyscraper, were driven on by immense engines that produced a furrowed expanse of foot-high swells in their wake.

Wren's speedboat squad caught up to it in minutes, thumping over the low Pacific waves at seventy knots, crossing its ruffled wake to come up close on the starboard side. There was no one leaning out shooting, no sign of gun emplacements hunkering in, not even any sound on the horn.

"Give me the hook," Wren shouted to Madrigal.

The speedboat rocked in the Seafarer's displacement, engine spluttering as the huge liner's waves lifted them in and out of four-foot swells, spraying sea foam in a constant rain. One of the Sicarios opened a wooden crate, pulled out a metal hook with a slim rope attached. It was handed along, almost lost over the side as the boat bounced and saltwater splashed in Wren's eyes, then pressed into his hand.

It wasn't heavy, a simple molded hook in mottled iron, linked to a slimline pulley threaded with a thin cord. That cord linked to a coil, which Wren took in his off-hand, and beyond that to a long rope ladder stowed in the crate.

He scanned the Seafarer's flank, looking for the lowest point to toss the hook.

"Lower-tier lifeboats," he shouted over the crash and roar of the speedboat thumping up and down, the occasional clang of their hull banging off the Seafarer's flank. He pointed. "Right there!"

The speedboat raced ahead. Wren tried to stand, found his vertigo triggered like a crushing black wall as the deck jittered and rolled underfoot.

"Hold it steady!" he barked and tried again.

The sky spun darkly. Hard to fix anything in his sights. He dropped the hook off to his right on a foot of slack then hinged his body upright like he was side-hoisting a kettlebell, sending the hook shooting upward. He lost it in the glare. There was a clang, a shout, then the hook came plummeting back at skull-cracking velocity.

It hit the water and sank hard. Wren reeled it in, head spinning. He rubbed saltwater from his eyes and focused on the bucking ship above. They couldn't do this for long, already taking on water from every wave broken against the giant ship's side. Wren doubled down, picked out the edge of the lifeboat he wanted to hit, thirty feet up, and levered his whole body to hurl the hook once more.

It climbed, hung, then at the last minute clipped onto one of the lifeboat's tarpaulin straps.

He tugged it and it bit, held. The line hung and Wren immediately began working it through the pulley. In seconds he had the rope ladder shooting up. The line tied off, then he was climbing.

His body swung and thumped off the ship. His feet missed the rungs. His hands slipped on the thin lines, spun on the plastic rungs. The sky and the sea rolled and the sun became a tumbling sphere edged with silver. Hellion spoke like a twittering bird in his ear but he bulled upward, forcing his hands higher, his legs step-by-step, until finally his fingers closed on the lifeboat's tarp.

He pulled himself over. Kneeling on the canvas jacket. Ropes led away up to the higher tier of lifeboats, above which lay the deck. Down below Sicarios clambered up the rope ladder in pursuit. The speedboat jostled on the waves like a fly-fishing lure, threatening any moment to sink. Off to the horizon lay Acapulco, its buildings lime-white as a Hollywood smile.

Wren jumped, caught the ropes leading up and shinnied higher, vertigo be damned. In thirty seconds he breached the railing and dropped onto the deck. Wooden flooring boards ran away in either direction, the white ceiling of the deck hung above, sky, sea, access doors with round portholes.

He drew his Desert Eagle, started toward the bridge. Madrigal called something from below but Wren didn't hear it. His brothers were here. He could feel it. Maybe X, maybe the Apex too. He shoulder-slammed through a door, glimpsed a map of the immense ship, and started up red-carpeted stairs.

Three stories and he emerged into a swimming pool area, eyes blinking against the sudden harsh glare. Everything was white. Deckchairs laid out around a rectangular pool, towels unfurled in places, bags, but no people. Felt like the Mary Celeste ghost ship, cocktails with their shakers still spinning, ice melting in the Mexican heat. Curfewed by the captain, Wren figured. He lurched on like a drunken guest, roving eyes raised to the forecastle. Another four stories, a large mirrored-glass window looking out, impossible to tell if anyone was looking down on him.

He slammed through a door and ran upstairs, past a games room packed with arcades, ping-pong, air hockey, all chiming noisily with not a person present. His thighs burned and he hit the top deck, saw the Bridge access locked behind a reinforced metal door. Terrorist- and pirate-proof, pretty much as he'd expected, and not a problem at all.

"Starboard-bow corner," Hellion said in his ear. Had to be checking the ship schematics.

He moved, found the chute leading up in the corner as promised, rungs recessed into the wall, and climbed. The hatch opened, putting him through the roof and out onto the roof of the forecastle. Twin large transmission arrays spun to either side. A cornucopia of satellite dishes.

He'd planned for an assault from the roof of a luxury hotel, so had the personal fast-rope gear and harness. Was packing .30 caliber armor-piercing copper jacket rounds to punch through the building's tough outer glass skin. Not so different here. All he had to do was find a place to latch on his personal fast-rope coil.

He clicked onto a truss for one of the dishes, outracing the nausea now. Staying just one step ahead. He stepped to the edge just as Madrigal poked his head through the chute, above the line of the roof.

"Jefe-" he began, then Wren hit the coil release and jumped backward. One bound and the bridge window was right there before him, broad like wraparound shades, tinted glass so he couldn't see anything but his own reflection in the glare of the setting sun.

He pushed off hard and fired three times fast as he swung out, enough to crack, shatter then burst the glass inwards. He kicked the fragments away as he swung in, paid out the line and thumped down off a dashboard of radar screens, levers and controls, found his feet and hit the coil release, Eagle up and trained in on two figures at the central wheel.

A tall Asian guy in his fifties, white short-sleeve button-down shirt with black and gold chevron epaulettes, captain's hat on the chair beside him and a gun to his head.

The guy holding the gun was mixed-race, washed-out brown skin with tight black afro hair buzzed close to his scalp, bright blue eyes and model-chiseled cheekbones, hiding his lanky frame almost wholly behind the body of the captain.

Wren took the rest of the room in with his peripheral vision: three figures laid out flat on the floor, white crew shirts with black epaulettes flecked with gold, blood pools glinting in the fading light beneath them. Looked like two shots in the head each, outright executions. Red alarms blared on the control screens, something about automatic cabin lockdown, and a banging came at the reinforced door that had to be Madrigal.

Wren refocused on the captain and the hostage-taker, let his spiraling vision split even further as he matched that face, those cheekbones, those intense blue eyes to a sepia-tone photograph snatched from the Apex's New York human zoo. Adding on nearly three decades, imagining the sag of time and the carving of wrinkle lines; not enough laughter marks and a beetled brow, as if all he'd done for thirty years was squint and frown.

No mistaking it. The resemblance was there, last seen at the bottom of one of the Apex's faith pits, faking death by asphyxiation for a celebrating Pyramid. Wren trained the Eagle on his face.

"Aden-Of-The-Saints," he said. "Hello, brother."

22

ADEN

A beat played out. The captain said something but Wren didn't hear it, lost in his brother's eyes. Happy to see him, in one sense. Chrysogonus was dead. Galicia was dead. You only had so many family members, and every one Wren had met so far was dead.

Once they'd played together, he vaguely remembered. Everything back then had been overshadowed by the cruelty of first the Apex and second Chrysogonus, but Aden had been kind at times. Taken a beating that was coming to Pequeño 3, maybe, or helped him gather the black stones from around the fake town that were his 'Essential Barometers' task, before the Apex got home and whipped anyone who'd failed to meet his standards.

Now Wren only had to look in Aden's eyes to know the whole of his story. Second fiddle to Chrysogonus from birth to death. Third fiddle to the Apex. Behind Galicia in eminence, deep in his father's shadow, and in Wren's too, maybe. A workhorse sent far away to Mexico to run the overseas zoo. A once-decent boy brainwashed and broken into this.

Aden stared at him with a gaze like bullets. Hatred.

Disdain. His lips pulled back in a snarl. The only way to stay that crazy was to hate harder than the rest, then use that hate to prop you up. Wren saw the end result coming before it happened. Had already seen this show play out with two lost siblings and wasn't about to watch it play out again.

He fired, punching a bullet that skimmed the captain's side without triggering the copper jacket, sluicing through skin and intercostal muscle to hit Aden in the chest just as he was in the act of turning his gun on himself.

Aden's gun discharged into the ceiling, then Wren was there, guiding the captain aside as his brother fell backward, again trying to level the gun at his own head. Wren grabbed for him, all his movements coming like splashes of oil paint on a broad canvas now as the concussion reared large, rendering the world to color and light, acting only through muscle memory. He dropped the Eagle and caught Aden's wrist in his left hand, caught the hot barrel of his Glock M11 in his right and twisted until something broke.

Narrow bones of the ulna and radius cracking like green sticks.

Aden cried out and brought a wild fist into play. Wren took it on the forehead, setting silver fireworks off in his head, then they were down on the ground together, Wren straddling Aden as he spat up blood and struggled to get free.

"Stop, Aden!" Wren commanded, taking a wild slap on the chin, getting bucked as Aden writhed. "Stop it!"

He punched the struggling man once, twice, just trying to get-

"Jefe!"

Wren spun, making himself sick. The bridge spun, the captain was gone. The secure door was open. Madrigal was right there, widow's peak leaning in, saying something that merged with whatever Hellion was saying in his ear.

"Find them," Wren said, couldn't hear his own words but

saw them ballooning out like long multicolored speech bubbles. "The rest of them. The captain knows. Take his team alive."

The bubbles splashed across Madrigal in a haywire rainbow, seemed he heard because he nodded. Wren turned back to his brother. Aden-Of-The-Saints. His beautiful face was splashed with blood.

"Where is he?" Wren demanded.

Aden gasped frothy blood, tried to laugh and only spluttered.

"The Apex, where is he Aden?"

"Ungrateful," Aden began, choked on blood, "son."

"I know my own damn name," Wren said between gasps, fighting for stability as Aden's face doubled. "Every one you all called me; little wren, ungrateful son, Pequeño 3, whatever. You're going to tell me where he is."

Aden laughed, gulped, gurgled. The bullet must have hit a lung. Even now filling up with blood, drowning him from within. Nothing Wren could do about that. "Little… brother," he managed. "I missed … you."

Nothing to say to that. Even if it was true, it wasn't true the way Wren wanted it to be. "Where's our father, Aden? Tell me something. Anything!"

"Anything," Aden gulped. "Do you … remember the desert?"

Wren leaned in. "Is that where he is?"

"The Pyramid… game. We'd play. Remember?"

Wren didn't. Or maybe he did. Pequeño 3 in the middle while Aden, Zachariah and Gabriel stood around the edges. The younger named Pyramid boys toying with the eldest of the unnamed Pequeños. Arranged in a triangle with Pequeño 3 in the middle, tossing black stones overhead and telling him to catch them. Climb the Pyramid to the apex, they'd say, don't sink to the tomb. Always Pequeño 3 stood at the center.

Always his older brothers tossed the stones too high for him to reach, laughing as he jumped and strained. '3's in the tomb', they'd jeer, 'never gonna be apex'.

"What about it?"

"You never… learned," Aden managed. "Never knew … your place. Always trying… to climb."

"Because there's only one Apex, I get it," Wren said fast, chasing the words like they might escape from him. "Where is our father, Aden?"

Aden coughed for ten seconds, twenty, the blood coming out bright and arterial now, frothy and aerated. He reached up his hand, the wrist broken and fingers jutting at an unnatural angle, touched it to Wren's chest.

"In your … heart."

Wren took his hand and twisted. Aden shrieked, gagged, coughed, swallowed. Only moments left now.

"Where?"

"Right at the … center."

Wren twisted his wrist, not thinking clearly. Aden cried out and laughed. "Where's the center, Aden? Where's X?"

Aden spluttered, smug eyes widening in panic as his breath caught, juddered. "In the f…"

"In the what?"

Aden gulped and caught no air, blew a feeble red gasp then tried again, managed to hiss out a few words.

"Walk in the fire, little brother."

Then he died.

Wren stared into his eyes throughout, watching the moment his soul escaped his body and headed toward whatever BS afterlife in some hellish 'tomb' the Apex had conjured up for his followers. The never-ending fight against the slavers. Freeing the slaves. Twisting children and spitting them out as…

Aden's eyes were vacant. No breath, no pulse. Just like

Tomothy-Whereof-The-Giants-Roam had died some thirty years ago, in Pequeño 3's arms.

Wren pulled back, shaking and nauseated. He lurched to his feet, tumbled over the control deck and dry-heaved as the vertigo hit and didn't let up.

23

APEX, TOMB

Wren sat atop the roof of the bridge as dusk set in over the Pacific, his hands shaking in his lap. The sky was beautiful before him, a fury of reds, oranges and yellows as the sun was gradually swallowed by the unfeeling horizon line. Eight hours of darkness and sleep until it reappeared and the cycle began again, rising toward apex at the summit of the sky.

Apex. Tomb. A cycle that ever ended.

By Wren's side his earpiece squawked. Hellion, B4cksl4cker, maybe Rogers, Maggie, Teddy. It didn't mean much to him right then. Riots. America in disarray. Maybe he didn't care.

That was a dark truth.

He thought about the light going out in Aden's eyes again. On some level, it had felt good, and that brought on the shame. A cycle like the sun, like that stupid game in the desert. Apex. Tomb. Little Pequeño 3 right in the center while his brothers laughed, teasing him for never figuring it out, just like they'd all been laughing at him for three decades, believing they were all dead.

Of course he'd understood the game from the start. The

very first time they'd taken him out to play. He'd always known he could never win, but winning against his brothers hadn't mattered to him back then. Everything in the Pyramid had been about winning, and Pequeño 3 was sick of it.

To play with his brothers mattered more. To make them happy, even if they thought it was through his humiliation. There were far worse things.

His palms stung. He held them up, saw the star-shaped scars where Galicia had plunged her stiletto blade through the flesh. Thinking about family.

He had children. Jake. Quinn. A wife, technically, still. Loralei. But she'd found another man, living in a duplex together with his children in Delaware. Secured by the Foundation. Wren could bring up his phone and watch a feed of them any moment he wanted. Spy-cams dotted through their house. In every room. Overlooking their yard. Cameras hacked everywhere in surrounding streets and through the little town of Frederica, so he could look down and keep them safe.

But what did any of it matter, if he was never going to see them again? So America burned. The Pyramid had died once already, at the Apex's command. He'd been the one to do it back then, setting all those people alight at his father's command, just like he'd killed Tomothy when the Apex ordered him to. They'd done it together. Just like he'd killed Aden.

So maybe it was all going to happen again. A cycle like the sun. Apex, tomb. He didn't know what any of that meant.

"Jefe," came a voice from in back. Madrigal.

Wren didn't turn. Knew what he was going to hear.

"We found only dead bodies. A room of torched computers. There is nothing."

Of course there was nothing.

"The port is calling. Federales are coming. We must go."

Wren said nothing. So federales came, it wouldn't matter. Lock him up in a prison, maybe he'd just escape. Maybe he'd stay. Stop trying to climb to the apex. Settle once for the tomb.

"You should go," Madrigal said. Like he cared.

Madrigal left.

Wren sat with his hands shaking, watching the dark sky curdle from pink to blue to purple to black. Stars emerged. Boats came out. Lights spinning, bullhorns calling cautions in Spanish. Nothing Wren needed to hear.

Hard to know what he wanted, now.

Two more of his brothers were alive still, out there somewhere. The third human zoo was a nothing now, just the final point in the looping dot-to-dot of some earlier plot, but nothing more. No X. No lead on the Apex. No way to stop the ALERTs from going off like missile bursts.

He was back to square one. Rubbed his thumping temples. Maybe he'd have been better off sitting this out on the Iowa farm. Watching the frosts come, the corn stalks decay, while the Foundation fell apart around him. Maggie had argued otherwise.

He smiled. What was a Foundation, if not the preparation for a Pyramid? Dig down for a tomb, build up for an apex. Of course, only one point in all the pyramid could be the apex. Everything else supported it. It was the one point that ruled over all.

The federales reached the ship's side. The New Dawn Seafarer's engines had wound down some time back. Wren hadn't heard much other than Madrigal since then, figured the passengers were all still locked in their quarters. If he wanted, it'd be an easy enough thing to evade the Mexican police. They didn't know what they were looking for. Wash his hands, melt into the crowd, disappear over the side. Take a lifeboat. No. That'd be too slow. Commandeer one of their speedboats.

He smiled again. Hands curling in on themselves.

With these hands he'd pulled the trigger to usher his brother on. On some level he'd savored it. Wasn't sure if that made him just as bad as the Apex himself.

Somewhere below the federales boarded. The dizziness receded. The earpiece bleated, and Wren slipped it into his pocket. No answers, no direction. He stood. Easy to fall, this high up.

Back through the bridge, he looked in on the body of his brother. Aden looked unpeaceful. The captain was there too, holding a stained towel against his side, staring at the body. He saw Wren, flung up his hands, said something fast in Spanish.

Wren waved a hand. "Lo siento," he said. "No te preocupes." I'm sorry. Don't worry.

His Desert Eagle had been set on the control desk. Maybe Madrigal's work. Wren looked at it. The captain looked at it too. Before he could do anything he'd regret, Wren strode in and swept it up. Easy. Tucked it into the holster and moved on.

He went down the stairs. You couldn't help but just keep on surviving. The federales were coming in around the swimming pool now, weapons raised. Wren ducked deeper. Took turns through the ship until he reached a low deck on the other side. It was quiet and still there, the darkness thick beyond the glowing white halo of the ship. Everything beyond that was the wild, and the wild belonged to him.

He broke a glass safety screen, worked the crank for the nearest lifeboat. Worked the second. The boats dropped on their lines, hit the water and tugged free of their ropes. Wren waited. At some point shouts went up. A federale boat pulled around. All eyes turned to some sad escape attempt.

Wren walked back around the midships. Found one of the federales' own rope ladders hooked to a railing and climbed it down to one of their boats. From below he didn't look any different from another federale, in tactical black. They'd all gone to the lifeboats, leaving one guy behind to watch the store.

"Hay alguna señal de él?" he called as Wren descended. Any sign of the guy?

"No hay señal," Wren responded, putting a little steam into it. "Vigile los botes salvavidas!" There's no sign. Keep an eye on the lifeboats.

When Wren dropped in beside him, the guy's eyes went wide. Not wearing the exact same gear. Not a federale at all. He swung his rifle but Wren slapped it aside, sent a meaty punch into the guy's jaw. He flew back against the boat's rubber edge and didn't get up. Lying there unconscious, he looked like Aden.

Wren leaned in, checked his pulse. Strong. That was good. Maybe he couldn't take another senseless death right now.

He sat at the tiller, fired up the engine and pulled away into the dark while the Mexican police scrambled around some empty lifeboats.

24

CENTROID

I t was around 11 p.m. by the time Wren climbed the steps to his Learjet at Acapulco International. It felt like he was wading through seaweed-clogged waters at the bottom of the Pacific. Distantly he smelled the acrid tang of jet fuel on the air, heard the muted sounds coming from a nearby passenger jet as baggage handlers threw luggage into the hold.

At the top of the stairs he stopped a moment, looked back, up and around, setting his vertigo spinning like a Matisse painting. A few lights on the concourse. The jet with its illuminated portholes like perfectly aligned bullet pocks. Vehicles flashing by on a nearby road. All the ships out to sea.

It was all nothing. No stars in the dark sky. No evidence in the zoo. No lead stretching out to X or the Apex.

His phone rang in his pocket, then force-connected before he could smother it silent. "Where will you go, Christopher?" came Hellion's voice, insistent like a bug. She'd know he was at the airport, at his jet.

"Home," he said, took the phone out and stripped the battery.

The jet taxied, launched, climbed, and Wren just sat in his chair staring out the oval window. Acapulco was bright, but all around it the dark of Guerrero province spread as far as he could see, overwritten with the afterglow of Aden's dying eyes. He felt the cost of that summary execution digging fresh pits inside and making him sick.

For nothing.

He didn't know what to do. Where to go.

Across the darkness he saw flashes of his brothers spread in their triangle, tossing rocks over his head. He kept jumping higher and higher but it was never enough.

He jerked awake with a gasp.

The jet's engines droned on around him. He got his breathing under control, surfacing from a nightmare. He hadn't meant to fall asleep at all, and brought his phone up, put the battery back in and scrolled through to the world map, where his route was drawn in red. 1:37 a.m.. He'd slept for a couple of hours, and still the vision of his brothers in their triangle shone like tracer rounds across his vision.

He killed the screen and sat in the semi-dark, trying to banish the past.

"In your heart," Aden had said. "Right at the center."

Dead.

He closed his eyes again, but now sleep wouldn't come. Too many phantoms in the air, too many mysteries locked in his dead brother's eyes. He reactivated his phone and stared at the map, watching the minutes tick by. In his messages feed there was a stream of past ALERTs gone out across the country. Dozens of them. The 42% rising for the Apex's lies, blowing up America for fun, for profit, for wild-eyed belief.

On the map the tiny icon of the Learjet jogged a pixel further northeast, stretching its red route from Acapulco a fraction longer. Somewhere over the Gulf of Mexico now, looked like the pilot had selected New York as his destination.

As good as anywhere. Another fallen zoo site. The red line blurred, doubled, and then he saw it.

Right there on the screen before him, as plain as day.

In your heart. Right at the center.

Instantly his heart began to pound. His mouth went dry and his vision tunneled to the screen like nothing else mattered. He reached one finger up to trace a simple geometric shape across the map, transposing Aden's last words and his last touch like a vast crosshairs.

Call it the center point of a triangle. The apex of a pyramid. X marks the spot.

He placed the call.

"Da, Christopher," came Hellion's flat voice this time.

"I think I've got something," he said, barely containing this new frenzy. "Can you bring up a map of North America?"

The sound of her keys rapped short and sharp like a drumroll. "I am looking at one. What is it?"

He tried to run the numbers in his head first: due west from the New York zoo, something like 2,400 miles across the country right along the 41st parallel, you pretty much hit the site of the second zoo, Seattle. Drop from there southeast all the way to Acapulco at the sagging belly of Guerrero, Mexico, and…

"Calculate distances from New York to Acapulco," he ordered, heart palpitating, "also Seattle to Acapulco."

Keys rattled.

"From New York it is twenty-two-hundred-forty miles. From Seattle it is twenty-four-seventy. Is this-"

A flash of red surged across Wren's vision. The concussion sending up a warning flare, but he couldn't stop now. Three locations, each virtually the same distance apart, made a clear symbol written across almost the entirety of the

United States. New York to Seattle to Acapulco and back to New York. Including or crossing almost every US state. Almost equilateral, but inverted.

An upside-down triangle. The Pyramid, fallen.

"The zoos make a triangle," he managed, feeling the weight of this revelation bringing the vertigo back. "Inverted. It can't be an accident. Nothing he does is by accident."

A second passed, followed by more clattering of keys. "You are correct, Christopher. It is slightly off-center, but is very close to triangle. What does it mean?"

A mark that America would burn, certainly. But more too. He remembered Aden's broken hand touching his chest. Bright red flashes burst in his head like fireworks.

"The center," he said, clinging to consciousness. "I need you to find it. The exact center of that triangle, by area, length, whatever."

A moment passed. "What am I looking for?"

"I have no idea. X. The Apex. His heart. Add it to your data matrices and dig until there's nowhere else to go."

"Working," Hellion answered.

Wren felt dizzy and sick. He stood up and held tight to the seat, turning the map of the US in his head, stepped out of his luxury seat like there was somewhere he might go.

"Oklahoma, somewhere," he guessed out loud, "maybe Kansas?"

"Approximate," Helion said. "I have centroid of this triangle, mathematical term for exact center."

Wren blinked, shuffled along the jet's aisle clutching seat backs. "Centroid. How is that calculated?"

"Middle point. It is created by intersection point of median lines. Line from middle of each triangle side to opposite corner, they meet at centroid. It is in south Kansas, southeast of city of Wichita, near small town of Medicine Lodge. This is Great Plains area."

Wren stopped at the service door and leaned against the wall, looking down over the Gulf's dark waters, fifty thousand feet distant.

"Medicine Lodge?"

"Yes. It is small town with one-thousand-seven-hundred population, seat of Barber County. Name comes from tree-trunk and branch shelter the native Kiowa people built in 1866, to celebrate annual sun dance."

"You've been reading Wikipedia."

"There is nothing else to know about this town, Christopher. This is centroid, but…"

Wren straightened up slightly, shoving the dizziness aside by force of will. "Does it cross with any data points in your matrix of the Apex? Somewhere he's been before?"

"Nothing I see yet. He has never been to this place, that we know. No Pyramid members have left trails near this place."

Wren blinked, rubbed his eyes, thinking back to the dying look in Aden's eyes. There wasn't just fear and anger in them, but also superiority. That little Pequeño 3 had still not learned his place. The exact kind of thing the Apex would do. Suddenly Acapulco made sense. The Apex had shown no interest whatsoever in Mexico, Canada, anywhere else before, but as a point of this immense inverted triangle? It was perfect.

Old briefings spun through his mind's eye like microfiche in a scanner, searching for some peg to hang this tiny, unimportant town on. "There was a cult in Kansas, I think, uncovered recently?"

Keys rapped down the earpiece. "Yes, I have it. Heaven's Fall. West Kansas. One man claiming to be 'Ancient Guardian', needed to have sex with young girls to secure their admittance to heaven. Murders followed, now he is in prison."

Could that be a lead? The Apex made a habit of adopting and co-opting smaller cults. There was no way this Heaven's Fall could have operated without his say-so, if he had any investment in Kansas at all.

Wren pushed away from the door. Wavering but straighter now as a fresh flush of adrenaline battled the nausea. He took the few steps to the cockpit and knocked on the door. It opened and Wren found himself looking into the weary face of a fuzzy-bearded young man.

"Yes, sir?"

"We need to redirect," Wren said. "I'll have the coordinates for a landing field sent through, but we're now heading to Medicine Lodge, a small town in south Kansas, southeast of Wichita."

The guy stared for a second. "The flight route's already logged, sir. I don't think we can-"

"We can," Wren interrupted. "Whatever it takes, I'll get. Whatever permissions you need are coming through right now. Turn the jet."

The guy gave a slight nod. Uncertain, but willing to find a way through. Crewing a private hire Learjet, the customer was always right.

"Thank you," Wren said and turned.

Red triangles flashed across his vision. Spread out across the country. One heart, one center. A raid, maybe, but on what?

"Are there any large compounds near Medicine Lodge?" he asked. "Militia. Biker gangs. Cults."

Keys flew. "I see nothing suspicious. No financial records for major construction. No large scale movements on satellite rewind. It is quiet, small town, lots of agriculture. Largest structures are malls and barns. Many barns."

Wren nodded. He'd have to find it, and fresh corollaries spun out from that notion. With the X-apoc hopped up to call in ALERTs when they saw him, there was no way he could just walk into Medicine Lodge and start asking questions. David Keller's campaign had made him a household name, debated endlessly on every news channel. If the 42% X-faithful figure held true, then some seven hundred people in Medicine Lodge were loyal to the Apex. It would only take one of them to set the town burning beneath another flash-mob riot.

"Can you get me an Internet blackout on Medicine Lodge?"

"Of course," Hellion answered. "Easy. But will take little time to arrange. Small town, remote location, we can provide this indefinitely, though it will be imperfect. We can block hardline Internet and phone traffic, but not radio, direct satellite links."

Wren grunted. Of course. If one of the X-apoc saw him, they'd find a way to get the ALERT out. That meant he couldn't do this himself, which meant he needed someone to run point. Open the questioning. Slip under the radar as much as possible. Candidates flashed through his mind.

Only one stood out.

"Get me Sally Rogers."

A moment's silence passed. "Agent Rogers is working to remain in the CIA," Hellion said. "We cannot pull her from this. She has essential role."

"The CIA's doomed if we can't stop X, Hellion. Doomed in any case, maybe. You know as well as I do, Congress are looking to shred the alphabet agencies. There'll be nothing left of them soon." He paused a moment, took a steadying breath. "Rogers won't like it. I don't like it either, but I need her more than the CIA right now. If I'm going to dig into Medicine Lodge, she's the only person I trust to be the shovel."

Another silence. "Christopher. This triangle, the centroid, it is… unscientific. The evidence is not here."

That didn't matter. Wren was feeling it. Aden's last words were all the evidence he needed. In the heart. In the center. Apex and tomb. "Until you have something better from the X app, it's our primary target. Everything bends towards cracking it." He took a breath. "And get me James Tandrews on the line. My real father. If anyone knows what this triangle means, it'll be him."

25

TANDREWS

"I n Kansas?" James Tandrews asked, after hearing Wren out. Sounded like he didn't believe it. "As far as I can tell, he's never been near Kansas."

Tandrews was Wren's adoptive father, and the FBI gold team leader who'd led the raids back when the Pyramid had burned itself alive. He'd been the one to discover Wren at twelve years old in the smoking ruin of the fake town, take him in and help channel all that trauma in a productive direction.

They'd hardly spoken in the twenty years since Wren had skipped out on formal adoption, except for a handful of times in the last year, when Wren was at the edge and needed help.

"It's a leap of faith," Wren said. "That's why I need your eyes on, James. Nobody knows him like you do. My team think this inverted pyramid idea is meaningless. Not scientific. But you and I know him. The Apex. Isn't this the exact kind of thing he'd do?"

Seconds passed, and Wren imagined Tandrews gazing out of his floor-to-ceiling windows into the dark Maine woods. Woken up in the middle of the night, and the old man had just taken it in his stride. A lifetime in the FBI would do that to you, Wren figured. Whether it was really happening or it was all a dream, you were always ready.

"I think you're right," Tandrews said. "The grand, megalomaniacal scale of this falls well within your father's psych profile." He paused a moment. "I never saw this inverted triangle, though. This upside-down pyramid. But it would match his egotistical MO. He's the Apex, and when seen from above, the apex of a pyramid lies right at the center. This triangle, everything your brother Aden said, it all points to the center.

"Medicine Lodge."

"Medicine Lodge," Tandrews repeated. "But what should you expect to find there?" He took a moment, thinking it through. Wren gave him the time. "Something ideological, I expect, though I've never seen the Apex use triangles in his iconography before. This may take us back to first principles." Another pause. "You're aware how the United States uses the pyramid symbology?"

"Sure," Wren said. "It's on the dollar bill."

"It is, along with an all-seeing eye. Now, that's a symbol open to interpretation, but many believe it to be the eye of Ra, Egyptian god of the sun."

Wren frowned. "And that would mean?"

"Who can say, Chris? That pyramids and sun cults are as American as apple pie? Maybe. There've been plenty of theories about that over the years." He took a moment, maybe winding himself up for a mini-lecture. "Let's begin with the purpose of a pyramid. It's primarily a tomb for a pharaoh. Immensely rich men and women, god-kings to their people. The pyramid enshrined their belief that, in death, they would continue into the afterlife with all their slaves, riches and family members intact. These tombs were hidden in the center of their pyramids, along with all their chattel and possessions."

"Like jet fuel," Wren said, picking up the thread. "Burning their past to reach take-off velocity into a new life. And that was the theory for years, right? After the Pyramid burned in the fake town, everyone thought the Apex had set himself up as some kind of modern-day pharaoh, going out on a booster rocket of his dead followers. Except we never found his body, because he didn't actually die."

"True," Tandrews said. "Which further suggests the fake town was only ever one step in a bigger vision. He didn't die because he had work yet to do. Perhaps this inverted triangle is that bigger work." Tandrews paused again, and Wren thought he heard the soft sound of slippered footsteps. The old guy pacing, getting the bit in his teeth. "Consider this. The pharaoh's tomb is just as central to a pyramid, as seen from above, as the apex."

That threw Wren for a second, but he caught up fast. "OK. Apex or tomb. Yeah."

"Yes, precisely like your childhood game. So what lies in Kansas? Will we find the Apex there himself, waiting for you? Or is this some kind of tomb, containing all his belongings, family members, dead followers, everything he wishes to take with him to the afterlife."

Wren thought about that. "His main booster rocket."

"More like his primary engine," Tandrews countered, sounded like he was getting on a roll, like he always used to in the Maine backwoods, teaching Wren the best way to trap a white-tailed deer or spit a New England cottontail. "A focusing point, as if with this triangle he could channel the entirety of America into one central spot, burning all our lives as his jet fuel."

Wren whistled low. "That is bigger. An inferno of souls." He thought a second longer, hearing again what Hellion had said. Unscientific. "Still, it's a big jump from a roughly sketched triangle to that."

"Perhaps not as big as you think," Tandrews said, and Wren could hear the gently chiding tone in his voice. "There are further links to Egyptian ideology than just this inverted triangle, Christopher. Consider what your father's mouthpieces have been saying in recent months."

Wren frowned. "You mean the X videos? Fear is a portal, walk in the fire, all that?"

"Exactly. This notion that hell is the site of some vast war, where we are all slaves to inhuman slavers, and he's the one setting us free through death?" More soft footsteps came, maybe the shushing of paper as Tandrews opened old files and began leafing through. "In Egyptian mythology, hell was called 'Tuat'. Every night the sun god Ra disappeared into Tuat to battle primordial chaos, and every dawn he emerged victorious to stamp order upon the world anew. Some call that a reincarnation, with every day the sun newly born, both father and son at once."

Wren frowned. "A son of the sun?"

"Quite."

"It almost sounds like the Christian belief in the Father, Son and Holy Ghost."

"Indeed it does. There are further ties to the Christian belief system, too, in his use of numerology. His three days in a desert pit matches Jesus's three days in the cave, before he rolled back the stone."

Wren took a long, low breath. Thinking about the hot dark of the pits, scrabbling for a way out with little Grace-In-Our-Times by his side. "That's crazy. That was a kind of rebirth too?"

"It is a confounding muddle," Tandrews allowed. "His Pyramid always was. A melting pot of different ideas borrowed from other faiths, adopted and adapted, bent in dark directions." He sighed. "The truth is, we still know so little about your father, Chris. One day he just appeared, and there are no records. It's not uncommon from a certain era, children born in the free-love sixties in various communes sprung up across the country. Cults had a field day in the wilds. We still don't know his birth name, where he came from, who his parents were, where he learned to do the things he does, or why."

A long silence settled between the two of them.

"I don't care why," Wren said. "Not anymore."

"No. But in the 'why' there will be answers. Think of it as his source code. And with answers comes predictability."

"Order stamped on chaos."

Wren could feel Tandrews smiling. "Every man's vision of order is different. For the pharaohs it meant a continuation, even augmentation, of their absolute earthly power. For you it means helping others who struggle with their pasts. For your father, perhaps it is some fusion of the two. Perhaps, even as he yearns for the absolute power of Ra, he also genuinely believes he is helping lost souls."

Wren snorted. "By making them kill themselves, and each other."

"All faiths call for sacrifice. The Egyptian god Osiris was cut up by his own brother into fourteen pieces before he was reassembled by his wife, which allowed him to become god of the underworld. Jesus died on the cross for all our sins, then walked free of his cave. You know sacrifice for some greater good is and has been accepted by vast numbers of people throughout history."

"Not when it's empty. Not when it's forced."

"I would never argue with that. But your father is an expert manipulator. His efforts have carried this nation to the precipice of self-destruction." Tandrews paused a moment. "I hope that at the center of this infernal triangle you will find not only the truth about your father, where he is and how to bring him down, but also some way to stop the feral spread of his lies."

Wren gritted his teeth. "Medicine Lodge."

"Medicine Lodge, and anything that leads you closer to the source."

26

HEAVEN'S FALL

6:33 a.m., and Kansas City burned below as Wren's jet came in to land. It looked like three large fires were spreading across the urban center, perhaps a mall, the town hall, maybe a vehicle pile-up on I-35. He checked in on his phone for the ALERTS. All were deepfake sightings of Christopher Wren. He watched the fires blazing until the jet banked left for its final descent.

Within minutes they touched down and Wren exited. His onward helicopter was waiting, a white private charter AW 109 seven-seater, pilot already in place, ten-thousand dollars by the hour.

"Where to?" the pilot asked.

He'd logged twin flight plans in advance. Now Tandrews' words echoed in Wren's head. Anything that led you closer to answers, and he knew he'd only get one shot at Medicine Lodge. Better to go in fully armed.

"Northwest," Wren said.

The helicopter took off, barely a five-minute ride over snow-spattered suburbs beneath glowering gray skies, long enough to think about the answers he needed.

Where his father was. Where X was. Why.

At five minutes the United States Penitentiary Leavenworth appeared ahead, looking out of place in the middle of the brown-green Kansan landscape; a Greco-Roman classical construction with tall white stucco columns, capped with an Italianate cupola dome.

USP Leavenworth was a medium-security federal prison nearly two-hundred years old, housing all manner of gang members, white-collar fraudsters, murderers and rapists along with one cult leader who'd done it all: the 'Ancient Guardian' of Heaven's Fall.

The helo put down on the pad inside the fence. A security escort trotted out to meet Wren. In minutes he was standing in the warden's office; all hashed out in advance, with calls to the governor via pressure applied through Rogers' connections; a guest investigator coming in on federal business.

The warden's office was reassuringly traditional: mahogany desk, teak cupboards well-stocked with leather-bound law compendiums, a brass globe, a potted fern. The warden by contrast looked furious. Top of the chain, she sat behind her desk like a dynamo ready to erupt; a broad-shouldered, crewcut woman with an ex-military bearing, effortlessly projecting an authority she no longer had.

"I cannot allow what you're planning," she opened. Pretty much what the governor had said too, when Wren had strong-armed him from the jet. "Any of this. Not you. Not here. Not now. "

Wren was ready for that. "If we don't do this now, we never will. Forget due process, ma'am. By this time tomorrow, America will be in pieces, and I figure there'll be nothing left for you to be warden of."

That broke through. "What are you talking about?"

"Turn on the news. You know about X and the riots. Did you know there's three raging downtown right now? I saw the fires as I landed." He paused a second, reading the woman. She didn't have the fiery eyes of an X-apoc devotee. Just a stickler for the rules. "For the one in city hall, they say I'm holding a tour group of kindergarteners hostage." He paused, looking piercingly at her. "Does that sound about right to you? It doesn't matter. What's real doesn't matter anymore. All that matters is how they feel, and how do you think those X-hatted idiots will feel when they find I'm not actually there? Are they going to turn around and blame X for lying to them, or are they just going to get madder, invent some conspiracy BS about false flag attacks and burn it all down anyway?"

The warden just stared.

"Forget the old rules. They're out the window. All that matters now are results. So put me in there with him. Now."

She gave the order.

In three minutes Wren strode into the maximum security Central Unit of USP Leavenworth. He was greeted by raucous hooting, insults and catcalls from the prisoners, raining down from three tiers of shuttered cells around the common area.

Wren met their wild eyes gladly. Their anger would only make his case faster. He sat down at one of the plastic-encased weld-molded picnic-style tables to wait.

They didn't keep him waiting long. Within a minute metal clanked as gates opened and closed, followed by the sound of shuffling feet, a prisoner in full restraints, handcuffs looped through belly chains to leg irons.

Wren waited as four guards escorted Aloysius Brick, senior Ancient Guardian of the Heaven's Fall cult, around. He was a skinny white guy in his forties, rusty ginger hair in ruffled sheafs atop an acne-bitten head, ears like open car doors, eyes close-set, potbelly working a bulge under his orange jumpsuit. He walked upright and disinterested until he saw Wren's face, then he gave a perfect double take and tried to run.

There was nowhere to go. Not in leg irons with a belly chain. All he achieved was thrashing in the guards' grip like a pillhead raving at a silent disco, and the cheap seats in the cell block tiers loved that. Wren waited as the guards settled Brick into a chair, as the hooting receded, then the two men looked at each other.

"You know me," Wren said, low and steady. "And you're afraid of me. Probably better for you if you hadn't shown that, Aloysius. But you did. Fear will get you every time. Is that why he didn't want you as a recruit?"

Brick's jaw opened, closed, opened again. "I don't know what you're talking about."

Wren gave it a second. Time for him to think about that. "You do. There's only one reason you'd be afraid of me, and that's because you know something about my father. Now you're going to tell me what that is, or it's going to get ugly in here."

Aloysius blinked, trying to get control of himself. "I don't know you. I don't know anything about the Apex."

Wren smiled. "Did I say anything about the Apex?"

It took a second for Brick to realize his mistake. When it hit, he sagged.

"Everything you know, right now," Wren said. "Hold out, I'll have them open up these doors and let the good old boys out. Way I heard it, they sealed your records. Nobody here really knows what you did in Heaven's Gate, so it'll be my parting gift to share the good word. All the kids you abused, Aloysius. I think the shoe'll be on the other foot pretty fast when they get down here, am I right?"

Brick's eyes dilated. Seeing the future and not liking it.

"You wouldn't do that. No way you could. There's systems here, and-"

Wren punched him in the face.

Not too hard. Not enough to break any teeth, his jaw, anything like that. Just enough to get his attention.

Brick rocked in the chair. Spluttered. He looked at the guards, but they didn't make a move to help him. He tried to rub his bloodied lip, but couldn't reach his hands up from the chain.

"One way to stop this from getting a hundred times worse in the next hundred seconds," Wren said. "Tell me everything you know, right now, about the Apex. I know he would've come to you on a recruiting call. There's no way he didn't, you setting up shop in Kansas. Try to bring you into the fold, I expect. It's how he rolls. Tell me about Medicine Lodge."

Brick's eyes widened. "Medicine Lodge?" Sweat raced down his cheeks now, blood stained his white teeth. "You mean, the little town, he…"

"Go on."

"I, uh…"

Wren watched the inner calculation taking place. Who to fear most.

"Eighty seconds. I'm right here, right now. Simple logic. I will make your life unlivable, right now. Help me out, I take him down and whatever gag-order threat he's hung over you disappears."

The decision clicked over. "Not only me," Brick said. "My flock."

Wren frowned. "What, Heaven's Fall? He'll kill them?"

Brick nodded.

"And they're still loyal?"

"Some."

Wren rolled that for half a second. Some cult followers always stayed with their leader no matter how dark it got. "I'll put a security detail on them, I promise. Now tell me about Medicine Lodge."

Brick took a breath, nodded, began. "Your father, he came five years back. It's like you said. Tried to bring us in. Vow loyalty. Talked about bigger things."

"Bigger things like tearing the US apart?"

Brick shifted uncomfortably.

"You were small-time then. He was planting a seed, hoping you'd grow to something bigger." Wren looked at him pointedly. "Lots of other cults went the same way. You've seen them on the news, getting broken. Yours never came to fruition, did it?"

Brick looked down.

"What kind of attack did he have in mind for you?"

"I got hints only," Brick said, wiping the drool off his chin with his shoulder. "Seemed it was religious. Turn people against Christianity. Get me to claim I was the Second Coming."

"Seriously?"

"Why would I make that up?"

Wren grunted. Religion was one fault line the Apex hadn't exploited in his efforts to split the country. Maybe this was evidence he'd wanted to, but it hadn't shaken out. "Vast egotism, maybe. One thing I can tell you, Aloysius, you're no Jesus."

There was a flare of anger in Brick's eyes, but it dwindled fast. "Maybe not."

"No maybe about it. I'm thinking you got too greedy, too fast. Did he sell you out, or did you screw up and get caught all on your own?"

Brick's expression darkened.

"He sold you out," Wren concluded. "OK. Means you weren't professional enough. You were an also-ran, not capable of going national. Some seeds were scattered on fertile soil, some on barren rock. You were a dud." He thought a moment. "So tell me about Medicine Lodge."

"I don't know anything about it."

"I don't believe you."

"Maybe some rumors. Nothing from him. I did my due diligence on the guy. Couldn't just hand my whole life over."

Wren nodded along. Plenty of other cult leaders had done just that. "So what did your due diligence turn up, four years back?"

Silence.

"Forty seconds."

"I put a tracker on his car!" Brick blurted. "One of his visits. One of my team."

Wren frowned. "Your team?"

"Of course. I wasn't stupid. Run a group like mine these days, expect the Feds to swing by. I had my kids in the rocks outside the compound every hour of every day. Any car pulls up, they plant a tracker, doubles as an immobilizer. We don't wait for the government to bring us down. We take the fight to them."

Wren grunted. "You had kids plant immobilizers? You trigger that at the wrong time, it's not just property damage. It's murder."

"I hear you've done worse."

No need to answer that. "So he went to Medicine Lodge. Right after you?" Brick nodded. "This is five years back. Where in Medicine Lodge? I'm hearing it's barely a one-horse town."

"No signal out there. I never retrieved the device. No idea where specifically. Just that he went there."

"And that's it?"

Brick shifted uneasily.

"Ten seconds."

"He had someone in the trunk of his car!" Brick said, then seemed to regret it.

"What?"

"I didn't hear her. The kids did. Told me later. Really spooked them."

Wren frowned. Disgusted, really, to think what this man had done to the people in his charge, but there was no point dwelling on that. "You think he was taking some victim to Medicine Lodge. Like a delivery?"

Brick shrugged. Getting some of his confidence back now. "Who amongst us knows the true darkness of the human heart?"

Wren snorted. "That the garbage you showered your congregation with?"

"All this and more, Christopher Wren. Son of the Apex. I see him in you, you know."

"Yeah," Wren said. "I'm a real chip off the old block."

27

TODAY

B y the time Wen strode back into the dawn light outside USP Leavenworth, smoke from the Kansas City fires twenty miles distant had blurred across the wan blue sky like furrows in an old man's brow.

America was burning.

The AW 109 helo was waiting for him in the lot outside the prison walls, but empty. Wren stopped at the cab, looked around. There was no sign of the pilot.

"Where is he?" he asked.

"Pilot is not responding," Hellion answered. "I do not have access to prison video feeds. Whole area is on comms lockdown until you are gone."

Wren grunted. "Did anything get out?"

"Nothing. It has taken much of our infrastructure to block this area, make it invisible. Many bot-nets crunching past communications in and out, like looped camera feed. No ALERTs. Whole prison is silent. This is big success."

Wren wasn't in a celebratory mood. Aloysius Brick's words echoed in his head. Four years back, the Apex had transported a woman in the trunk of his car to Medicine Lodge.

Why?

Tandrews was right about that. The 'why' was everything.

"Agent Sally Rogers has arrived outside Medicine Lodge limits," Hellion prompted. "A strike team is ready. Comms blackout prepared. Can you pilot this helicopter?"

Wren looked around a final time, taking in Leavenworth's classical limestone walls and verdigris cupola dome, like something his namesake architect would have put atop the St. Paul's cathedral in London. A worn baseball diamond for the prisoners off to the left, tree-lined roads with a couple of penitentiary workers' homes across the way, and beyond that just empty fields of grass stretching to the horizon. No sign of the pilot at all, like the land had swallowed him up.

A freak-out, no doubt. He'd seen the spreading smoke, tried his phone and couldn't get a meaningful line out, then panic hit and he ran. Wren was grateful he hadn't taken the helicopter. Maybe some small vestige of order remained, but not for much longer. Property rights would be first to go.

"Can you pilot this helicopter, Christopher?" Hellion repeated.

"Maybe." Wren opened the cab door, took a look inside. The key was in the ignition, the dashboard lit up ready. Standard-looking cyclic, collective, throttle, anti-torque pedals. He'd flown bigger helicopters. Last time he'd been in the cockpit was a year back, when he'd used one like a can-opener to slit Somchai Theeravit's mid-century modern Alaskan mansion open, get to the goodies inside.

He leaned in, tapped the dials. Plenty of fuel. Easily enough to get him to Medicine Lodge, two-hundred-seventy miles distant. Four hours by car, one and a half by air.

He climbed in and started the blades. Within minutes he was at six-thousand feet with the blades at a steep forward angle of attack, all the land spread like a patchwork map below and the smoke of Kansas City fading in back, roaring southwest.

For an hour and a half he barely thought. Watched the navigation computer as it charted his progress. Listened to the odd radio report of riots spreading across the country as fresh ALERTs popped like Russian missile strikes in some grand game of mutually assured destruction.

Like a spell. A triangle his father had etched like some vast hieroglyph across the country, aiming to focus all the pain on Medicine Lodge and turn him into a god.

It didn't matter that none of it was real. Egyptian pharaohs. Afterlives. Slaves that served you forever. What mattered was that people were willing to believe it. And there were always people willing to believe, for a shot at belonging to something bigger than themselves.

He placed a call, routed through the helo's headset, switching off all monitoring from his hackers. The phone on the other end rang. Three times. Four. When it picked up he felt his heart almost stop.

"Yes."

Her voice. Loralei. His wife. A woman he'd loved so fiercely it'd given him the strength to finally leave the CIA behind. Drop the crutches of the past and try to become the family man he'd always aspired to be.

Too late.

"Who is this?" she asked.

Wren tried to speak, but the words wouldn't come.

"Chris?"

Wren crushed the phone to his ear. It killed him that she'd guess that. It killed him more that she didn't sound angry. Maybe concerned. Maybe afraid.

"It's me. Lor."

There was no response for a moment. Wren thought

maybe she'd hung up, began to panic, but then he heard it, the distinctive catch of her breath as she tried to disguise tears.

He'd only known her to cry twice in all the time he'd known her. Once when she'd told him she was pregnant with Quinn. Their first child. Tears of happiness, fear, excitement. They'd shared them together, even as they'd gone on for what felt like hours, riding her body in waves. A second time, they hadn't been shared with anyone. They'd been near-silent and alone, and he'd witnessed them like some thief-in-the-night voyeur, through a spy-cam his Foundation had installed in the den of her Delaware duplex.

It hadn't been any kind of moment, as far as Wren could see. No fight with the man she'd taken up with for the last eighteen months. No trouble with the kids. There'd been supper, bath time, bedtime stories. A kiss with the guy, tell him to go on to bed, then she'd gone downstairs to watch TV.

Except she'd never even turned the television on. Just sat on the couch and shook, then those silent sobs had begun. Like she was holding up the weight of the sky all on her own. Like the dam was finally bursting on a year's worth of pain.

Wren had wanted nothing more than to call her then. But it wasn't his place. He'd caused all this, after all. His lies for over a decade. His job. His past. His father. All he could do was watch until it grew too much, then he shut down the cams and left the woman he loved to her own private pain.

All that came rushing back as he heard that muffled sound again now. The joy of their first child. The pain of their separation.

"I'm sorry," he said, the words passing through him like a summer storm. "For everything. For how bad things are now. I'm sorry I let it get so bad, Lor."

Moments passed. Her breathing steadied slightly.

"You're sorry?"

He braced. Expected another tirade. A knife wagged in his face, a demand that he never call again. He had accepted the limit of the restraining order she'd placed against him. He'd do it again, whatever she demanded.

"So much. For all of this. I just… I wanted to-"

Words abandoned him. The truth was so many things. He wanted to hear her voice. He wanted to make promises he didn't know he could keep. He feared all the ways she could crush him again.

"Chris," she went on, "as far as I can see, you're the only one fighting it. I'm watching the news, and the things they're saying about you?" She paused a moment. "I just don't believe it. They're all lies. This X? It's crazy. It's your father. I know that now. I see that. I'm the one who's sorry. I need to-"

She stopped, and Wren felt his heart teetering like he was about to hit aortal flutter, fit to pass out.

"I-" he managed, but couldn't squeeze any more through his tightening windpipe.

"Let me get this out," Loralei pressed on. "It's… I should have given you a chance. Maybe. I don't know. But you're not, ah, who has the words!? I know you're not bad, Chris. I know you love us. Me and the kids. You hurt us so much. But with all this going on, I just…" her breathing grew erratic. Wren felt like he hadn't taken a breath in minutes. The helicopter could be falling from the sky and he wouldn't even notice. "I'd never seen the full size of it. You never told me, so I guess I can blame you for that too." She laughed through the tears.

Wren sucked in a breath, trying to speak.

"Hush!" she ordered, sharp like she'd always been before, when she'd wanted to make him laugh. "Let me finish. Now I see it. How he's coming for you everywhere, coming for us all. Across the whole country, city after city. I can see them marching in the street outside right now! People I know, decent people, they're going crazy. Dressing up in his colors, waving his flag, talking about walking in the fire. It's... I don't know what to do." She sucked in a gulp of air. "The kids are inside. We're all safe, but who knows, really? This is bigger than any of us. If one of their mobs hit this neighborhood, I know there's nothing I could say or do to stop them. We'd be helpless. They'll burn us alive and think they're saving us. This is way bigger than you or me, and now I see it always was. The Apex, right? He sent me that email at the start, he's the one who broke your cover. He shattered us. He did this. And I was so mad at you, I never once thought why."

Wren's eyes blurred with tears. Couldn't help it. Felt like an incredible weight was lifting off his shoulders.

"That bastard!" Loralei said with unexpected vigor. "Now I see he wanted you isolated. Ineffective. I never listened, I was too hurt, and you've lots still to answer for, but I know you're still the Chris I knew. That agent, Sally Rogers, she told me you'd let her take you in, put you in that CIA prison." A pause. "That's the right thing, Chris. It means you weren't ever as bad as I feared. So now I wish I'd given you that chance. To explain. To make it right. I wish I hadn't let him manipulate us. So I'm sorry for that."

Wren couldn't believe what he was hearing. Finally found his voice. "You don't have to be sorry. It was all me. I should've-"

"You're damn right you should've!" Loralei snapped, followed by pained laughter. "We'll talk about that plenty, don't you worry. If anybody's sorry here, it's you. You screwed up with us so bad, Chris. But I see it now. All this X stuff, I get it. What you were up against. What was driving you." A pause. "I want you home."

That was a punch in the heart. Ten seconds passed. Twenty, more, and he couldn't breathe. Everything he'd hoped for, and it had only taken the imminent end of American civilization to bring it on.

"I'll get you," he finally settled on. "I'll send my best people. They'll pick you up now. The kids. The guy too, if you want. Ship you securely out of there. It's all going to fall apart, Lor. I'm trying to stop it, but…"

"I know you are, honey."

That 'honey' broke him further.

"There's a place," he went on, desperate to get the words out while he still could. "The safest place I've got, maybe the safest in the country. It's called Little Phoenix. It's a kind of headquarters for my Foundation. Remote, reinforced, capable of independent living even if the world around it goes mad. I trust everyone there implicitly. You'll be safe."

Now she was crying again. "We'll go. We're waiting, Chris. Just do what you need to do. End this as soon as you can, and come home."

He squeezed his eyes tight shut, gritted his teeth like he was bulling through the worst torture he'd ever felt in his life, like he was back in the Apex's pit staring down the barrel of emptiness forever.

"I will. I love you, Lor. Tell the kids. My people will come for you soon."

He hung up. Couldn't take anymore, not and still focus on the job ahead. The work to be done.

The tears dried in his eyes. His breathing grew under control. He gave the order through Teddy for an urgent pick-up from Frederica, Delaware. His wife, his kids, and the guy too. Then he issued the ruling wider. All points evacuation to Little Phoenix, Arizona. The last safe place in America. Hunker down and try to weather the oncoming storm.

By the time it was all done, he was back in the headspace

he needed to be. Dead brown fields ripping by below. Rogers and a team waiting up ahead. Medicine Lodge fifty miles further. The dashboard clock clicked over past 9 a.m.. A weather warning slid up on his phone, said a heavy snowstorm was brewing over southern Kansas.

It was all going to end today, one way or the other.

28

FATHERS

Wren brought the helicopter in low over barren fields shorn of grain sorghum, wheat or soy for the winter, like echoes of the Iowa farm. Southern Kansas, close to the Oklahoma border and flatter than an ice rink, almost as sparsely populated as the surface of the moon.

Wren felt it in his gut. The dry cold in the air buffeting through the slitted cockpit window. No Interstates within a hundred miles, no railroads, no real airports. Quiet fields, big sky turning black with the gathering storm, small towns. A vision of another world, like the clock had wound back to the Wild West and any minute he'd see cowpoke rustlers pushing a cattle train across the great plains, Wild Bill Hickock surging out with his lawmen, Wyatt Earp following up with a jail stagecoach.

Intermittent structures flew by below. Ruined homesteads and storm-battered old barns, showing Bleeding Kansas' history as a Civil War-era holy grail. Chase that with decades of sharecroppers tilling life from the clay soil, then rip it all up with the great Dustbowl, as mass migration West left family lands to be swallowed up by the big banks, handed off to become the current system of factory farms.

Now there was only the occasional vast tractor squatted beside a field like an alien dropship, enormous plow spreading like an iron river delta, broad enough to do the work that once took thousands of men. Immense tin sheet barns stood clumped at the center of vast networks of fields, fringed by green fern-like sprays of coppicing; trees sprung up around shallow curling arroyos.

The history of America written in the scars of the land.

9:40 a.m., and Wren glimpsed his team up ahead as blots of color beneath the glowering sky. A white semi-trailer parked at the desolate side of the road, ten miles out of Medicine Lodge, with Sally Rogers at the front by a Ford F-150, her vehicle of choice, branded in blue and silver. Impressive work for a rip-off sprayed up by his junkyard mechanic Alli, flown in specially out of Arizona.

He put the helicopter down by the truck, killed the engine and took the keys, then ducked out of the cockpit as the blades wound down. Agent Sally Rogers strode across the low mound of raw dirt at the side of the road toward him, looking every bit the part.

Pale blue shirt with shoulder straps, embossed metal insignia studded through the collars, navy tie tucked in at the third button down, silver badge on the left shirt pocket, gear strap worn like a bandolier, Glock 19 at her hip, navy pants with a powder blue ribbon sewn down the outside, and to cap it all off, a broad-brimmed Stetson cap almost completely obscuring her straw-blond hair.

A Kansas Highway Patrolwoman, no two ways about it.

"Boss," she said, and her intonation along with the pale cast of her face said it all. The same vertigo sense of teetering over a vast drop that he'd been feeling for a week now. America in free fall.

"It's good to see you, Sally," he said, and that landed harder than he'd expected, brief emotions splashing across her face before the professional mask reset. He never called her Sally. "I wouldn't want anyone else with me for this. Thank you for coming."

If anything she turned paler. Regardless, the hand she held out to shake was rock steady. "I wasn't going to at first," she said. "I felt sure we had this. The riots, upheaval, X." She raised her arms, gestured around. "On TV, from Langley, even seen from a crowd control helicopter, everything looks different. You mistake chaos for an outlier, mistake order for something inevitable, like it's our natural state." Her eyes took on a faraway look. "But it's not, is it?"

Wren didn't say anything. Figured the question was rhetorical, something she'd share if she needed.

"I talked to my folks, Chris," she said. She rarely called him Chris, either. Seemed they were both feeling it. "My dad joined them." Her voice caught. "My mom was in pieces. She'd been holding out on contacting me, didn't want to 'worry me'. Apparently he left the house way before dawn, when one of those flash mobs was called. He's seventy-three, Chris. Now he's out rioting somewhere in Poughkeepsie. It's..."

She trailed off. Wren put a hand on her shoulder. Strong, but she was shaking for all that. His cue.

"It's not his fault."

"That's just it," Rogers said, and now Wren saw the anger burning through. If she was shaking with anything, it was rage. "It is his fault. It's mine and my mom's too. He's been spouting off about X for months, trying to convince us to 'save our souls' before it was too late. I pushed back some, figured that he'd have his fill of it soon, figured it was mostly harmless crackpot nonsense, but maybe I just told myself that. Like a cancer, you know? It's easier to ignore the warning signs than dig in for chemotherapy."

Wren grunted. About all the response she needed. There'd be time for recriminations later.

Rogers shrugged. "Yeah. Truth is, he's always been one for conspiracy theories. I used to find it amusing. Not so much, now. He shoved my mom aside, apparently. Took his rifle. He's still a crack shot, used to be a Navy marksman. This X BS, it's..." she trailed off, bit her lip, firmed up her demeanor. "It's dangerous. Lethal. I can't believe he did that to himself, but then I can. It's our job, right? Warding off self-radicalization, the new vector for terror, and we're all responsible. All of us who humored him, looked the other way." She took a breath. "Now my mom's home alone, terrified at every loud noise, watching black X flags parade by in the street. I've tried calling my dad, he's not answering. I'm thinking any minute I'll see him on the news."

Wren nodded. "You're furious. I get it. And you're not sure who to be angry with."

She laughed, almost lost control but caught it. "You're damn right I'm mad. But place the blame where it lays, I say. Your father's at the root of all this. No offense. That's why I'm here."

"No offense taken. Your father needs help, Sally, just like any cult devotee. My father needs a long fall from a short rope. Right now we focus on only that." He pointed off in the direction of Medicine Lodge, where the storm skies were darkest. "You're going to be my face in there, my voice, my eyes. We have to play this right. Spook this town, it'll snap shut like a mantrap. We need something from these people…" He took a breath, looked off to the side. "Hellion, Medicine Lodge is on a comms blackout?"

"It is," she answered sharply in his ear. "Invisible. ALERTs blocked. Incoming and outgoing calls spoofed. It is energy intensive, but we are spreading the burden. This should last several hours before it is noticed."

Wren looked back to Rogers. "Several hours. He's here, Rogers. Final hurdle. Let's dig the bastard out."

Rogers nodded sharply. Call that properly motivated.

She started toward the F-150, painted in its Highway Patrol colors; better than unmarked FBI for rolling in and asking questions of small-town folk. Take national politics off the table. They'd be less likely to close ranks. Wren had prepped the cover story, too. They had a photo of the Apex not publicly shared, not sought for any crime, nothing that should activate any X recognition, and a cover story with him as a potential victim of wire fraud. It should be enough to bypass any X BS long enough to get some answers.

Wren followed Rogers over. She popped the lid of a large equipment box, dug out a second Highway Patrol uniform and held it out.

"I doubt it's your size."

"Maybe not the hat," Wren quipped.

Rogers briefly cracked a smile. "You have got a big head. Come on."

Wren chuckled, changed there at the roadside. The navy pants almost split at the thigh, but that was fine, his job was mostly to sit in the car and keep his head down. The shirt barely buttoned across his chest, but the tucked-in tie covered that up. The hat fit well in the end, perfectly shading his face.

Last he looked to the team. They'd been spun up on a dime, standing now by the semi and fully kitted out for tactical suburban warfare. Doona, Henry, Mason despite his various broken bones, plus Abigail and Luke, who'd helped save Steven Gruber back in their battle with the Ghost. Abigail was a brilliant triathlete and cult survivor, Luke was an ex-State Congressman who'd been kicked out of office for taking bribes. Alli slouched nearby with spray-paint burn on her dungarees, looking surly as ever.

That cheered Wren up. He strode over, shook hands, patted shoulders, gave encouragement.

"You look like a dead dog on a stick," Alli said. Wren beamed. Half her head was shaved close, the other half was bleached blond in a topknot, and there were numerous jeweled piercings in her face.

"I feel like it. You look like a badly inlaid brooch."

She laughed, punched him in the shoulder. Same old Alli. "Great work on the Ford," he said. "I'd never spot it's a fake."

Alli looked offended. "It's not a fake. Same model of Ford, exact same paint the Stateys use, exact same spec. Ther own mechanics wouldn't know the difference."

Wren beamed. With a team like this, how could they fail?

Henry was waiting with a serious look on his face. "On your order, Corporal. We'll be there in minutes."

Wren nodded. Looked over his select team a moment longer. There weren't a lot of them, next to what the Apex had to be packing. A handful only. But he wouldn't trade them for the world.

"I know it. Godspeed to us all."

Rogers climbed into the F-150's driver's seat, kicked open the passenger door and Wren stepped in after her. She hit the gas and pulled onto the road leading toward the heart of it all.

29

MEDICINE LODGE

They entered Medicine Lodge from the north on Well Road, driving in silence into a flycatcher grid of generous grass-laid blocks, each filled with a handful of spacious ranch-style family homes.

Picket fences. Well-groomed yards. White-painted stones lining a row of old-growth elms. No snow on the ground, though the forecast said the storm was imminent, with mottled dark clouds yawning overhead, like some great beast ready to bite down and scoop this town, this state off the face of the Earth.

"Looks like my hometown," Rogers murmured, weaving toward South Main Street.

Wren said nothing. Maybe this *was* his hometown, or at least his father's. Everything about it spoke of ease, tradition and comfort, though he felt none of that. The X icon was everywhere, on black flags hung from windows, on lawn signs, on truck decals. A woman walking her dog had a cap emblazoned with a bejeweled X.

"They're crazy," Rogers muttered, tracking the woman briefly. Even the dog wore an X on its doggy jacket. "Like it's the World Series."

Wren focused on his breathing, on managing stray flickers of vertigo.

Rogers made the turn onto Main Street. It was a broad red-brick paved expanse laid out like a cowboy town of old, enough for four lanes abreast though there were no markings. No need. Barely half-a-dozen vehicles troubled the thoroughfare, cruising slow like old-time stagecoaches.

Tall federal-style townhouses spotted the avenue, stark red brick fronts decorated with sharp white chevrons, hosting the lawyer, the town's one fancy restaurant, the bank. Rogers slow-rolled like they were cruising johns. Interspersed amongst the older structures were newer, stubbier buildings with Old-West false fronts like a long line of saloons.

An auto shop. Internet services. A place with only 'TREASURES' written in whitewash on the window. Plenty more X symbols.

"Up here," Wren said, nodding toward a place called 'Larks', the town's only breakfast diner.

Rogers pulled in easy. No siren. She killed the engine and turned to him, they exchanged a look, then she stepped out. Closed the door, took a few steps, spoke. "You hear me?"

"Loud and clear," Wren answered, receiving through his earpiece.

"Getting video?"

Wren tapped his phone to activate it, set the screen low on the dash and saw from Rogers' bodycam. "Got it."

"Then in I go."

She turned and walked up to the Larks' entrance, Wren tracking her. Looked like 50s diner style inside. Lots of chrome, baby blue bar, glossy red Bakelite two- and four-tops, neon signage in back. The door pushed open and Wren split his attention to the bodycam footage.

The diner had black and white tile flooring, mirrors in back, a gleaming soda fountain next to a cake rack. Real retro. There were two customers sitting along the bar, both tucking into blueberry waffle mounds, one of them wearing a black sweater with large white X's hand-painted on the arms. Rogers stiffened slightly. The guy had his phone right there on the bar; useless for calling in an ALERT, with Hellion's comms blackout in place, but all he had to do was run out on the street and shout it out, that ought to do the job.

Wren itched to warn Rogers, though of course she'd know to play this thing below the radar. Paramount to all of this was not turning the town into a mantrap.

Wren studied the guy as Rogers kept on toward the bar, not breaking stride. He looked thirties, burly. He glanced briefly as Rogers came by, then turned back to the TV in the corner, showing the fires in Kansas City. Maybe waiting for the call from X to come.

Behind the bar stood a sun-weathered woman with straw-blond hair, maybe late fifties, white apron over denim shirt, long dangly earrings, polishing glasses while idly watching the news.

"Help you, hon?" she asked with a true Kansan drawl.

"I'd kill for some good old cream soda," Rogers said, and Wren imagined her flashing a smile, "but maybe when I'm done here. For now I'll just take a coffee, black, plenty of cream."

The woman smirked, nodded in Wren's direction through the glass. "Take your coffee like you take your men?"

Rogers laughed low, just girls sharing a little smack talk. "That one's a rookie. Disgraced himself one town back, started talking up the Wildcats, Kansas State."

The lady blew air out of her lips, flipped a cup, expertly hoisted a chrome coffee pot and started the pour. "Them's killing words out here. What town were you last?"

"Harper. Blackwell before that. And it ain't barely ten yet."

The coffee sloshed satisfyingly, followed by an unhealthy dose of cream from a huge tin pitcher. "They sure keep you Stateys busy. Anyone knows the South, they know we're for Barclay. Maybe a small college, but they're religious, got fight."

Rogers smiled, raised the coffee mug like she was saluting. "I hear that, ma'am. Except last I heard, Barclay's got no football program. Soccer, they have. Basketball. Maybe that's what you mean."

The lady grinned. Wren hadn't done the research, hadn't even realized that was a test. "You ain't disgraced yourself yet, girl. How's that coffee?"

"Beats Harper hands down," Rogers said, smooth as hot licorice. "Now, Blackwell I'm yet to try, but I'll be sure to share notes."

"Ask them tightwad bastards for cream, they'll give you spit and shoeshine for your trouble."

Rogers laughed. "The old boy in the Main-Street diner there, he didn't look too friendly. More like a bobcat waiting to strike."

The lady laughed. Held out a hand. "Name's Linda. I seen that old fella. I don't often head out that far, but they got the mall. He has a real wily look."

"The good Lord treats some men mean and keeps the rest keen," Rogers said smooth, then shot a glance to Wren. "Others he just hits with the stupid stick all the way down."

Linda cackled.

"All right now," Wren said low, but Rogers ignored him, took Linda's hand and shook.

"Sally Rogers," she said. "Field Supervisor, pulled rookie-training duty all this month."

Linda nodded at Wren. Both seemed to be enjoying this. "He's watching you real close, that one. Intense, like. You got him the whole month?"

Rogers sighed. "He's first place in a carousel of hard-chargers. Or that's what they think, anyhow. What a ball-ache."

"Men," Linda lamented.

"Amen to that."

Rogers took another glug, smacked her lips. Wren began to wonder if she was ever going to get to the point.

"So what brings you to Medicine Lodge, Sally?" Linda asked. "Especially with this storm about to blow overhead. You best not get out of town too far, they say it's a bad one, gonna dump ten inches of snow in three hours."

Rogers whistled low. "How about that? I guess this'll keep. Fact is, we had a BOLO a few days back, track and find, but it's not urgent." She took a look meaningfully around; at the guy with the X arms, at a small X badge on Linda's apron. "Seems you're all good folks here, though, you have this town in hand. I'll just write it up. It's a cold trail anyhow."

Wren glanced over at the guy by the counter. He wasn't looking at Rogers. He was staring directly at Wren.

"You say that, hon, but we got our weirdoes here too," Linda said low, leaning in. "Folks who don't know which side of the egg's got the yellow, you get my drift?" She paused a long moment. "You hunting a murderer?"

Rogers laughed. "That'd be something. Nope. It's training-wheels time, caught a bad traffic stop on a stolen vehicle outside Wichita, led to some further fraud charges. You'd think with all this going on," she gestured to the TV, "they'd have us on something bigger, but the State's split on which way it's going to flip, if it comes to that."

Linda nodded thoughtfully. "And you?"

"Oh, no question," Rogers said. "Like I said, I see only good folks here. I'm a patriot. State police ought to be pulling for what's right."

Rogers glugged more coffee. Linda seemed to be coming to some kind of decision. Opened her mouth to speak, but Rogers beat her to it.

"Fact is, we've got the guy who lost his truck, know he's been associated hereabouts, but nothing concrete. We need to check in, let him know the goods are recovered and be sure he's not getting defrauded further. Simple as that."

Linda licked her lips. Maybe starting to believe this wasn't X-related, maybe worth homing in on for some good gossip. "You got a name, a photo of the guy?"

"No name, but a bad photo. You sure it's no trouble?"

Linda was practically salivating. "If anyone in this town knows, it'll be me. I been here all my life, run this place thirty years."

The camera shuffled as Rogers pulled out the doctored photo of the Apex, digitally shifted from Keller's campaign stage to a standard white backing, like a DMV mug shot. Even a hardcore X-apoc wouldn't know who it was, judging from the X videos of him as a much younger man.

"Here's the guy. He's kind of a looker, for an older fella."

Linda took the photo. There was something for a second, some kind of stray knowledge fleeting in the depths and rippling across her face, but it disappeared fast. Wren thought for a second she was going to clam up completely, but that's not what happened.

"That guy, he's bad news." Linda pushed the photo away like it was poison oak. "I never met him, barely even seen him, but folks know. You say he was a victim of carjacking?"

Another test. Rogers played it perfectly. She'd never said carjacking. "Unknown at this point. Some delinquents in a car registered to him, is all I know, routine traffic stop." Her head tilted slightly. "Why, you think I need to be careful? Maybe he's mixed up in this fraud too, not just the victim?"

Linda nodded wisely. Another test passed. "I bet you

always are careful. But you go looking for that man, I reckon you bring more than a rookie with you, y'hear?" She leaned away. "I wouldn't bother, though. He ain't been through town in years, least I know."

Sally nodded, folded the photo back into her breast pocket. "Well, any idea where he moved on to? These itinerants, mayhap non-believers, they're a plague. One minute they're greasing fools for their pension, the next they're locking kids up in the basement, starting a livestream."

Linda's eyes widened slightly. Another great play. Offload the responsibility to some other town. Raise the stakes at the same time, but in a totally different direction, just following up on what she'd already said.

"A livestream?"

Rogers nodded toward the TV. "You see how it is out there. What people will do these days just to get their kicks. It takes good folks standing up to set things like that straight."

Wren had to admire that. A masterful piece of work. Feeding into the X madness and letting Linda fill in the gaps, letting the guy in the X-shirt know she was no threat, even figure they were all on the same side.

"You're right on the money there. Well, last I heard, that man headed west. He was tied up with some church out that way. First Corinthians, I think."

"I don't know it."

"You wouldn't. It burned down some, oh, three years back? They had charitable projects through the area, though, a roaming ministry, as I heard it, but not anymore. I ain't seen him in years, like I say."

"Sounds all the better for you." Rogers took another glug of her coffee, knocking the rest of it back. "Well, I've got a good start on my report here, I figure. Thank you, ma'am."

Linda looked uncertain. Maybe already suspecting she'd

said too much, cooperated too easily. "You ain't gonna put my name in your report, are you?"

"Are you kidding, and end up sharing this coffee with the other Stateys?" Rogers grinned. "Not a chance this side of the almighty's fire, Linda."

Linda smiled. "Well, you stay safe out there, Sally. It's strange times, what with the storm coming and all. Of course I don't just mean the weather."

"I hear that, and it surely is," Rogers closed, tipped her Stetson then looked around to the man with the X on his arms. "Y'all stay safe here."

The guy's gaze followed her out, then lingered on Wren until she got behind the wheel and pulled away.

30

FIRST CORINTHIANS

"Hit on the first try," Wren said. "What are the odds?"

"In a small town?" Rogers asked, rolling slowly south on Main Street. "Pretty good."

Wren nodded. Small towns, everyone knew everyone else. The human record went long, and the diner was always a center. Right alongside the bar, if the town had one, and the church; the real storehouses of a place's oral history. Not the things that went in the books or appeared in the paper, nothing so tectonic. This was the language of impressions, slights, grudges and generational feuds. Tap into that and a waterfall of knowledge would pour out.

"First Corinthians," came Hellion's voice in Wren's ear. "I can find no record of this church."

"Figures," Wren said, then turned to Rogers. "You did great, by the way."

Rogers looked at him, flashed an almost cheeky smile. "I've got moves. You seen all the X stuff in there? They love them some craziness."

"Cancer spreads from the middle," Wren said low. "No

mirrors in a place like this, no different folks to reflect you back in a different light, show up the crazy."

"Cancer," Rogers repeated, then brightened. "There were plenty of mirrors in that place, though. About every surface was chrome."

Wren snorted. "Not really what I meant, but point taken."

They pulled up to an intersection, where an old guy was doddering slowly across the street aided by a walking frame. Rogers blipped her sirens briefly, gave him a neighborly wave. They waited.

"So, five years back," Rogers said. "Coincidence, or you think she saw our guy, ferrying some victim in the trunk of his car, as per Aloysius Brick?"

Wren thought back to Brick in the Penitentiary, eyes going misty as he remembered the 'good old days' of Heaven's Fall. "It's never a coincidence with the Apex. I think your girl Linda knows more than she's saying. But we can't force it."

Rogers nodded. "That guy at the bar had a hard-on for you. Maybe he knows something too."

Wren shrugged. "State troopers. Maybe he got a sense who I might be. Through two layers of glass, though, wrong outfit, hat shading my face, I think we have some leeway. And if First Corinthians leads nowhere, we come back and pump him like a fire hydrant for all he knows."

The old guy cleared the crossing. Rogers gave a thank you blip of the sirens.

"So where to? Drive west, looking for burned-out old churches?"

"Sounds about right to me. Hellion?"

"I am completing scan of west region, Medicine Lodge," came her Russian-accented voice in his ear. "I see what must be burned church. Drive west, Sally Rogers, I will direct you."

"Gotta love an eye in the sky," Rogers muttered under her breath, and pulled right.

The townhouses and false fronts of Main Street swiftly bled back to ranch-style homes, which soon became nothing but grass, trees and fields, their winter colors muted further by the black sky. Hellion directed them on a few turns heading further from the beaten track, circling around outcroppings of robinia and birch trees grown up around curlicue arroyos; signs of water turning on flat soil as it tried to find a level.

Ten minutes passed, twenty. They rode through fields, now, fenced-off for cattle. The grass was close-shorn, and large yellow hay bales stood like watchmen surrounded by chewing cows.

"To the right, in this field," Hellion said.

Rogers pulled up on the verge. They both looked out over a field of stubbled grass. "I'm not seeing anything," she said.

"Do you see those trees?" Hellion asked. "Clustered around small stream. Church is within the center."

Wren pushed the door open, started out into the chilly air. Felt like the temperature had dropped well below twenty degrees in the last hour. There was the faint hint of a gravel track spreading forward through the level grass, but clearly disrupted and picked over by four years of grazing. A path to the church. He straddled the fence and started on a beeline for the trees through a gathering of cows, Rogers following close behind.

"You should know, there is movement back in Medicine Lodge," Hellion said in his ear.

The cold air stung Wren's cheeks, burned his throat. Still healing from smoke inhalation back in D.C.. "What kind of movement?"

"The man in the diner, he is gathering others. They are armed."

Wren cursed low. "How many?"

"Four so far. They are all X-apoc, Christopher. They wear this openly on their clothing."

Another curse. "Have they tried to trigger an ALERT?"

"Not yet. I will block it if they do. I cannot predict further, but this man certainly heard your current destination. Perhaps they will come. You should be fast."

Wren wasn't worried about that. In a firefight with civilians, he liked his and Rogers' chances two against four. It could even be a blessing in disguise. Out here in the middle of nowhere was the perfect place to run a no-holds-barred interrogation. But many more than four, and if they were all armed? That might be a problem.

"Put the team on alert, send them circling this way. If there's more than four, we'll bring them in. Otherwise, just give us the head's up when they're near."

"Now there are five."

Rogers laughed.

"OK, so we hurry," Wren said, and started to run.

The gravel crunched. The cows parted as they neared, lowing loudly. Thirty seconds later they hit the tree line. Tight-knit trash saplings had woven thick around a few tall robinia trees, between them hiding a shallow trough in the grass; the path of rainwater curling like a crop circle. Wren pushed through, stepped over the dried-up waterway, passed another veil of low saplings into a green-encircled clearing, and there it was.

"Holy moly," Rogers said by his side.

As a church there wasn't much of it left. A few wall risers where the damp ground had seeped up and tamped down the flames, no higher than Wren's shoulder, fire-bitten edges rounded by five years of rain. The remnants were black but showed through hints of silver birch underneath. The wooden flooring was a fire-ravaged pit, and at the center where the blaze must have raged hottest was a jagged ring of soil showing, sprung up with weeds, ferns and more spidery robinia, straining for the sun.

Wren strode closer. Around that inner ring of soil some floorboards remained, scorched but saved by how snugly fitted they were to each other. Looked like expert craftsmanship, even holding together still. Scattered atop the boards and slurried at the edges was a papier-mâché paste of old wood pulp, interspersed with the dull blue and black of leather Bible bindings. In places the hollowed-out frames of chairs remained, black with char and tumbled where the fire's draft had swept them.

Rogers cursed.

Wren stepped through the entrance, little more than the ten-inch stubs of a doorway to either side. Underfoot a mosaic of oxidized steel roof tiles slid uneasily. Off to the right lay the crumpled church tower, the most intact part of the structure remaining. Half in the arroyo, the top portion appeared to have survived the fire unharmed. Silver birch, red roof shingles, square box design leading up to a copper cross, one of its arms embedded in the earth.

Wren pointed. "Strange nobody came for the cross."

"Strange they just left all this here," Rogers countered. She stepped over the wall and stood in the midst of a heap of charred furniture, holding up what looked to be a moss-sodden yellow jacket.

Wren frowned, stepped closer. "That wasn't in any fire."

Rogers shook it, handed it over. Wren handled the jacket, opened it up. Moss shook free, maybe a few years' worth of growth. In places the yellow was faded, but in the folds where it had been lying upon itself the fabric was bright still.

"You think it's hers?" Rogers asked. Didn't need to say any more than that; they both knew who she meant. The girl in the Apex's car five years back.

Wren surveyed the rest of the church, mind racing to the contents of Paul's first Epistle to the Corinthians. As far as he remembered, it was a message to the people about immorality, focusing on division amongst the people, sexual impurity and the doctrine of Christ's resurrection. In particular, though this portion was considered by some to be a latter-day addition, there was a section mandating the silence and subordination of women at church.

A melting pot of ideologies, just like Tandrews had said.

"Maybe," Wren said, casting his gaze wider, holding up the jacket. "Why else would this be here?"

He looked past the low saplings in the center, to the fore where the altar lay on its edge, hardwoods only partially burned, to the edges, over the slippery roof tiles and the rain-matted wattle of Bibles, leaflets and hymnals.

"Could be kids," Rogers hazarded. "It's a great place to make out."

"I don't think it's kids. Look around. The whole place feels staged somehow."

"How so?"

"There's no other trash," Wren began, scouring the floorboards. "No beer bottles, cans, cigarette butts, plastic bags, graffiti. If it was kids, this place'd be a dumping ground."

"That is strange," Rogers allowed.

Wren strode up to the burst of saplings in the center. They caught a narrow halo of light directly from above. The rest of the church lay in shadow, but not here. Had the tower been erect, it would have caught that sunlight on its spire most of the day.

He toed the earth at the edge of the floorboards, where the firmly slotted wood gave way to soil, and felt a wash of vertigo rushing over him. The line was clearly demarcated, not worn away into crumbly charcoal as he'd expected.

"These boards didn't burn in this pattern," he said and looked up, sending dual visions battling across Rogers' face. "This close together, they'd never incinerate so perfectly. They were cut."

Rogers stared. "Cut?"

There wasn't much more to say. From a top down view, you couldn't tell which parts of a pyramid were which. He pointed off to the side, where the turret and its cross lay unbroken. "Apex." He pointed at the dirt by his feet. "Tomb."

Rogers paled. "You think she's buried right here?"

Wren was already rolling up his sleeves. "Only one way to find out."

31

YELLOW JACKET

They wrapped sharp-edged roof slates in their Highway Patrol jackets and dug. The metal cut clean, but given the near freezing temperature, it took time to chip into the hard soil. Minutes passed as Wren chopped through wiry sapling roots, Rogers battering out divots beside him. Inches at first, giving way painstakingly to a foot of clearance.

"Seventeen X-apoc," Hellion said abruptly in his ear. "All armed. They are coming in five vehicles."

Wren laughed. "Seventeen?"

"This is correct, Christopher. They are serious."

No doubt. Seventeen was too many, maybe even for his whole squad. Still, if the 42% number was accurate, then seventeen was just the tip of the iceberg.

"Too many," Rogers said. "Even if they're all raw civilians, never been out on the range, and I doubt that. They'll have trained, as per the X app. We'll be over-run."

"Twenty minutes yet," Wren answered, and kept on digging. Everything could change in that kind of time. "Are the team in position to intersect?"

"They are still en route to you," Hellion answered, "perhaps twenty minutes also."

Wren laughed again. "Give us a proximity alert. Their job is to hold these idiots off, not engage in a mass shootout. No unnecessary risks."

"Understood."

The slate-shovels rose and fell. Wren's slate cracked and he swept up another. His shoulders burned from the vibrations, the healing wounds in his palms ached with every dropped blow. Digging a pit down to the foundations.

Five minutes. Ten. A cloud passed over the sun above, sending shivers up Wren's spine. Moments later a single flake of snow drifted down to rest on the hard pack undersoil.

Rogers laughed.

"Faster," Wren said.

More snow fell. They took it in turns to scoop out the hole, a three-stroke motion like a rail-tacking team, laying the beam down, setting the tie, hammering it home. Chop. Chop. Sweep.

Several feet deep already, several wide, hammering like a twin cylinder two-stroke engine, up then down.

"They are one minute out," Hellion said.

"Our team or theirs?" Wren grunted between strokes.

"Both."

He hammered deeper, like he was digging a route back to the past. The sound came of approaching engines.

"They are beside your vehicle. Henry's team are ahead, circling in behind tree cover."

"Hurry your ass up, Henry," Wren commanded, sent another downward stroke, and this one hit metal with a clang.

He looked up at Rogers. She dropped her slate and started clearing the dirt with shaking hands. A small patch of tarnished tin emerged.

"Here," she said, pointing at a thick knot of roots and

earth. Wren brought the slate down with all his strength and mass. The root network cleaved clean through, a five-inch chunk of soil broke off like an iceberg calving, and Rogers lifted it, tossed it aside. "Here," she pointed to another likely spot, and Wren brought the slate down again. She turfed and cleared, dug around in the loose shale.

"I can feel the edge," she said, then pointed again.

"They are coming up the field," Hellion warned. "Henry is asking to engage."

"Fire to draw them off us," Wren commanded, slammed the slate down. "Do not get shot. Avoid aiming to kill, if you can. Don't expose yourselves."

"Understood, Corporal," came Henry's sharp response.

The first shot rang out. A wild chance fired through the tree cover which ripped a hole in one of the church's low standing walls.

"Henry," Wren urged, brought the slate down again.

"Incoming," Henry answered, followed by the incredible crack of his M25 firing an M118 Special Ball. "One down, should be non-fatal."

After that the air became a storm of bullets, gunshots sounding like a ceaseless roll of thunder, slugs tearing through the trees and shredding the church walls.

"Keep their heads down," Wren barked into the chaos. "Just buy us time."

"Yes, sir," said Henry, and another Special Ball crack rang out, this time echoed by a substantial explosion. Had to be Henry finding the range of their vehicles' fuel tanks.

Wren and Rogers worked throughout like an artillery loading team, her targeting, him letting rip with the slate.

"X-apoc are trying to press ALERT," Hellion said. "I am blocking actively."

The slab of metal was exposed on one corner and down most of one side now, looked at least three feet long and maybe the same wide, maybe a third of it cleared. "Tell me they're not getting through," Wren said.

"Comms blackout remains, but now they see this. Our spoof response is giveaway. I have them radioing on shortwave, perhaps out of blackout zone."

Wren cursed, brought the slate down, Rogers cleared it. "Reinforcements. You can't block shortwave?"

"I cannot, Christopher. This will get out."

The ALERT would escape. The flash mob would come.

"I'm hit!" came Doona's voice.

Wren brought the slate down so hard it bit back through his jacket-grip, slitting into his palm. He cursed, reared back and looked through the screen of trees. Beyond the green he could loosely pick out the row of silhouettes advancing steadily, a floodtide of X-apoc maybe fifty feet out.

"Get her out of here, Mason. Henry, kill their vehicles and go."

"Retreating," Mason answered. "Get out too, Christopher."

"Boss," Rogers shouted, jerking his attention back down. "Help me."

He looked. She had her fingers pried tight under the corner of the metal cover. He swiftly repositioned, wedged his fingers under the lip beside her with his legs coiled, then together they strained. Half the cover was still coated with several foots' worth of soil and saplings, maybe a half-ton of mass embedded in the wider root system.

"Heave!" Rogers commanded, and they heaved. Wren's legs burned as he fought through the deadlift, breath coming in sharp pants and vision swirling with bright colors as bright white roots popped out of the soil like straining stitches.

Not enough.

"They are twenty yards out," came Hellion's voice.

"Now or never, Corporal!" Henry shouted from in back.

Wren chanced a glance, saw Henry hunkered down by the church turret.

"Heave!" Rogers ordered again, and they both lifted with all their strength, legs thrusting, arms drawn to the limit. The metal sheet lifted some three inches, soil tilting to the edge and roots spraying like snapped elastic bands.

"They are on you!" Hellion shouted, matched by a crack from Henry's M25. Wren was distantly aware of a man falling back through the screen of trees, head exploded. More were coming. Everything looked red.

"Heave," Rogers ordered once more, and he gave it everything he had.

Now the whole ground hoisted up with a dislocating wrench, and Wren staggered forward as it tipped, almost stepped into the shallow pit beneath, instantly lightheaded as the pressure came off. Rogers caught him, another Special Ball rang out, then she had her Glock up and was joining Henry in fending off an incoming wave.

Wren was left staring into the pit alone. Maybe five inches deep at the edges, though it deepened sharply toward the center. Within lay the contents, like some kind of ancient display case ornately laid out in a museum. No mistaking what he was seeing.

Yellow-white human bones laid out in an inverted triangle. Perfectly aligned. The bones of both legs; femurs, tibias and fibulas made up the two downward-angled sides. The bones of both arms; humeri, radiae and ulnas made up the top bar. In the center of that triangle lay a rib cage, with the pelvis atop it, and nestled atop the pelvic girdle lay the skull, facing down.

Wren's vision popped and tripled. There was not a scrap of flesh remaining, as if the bones had been bleached before burial. A perfect inverted pyramid, with the heart, womb and skull at the center. Apex. Tomb. Everything. A fellow human's skull forced to stare down into hell forever.

Wren reeled backward.

"We have to go," Rogers shouted.

Wren heard her and knew she was right, but that didn't matter now. With unconscious precision his hand went to the Highway Patrol-issue Glock 19 at his hip, drew it smooth and was already striding forward.

"Chris, no!" she shouted.

"Christopher's AWOL, cover him!" Hellion bawled through the earpiece, but Wren wasn't listening. Only seeing his father again, standing over one of his pits and burying people alive, with those same people thanking him for the opportunity.

Everybody was responsible.

He broke through the tree cover shooting. Seconds passed before the X-apoc realized what had hit them. Maybe a dozen of them remained, advancing in a line. Wren saw their faces in flashes like special effects in the X app, allowing him a focus he'd never quite felt before.

The Glock bucked in his palm.

Two down in a second. Three down and half of those remaining broke ranks and ran when they saw who it was. The fabled Wren. Five turned on him and fired back.

Rogers burst out beside him, took two more. Special Balls rang out. Wren saw X wherever he looked, his morphing face atop these men and women, wearing their insignia, playing their games like no one was going to get hurt, when everyone knew what the wages of sin brought.

They knew. The kids back in Louisville had known. The man who'd shot the reporter. They all knew. They were all responsible. He saw Rogers' father out there. He saw his own. Doona limping up from the side. Mason striding through gun smoke like some battle angel. Bullets tore into the earth around him, spraying wild.

He sent back only precision. Chest, chest, head. Femur, radius, ulna. Imagined digging pits with meticulous care, bleach-stripping away the flesh and burying them all facing down, wondering what that really meant.

Taking everything away, even in death.

The Glock clicked empty. He looked up, dizzy on his feet. Snow was falling thickly now.

"Boss," came a shout. He turned. Rogers was there. She mouthed something but he couldn't make out the words. To his left the field was strewn with bodies. Some groaning, others still. A vehicle tore away.

"We got all of them," Rogers said, standing before him now with her hands on his shoulders, trying to focus his eyes on her. "We're clear."

They weren't clear.

Wren shook free and stalked the battlefield, barely hearing as Hellion reported the worst news yet. "They got a shortwave message through, Christopher. An ALERT has gone out from nearby town of Harper. I see hundreds mobilizing already. Thousands. One hundred mile radius, maybe more. You must get out of Medicine Lodge."

Wren kept walking until he found what he was looking for. The guy from the diner. He dropped to one knee, put a thumb on the guy's eyelid.

"Where is he?" he demanded.

The guy cried out as Wren pushed. Getting his attention. Was already carrying a wound in his belly, maybe not long left for this world.

"Who?" the guy bleated, one eye roving.

"I know who you think I am," Wren boomed, pushed his face in to fill the guy's field of view. "What you think I am. The biggest jailer of them all. So believe that. I have you right now. Your soul. Tell me what I want or I'll never let it go. Where is he?"

The guy's eye was nothing but terror and pain. "I, I, who?"

Wren didn't let up the pressure. "The man behind First Corinthians. Where is he?"

"First Corinthians," the guy managed, confusion spinning through the fear like a mad top. "That guy? He's further out." He swallowed, sobbed. "Man, you gotta-"

Wren pushed.

He screamed. "The guy, he ran this place! He ran all the Corinthians stuff. He's got a farm!"

Wren leaned in close, made sure all the guy saw was his face. "Where?"

"I ain't been there! It's…" his eye whirled. "Anastasi Street, I heard! Way out, big place, you can't miss it."

Wren waited.

"Yes, Christopher," came the harried voice in his ear. "Anastasi Street exists. I see several farm buildings gathered. A compound."

Wren let go, stood. Was about to walk off but something made him stop, turn back to the guy.

"Face down," he said.

"What?" the guy managed.

"Face down!" Wren commanded. "That's how you die, looking into the earth. Now!"

The guy rolled. Set himself belly down. Bleeding into the cold, snowy dirt.

Wren looked up. Saw Rogers staring at him, Henry, Mason, Doona, the others. Judging. He didn't care. Everybody made their decisions, and everybody had to pay.

32

FACE DOWN

T he F-150 raced at sixty miles an hour down the straight country road through thickening snowfall, headed west for Anastasi Street. Wren could feel Rogers seething by his side.

"No unnecessary risks," she said through gritted teeth.

Wren said nothing, focused on cleaning dirt out of the cut in his palm with an antiseptic wipe, wrapping it in bandages.

"You said it," Rogers pressed on, flashing him a murderous look. "No unnecessary risks, so what the hell was that? Solo charging a superior line? Then get the guy to go belly down. Why?"

Wren turned to her, turned away. "You saw that grave."

"I didn't see a thing. I was covering for your ass. She was in there?"

Wren let out a long breath. Not keen to revisit the contents of that grave, but Rogers had to know. "She was. Bones of her arms and legs laid out in an inverted triangle. Pelvis and rib cage stacked in the middle, skull on top facing down."

Rogers didn't say anything for a long moment, then let out a frail-sounding, "Oh."

Wren gazed out the windshield. The sky was a black ceiling, pregnant with mass. The wind was picking up harder, slashing snow against the glass, forcing the wipers to work hard to keep up.

"How's Doona?" Wren asked.

"She'll live," Hellion replied. "Calf shot. They are stabilizing her. Christopher, I am sending them next to a jet north. Many more X-apoc are coming. You will not be able to shoot them all down like old-movie gunslinger."

He grunted. Maybe that was funny. Striding out into gunfire and surviving. Some ridiculous kind of thing to do. He turned to Rogers.

"You think he deserved better?"

She looked his way, refocused on the road. "That guy?"

"That guy."

She thought for a second. "No way he was the one buried that woman there."

"Agreed."

"So you just punished him for crimes he didn't commit."

Wren was ready for that. "You're thinking about your father."

She half-laughed. "You're damn right I am."

Wren steeled himself. "I'm done babying these people, Rogers. That man sucked down lies for months. He gulped them greedily, just like your father did." She opened her mouth to protest, but he sped on. "If I can save a man like that, like your father even, I will. It's what the Foundation's for. But at some point they cross over and become enemy combatants. About the time they take up arms and start shooting, I'd say." He paused a second, catching his breath. "This is not a game anymore, this is real. Self-radicalization's a bitch like that."

Rogers said nothing.

"He picked a side. This is a war. I'm all out of mercy."

"When were you ever merciful?"

Wren thought back to Diego Helmuz and the kids in Louisville. "You should have seen me yesterday, in Kentucky."

Rogers snorted. "What were you, handing out candy at the Vantasy Con? Way I heard it, you got that whole place set on fire."

"Oh, I got it all on fire," Wren countered fast. "Haven't you been watching the news? Every one of these X-apoc outbreaks, it's me. My atrocities, my fault, so they can heap up all their hate in one place. I'm chief jailer to these people, setting their souls on fire, so why not play the role they want?"

"You're not their jailer."

Wren laughed. "Maybe I am."

"What?"

"Just something the 'Ancient Guardian' said in Leavenworth. He saw my father in me. Maybe he's right."

Rogers snorted. "Well that's bullshit. He may be in there, but you aren't all one of anything. Just like me, just like that guy you put on his belly, just like my dad. We're all imperfect little angels."

He took that on the chin.

"And why's it always about your father?" Rogers went on. "I'm sick of that bullshit, too. Who's your mother, Wren? You ever ask that question? Coffee's different with a little cream. Maybe she's half the bad, maybe she's half the good. You don't know a damn thing."

Wren looked away. Couldn't argue with that, and as the heat faded a little now, things did look different. He brought up his phone and transferred the line direct to Henry.

"Henry," he said.

"Yes, Corporal!"

Wren took a breath, didn't look at Rogers, spoke

through clenched jaw. "When Doona's stable, do what you can for the others. The X-apoc. Seal wounds, put them in a vehicle, heating on. They'll die out there in this storm otherwise."

Henry said nothing for a moment. Probably trying to square this with the Wren he'd just seen.

"I know," Wren said. "They're the enemy. But they're also us. It's not like Afghanistan. We can't kill our way to victory. Not that we ever could there, either."

Another second, then a bright, "Yes, sir," came back.

Wren ended the call. Looked at Rogers. She nodded once. That would have to be enough.

Back on his phone, he scrolled through to the darknet, thinking ahead. Their cover was definitely blown. Medicine Lodge was in the crosshairs now, and the Foundation boards were wild with speculation and anger: about X and the X-apoc, the attacks, where Wren was and what he was doing, what they should be doing to support him. His last orders had been to lay low, relocate to Little Phoenix where they could, and it seemed they were struggling with that. De-escalate. Avoid friction, try to keep the X-apoc from triggering. It was hard to stand by and do nothing while the crazies were out setting innocent people alight.

Wren knew that all too well. Anger made you vicious.

He took a breath, fingers hovering over the touchscreen keypad. About to make the decision and cross over. It was one thing to tend the wounded. It was another altogether not to fight in the first place, and there was no point pretending any longer. You couldn't de-escalate a mustering army with decency and reason. All you could do was meet it on the field.

TO FOUNDATION MEMBERS IN KANSAS - RALLY TO MEDICINE LODGE NOW, READY FOR BATTLE. THE X-APOC ARE COMING IN THEIR MASSES. OUR

GOAL IS PRESERVATION OF LIFE. ALL MEANS ARE JUSTIFIED.

He fired it off. Started on the next.

TO ALL FOUNDATION MEMBERS – RALLY TO YOUR STRONGPOINTS. HOLD BACK AS LONG AS YOU CAN, BUT THERE MAY BE NO AVOIDING THIS. PREPARE TO FIGHT FOR YOUR COUNTRY AND YOUR LIVES.

He sent it.

Long seconds passed. A minute maybe. He heard the tiny squawk of Rogers' earpiece, receiving a barrel-load from Hellion. Watched her knuckles whiten on the wheel, teeth gritting, then she spun to him.

"The hell you just did?"

"Watch the road."

She cursed. "Answers, now, Chris! Sounds like you just ordered your people to prepare for open warfare across the country."

Wren looked at her, sad for her loss. Her father was already a casualty. She was struggling with the man he had become, and Wren knew exactly what that felt like.

"You've seen what they do. They hit a place based on some deepfake footage, make up some crimes I committed, then shower violence on everyone nearby when I'm not there."

"Fires," Rogers dismissed. "A few deaths."

"More than a few deaths," Wren countered. "The count's in the hundreds nationwide, and all those were for fake crimes I didn't even commit. But look where we are now, Rogers. I just saved a dozen X-apoc fighters so they can report in. They won't need to deepfake anything. I really am here. I really did shoot them. They're going to hit Medicine Lodge and wipe it off the map, just because it happened here."

Rogers' grip on the wheel tightened. "I don't buy it."

"Because you're torn. I get that. But the country's about to cross the Rubicon. Open warfare's three heartbeats away. We either stand by while they massacre the whole town, women, children and babies all, whether they're in X onesies or not, or we take a stand. Once that's done, it's going to go the same way across the country. This place is the trigger, and there's no avoiding it. Unless you think fifty-eight percent of the whole country can somehow retreat? Up to Canada, maybe? Cede the country to the Apex, so he can burn what's left for his afterlife slaves."

Rogers stared hard, like a pressure cooker nearing its limit, then let out a loud burst of cursing.

"I'm sorry, Rogers," Wren said. Staring out into the snow as if he could see all the way to Anastasi Road. "For now, your dad's gone. He made his choice. Now do what you told me to, and start thinking about saving your mom."

She slapped the wheel once, twice. Cursed him out. Slapped it again.

Nothing to say to any of that.

The snow fell and she drove faster.

S eventeen miles west and a handful north, the snow grew thicker and the farms grew bigger, fences receding far away into the streaking snowstorm as the black skies opened and the snowstorm let rip. Wren half listened to Rogers talking to her mom, the signal barely crackling in through the storm, and half tuned to Hellion and B4cksl4cker talking on a side channel.

Rogers was alternately begging, advising and commanding her mom not to go out and look for her father. Not to mock up some X gear, not to pretend she was a member, not to go march in their fiery riots unless she wanted to be made complicit in murder and risk death in a firefight with government and Foundation forces.

"Stay at home," Rogers urged, eyes shining as she kept the Ford barreling into the crazy snow. "Mom, just stay at home."

In the other ear B4cksl4cker was relaying orders from Teddy through to Hellion as she prepared to run field-marshal on the largest battle of her long wargaming career. As a StarCraft maven, winner of the top awards for online battling when she was only fifteen, with the eye-watering stat of four hundred meaningful actions per minute, she'd developed an awesome ability to multi-task a war on dozens of simultaneous fronts: units fighting at the front lines, units gathering resources at the back lines, units building new weapons, units on first aid, units setting traps, all blurred into a real-time strategy that moved with the enemy like a living thing, like weather.

All that made for a management system so complex and interwoven that commentators often spent months breaking down every one of her myriad brilliant moves, all made in real time, putting a dozen gambits into place every second, monitoring and following through only on the best.

This was bigger than anything she'd ever attempted before. B4cksl4cker was already spinning up dozens of AIs to automate whole sections of the country under her control. Foundation forces in Florida. Foundation forces in Milwaukee. Foundation forces everywhere. Their strengths, their training level. Breaking them into units, setting them up with leaders, assessing their resources, preparing them to go headlong into battle against the X-apoc.

Civil war. It was real.

"We will not be able to help much in coming hours," B4cksl4cker's deep voice came in Wren's ear. "Jets are already waiting at all surrounding airfields for you. Perhaps pilots will wait. Some are Foundation fringe, so we are hopeful. We are also paying very good rate. But..." he trailed off.

Nothing more needed to be said. The larger battle was in the hands of his hackers now. A couple of millionaire kids, really, in charge of the fate of America. Five years back when he'd dug them out of international hacking schemes, blackmailing North Korea with Russian intel, holding Belarus hostage with a Venezuelan cryptoworm, he would never have seen it coming to this.

"Compound is ahead," B4cksl4cker said. "Two miles off road. Good luck, Christopher. I hope this will help end war."

"Me too," he answered. "Good luck."

The line in his ear went dead. He looked at Rogers. Seemed her call to her mother was finished.

"This is crazy," she said.

"She's safe?"

"As anyone, now."

Wren could feel her twisting inside. Overtaken by fear, betrayal, anger. Maybe trying to decide how much of this to lay at Wren's feet.

"We get the Apex, this thing ends, Sally. Force a confession live on the Internet. Half the X-apoc will fold in the moment, a quarter will probably lay down arms under duress, the last batch will get smoked out and jailed. It will happen."

She laughed. "He'll never confess."

"Then a humiliation. Put him in cuffs and frog-march him out of there in Federal custody. Shut down the X app for good. No more ALERTs. No more BS in the air. I guarantee, those people will look up from what they're doing and just wonder what on Earth it's all for. Like an epiphany. I've seen it before, and I know we can break his hold. Even on your father."

Rogers grunted, then yanked the wheel right. They dumped through a shallow ditch with a thump, smashed through a wooden fence then peeled out across a field.

"Dead ahead," she said.

Wren couldn't see anything yet through the driving snow, but brought up his phone maps app. B4cksl4cker had already pinned their target, and now the dot that represented their vehicle was racing diagonally toward it. Wren zoomed in. On the map it looked like an industrial farm complex: a huge warehouse barn, several long battery-like outhouses for cattle, one of those massive tractors, a square residential block.

"I never saw your father as a farmer," Rogers said.

"He's a farmer of souls."

Rogers stared at him. Didn't look ahead, didn't need to, plummeting forty miles an hour over an open field. "And the crop's ripe, is that it?"

Wren met her gaze sincerely. "Bursting at the seed pods."

For a second he thought she was going to curse him out, but the moment broke with a couple grunts of laughter instead.

"You're a weird guy, Boss," she allowed.

"Coffee in the cream. Now eyes dead ahead, lieutenant. The Apex awaits."

She laughed again. Wren allowed a smile. With the country falling apart it hardly felt right, but what else were you going to do?

"Pull right," he said, watching the maps app. "Let's come in around the back of the barn. Snow will provide cover."

Rogers turned the wheel. Wren held up the phone so she could see, and she navigated by the screen. There was nothing visible through the snow until the last minute, when the towering aluminum side of the barn appeared to the left. Rogers slowed until they reached the corner, then halted and killed the engine.

"No backup for an hour plus," Wren said.

"Just the two of us," Rogers said. "We've got shotguns in back."

"Mossberg?" Wren asked.

"Tactical."

Wren held up a fist. Rogers bumped it.

"Let's go."

34

ANASTASI

I n two minutes they were fully tooled up with fresh gear over thermal jackets: black Mossberg 500 12-gauge shotguns, with 00 Buckshot cartridges in a quad-hold chest strap ready to speed-load; pistol ammo bandoliers for their Glock 19s, six magazines each packing Gold Dot G2 rounds; Kevlar-wrap level III+ front and back plate body armor; high-cut IIIA ballistic helmets with night-sight mounts; fresh earpieces with subvocal throat-mics; a strip of flashbang and percussive grenades.

"You have thermal binos?" Wren asked.

Rogers rustled in a box, all equipment dumped from a Foundation storehouse into the back of her F-150. "For the snow?"

"Anything will be better than zero visibility."

She came back with a pair of HD 640 thermal monoculars. They fastened them into place on the helmet mounts. Wren nodded, raised his shotgun. "You have left, I'll take right."

"Pincer movement, got it."

They broke.

Wren rounded the corner of the barn in seconds,

advancing steady and smooth, scanning the wall of snow ahead. Even with the monocular live, the raging flurries cut his visibility down to maybe ten feet. His heart thumped. Across the yard he could just about make out the long outlines of the cattle outhouses.

No sound, no movement. He reached the barn's edge and cut left around the front, found a door, tried the handle. Locked. He pulled a folding pry bar from his gear belt, wedged it into the jamb with a firm thump of his palm, then yanked.

The lock creaked, the frame warped and the door popped open.

"I'm in the barn," Wren subvocalized into his throat-mic, and slid easily into a narrow tin-walled corridor. He smelled diesel oil and molding hay on the dry air, heard only the masking shush of fat snowflakes driving against the walls. Five steps on and he hit an opening into the barn proper.

It was dark and cavernous inside, no electrics lit, hardly any natural light filtering past the falling storm through corrugated plastic panels high in the roof. Just enough to make out a ramshackle assortment of farm machinery.

Wren strode forward steadily, wary for traps, working a path between various oversized threshers, harvesters, milling boxes and seeding trailers. The monocular performed better here, showing only cold in sharp blue vertices. No signs of life. Fine dust in the air caught the gray light rinsing in from above, making the space feel oddly unreal, like a monochromatic dream.

Wren reached the rough middle of the barn, rifle sweeping. Ahead implements hung on the wall beside tatty denim overalls. Tall stacks of baled hay climbed toward the metal beam rafters, feed for the cows. An old tractor sank on deflated tires in a corner, next to a metal workbench neatly laid out with various mechanic's tools, a few long gas canisters, a sawhorse.

No hostiles, though, no triangles, no pyramids. No sign of a trapdoor leading down, no heat signatures below his feet signaling another human zoo packed with captives. Wren didn't know what he'd expected, but it wasn't this.

"All clear, Rogers," he said. "There's nothing here. It's just a barn."

"Understood," she came back. "I have eyes on the cattle outhouses. Nothing here either, except cold cows."

Wren pushed back against the sense of his heart sinking. Cold cows. All signs suggested this was a normal working farm. Whoever ran it would have no time to also run an international cult bent on bringing down America. He let his rifle barrel drop, lifted his monocular, felt all dressed up with nowhere to go.

Trespassing in some random farmer's barn.

What was their lead here, anyway? Some dying guy who'd picked Wren out from a diner, another X-apoc loser? The X-apoc were civilians off the street, not drafted for their proximity to the Apex. The guy was most likely a nobody, maybe worked in the local library, wrote out late tickets on books on loan too long.

What did he really know about any of this?

Wren cursed under his breath. Maybe this took them right back to the drawing board. He checked his watch, twenty minutes gone. The X-apoc weren't going to wait on him, and every wasted minute brought the war closer.

Too early to give up on the lead already, though.

"Meet you at the house," Wren said.

"Roger that."

The main barn gate was locked with a thick padlock and chain, so Wren went back the way he'd come, through the popped door and out into the raging storm. Ten yards from the barn and all hint of where he'd been was concealed by thick gusts. No sign of where he was going, either, lost in the whiteout. For twenty seconds he jogged in total solitude, then the house loomed out of the semi-dark.

Clapboard siding, one dim light on upstairs, looked like a swing set off to the left. Wren bumped into a low white fence, invisible in the storm, and vaulted it. Feet trudged down in the soft loam of a flowerbed. That didn't feel right.

"At the door," came Rogers' voice. Almost a shout now, to be heard over the pummeling wind. Wren crossed the garden and met her by the front door, barely more than a gray ghost in the white until he was upon her.

"I'm not feeling this, Boss," she shouted over the wind.

"I know," he answered. "Vehicles in the driveway?"

"Two. Looks like someone's home."

"Upstairs," Wren agreed. "We go easy, full alert. In three."

Wren stepped back, counted two then put a hard front kick into the front door's lock plate. It sprayed open, bolt tearing back through the frame, and Rogers was first in, Glock raised. Even over the roar of the storm any inhabitants must have heard that.

"FBI!!" Wren shouted and sped down the hall, watching the patterned glow of heat resolve through the monocular.

There was a wood fire burning in the den, two sofas laid before it, rug, coffee table, assorted kids' wooden block toys spread on the floor, a cup of coffee steaming on the pass leading into the kitchen.

"Clear," Rogers called, patted Wren's shoulder from behind and he fed through into the kitchen. Nobody there, though the washing machine was on a spin cycle. He cleared the utility, circled back to a study, dining room, downstairs bath, all empty.

Rogers led the way up the carpeted stairs, switching to her Mossberg now. Up to the landing, where five doors led off.

Whoever was in the home must have heard them by now. Wren nodded left, started dead ahead, and just then one of the doors opened.

A slim guy stepped out, unarmed, late twenties, wearing a threadbare dressing gown, googly rabbit-face slippers on his feet, eyes widening on Wren and Rogers. Behind him Wren saw a woman holding a baby, curled up against her chest in a cuddly pink one-piece with unicorns.

Not at all right.

Wren lowered his shotgun to the side, not all the way but enough to take the worst of the threat away.

"Where's the Apex?" he asked. Not as rough as he could. "Where's X?"

35

MARKS THE SPOT

The guy just stared. Trying to compute two people in full tactical gear on the upstairs landing of his house.

"X…" he repeated, trailed off, voice a little high, eyes darting between Wren and Rogers. "Like, X marks the spot?"

That log-jammed Wren for a second. "X," he tried again. "From the X app. X-apoc. The Apex."

The guy looked more bewildered by the second. "I, uh. X-what? I don't, uh, know what you're asking me? I want to help. What is, um…"

Wren shot a disbelieving glance at Rogers. It didn't look like acting. It looked like some sweet domestic scene. He spun back, lowered the shotgun all the way.

"This is Anastasi Street?"

The guy nodded vigorously, looked glad he could finally contribute something to the exchange. "Yes. Anastasi Street. Listen, I'll be happy to cooperate with any lawful duties, I just-"

"We're looking for the man who ran the First Corinthians church. We were told this was his place."

The guy's jaw opened, closed. "Um, first what?"

Wren took another second. The guy was young, but not that young. Anyone from Medicine Lodge would surely have heard of First Corinthians, if it was everything Linda back at the Larks diner had said. Churches, outreach, charity work. But then there was the baby. Under a year old. Given how time-consuming a newborn could be, it was totally possible they'd never even heard of X or the Apex. Add to that, this place was clearly a factory farm, and the guy's accent was slightly off.

"You're not from around here, are you?"

The guy nodded eagerly again. Something else he could contribute. "No. I, I mean we, we've been here just six months. Same time as the baby. I, uh, we took a position. I've got papers and everything."

"You're the farm manager."

"We are," the guy said. Looked momentarily grateful. Shot a look back to the woman. "My wife and I. So, uh, can I ask officer, if you are an officer, I'm not sure that's the right term, but what's this about? There's nothing here, it's-"

"Managing for who?"

The guy blinked. "It's a company."

Rogers cursed low.

"What company?"

"It's called Riker foods? I'm sure you've heard of them. They're one of the biggest, um, producers in the state." He paused. Wren stared. "They make cornflakes," he added.

"We missed the guy by years, maybe," Rogers said quietly. "Or it was all BS from the start. This was never the place."

Wren felt the lead getting frailer by the second. Without it, they had nothing. His eyes darted around the space, looking for something, anything to hang their next step on.

Nothing came.

Vertigo hit. He started thinking about what came next.

Track Riker back through financial records, try to sift some link to First Corinthians, the Apex? Without Hellion or B4cksl4cker to run that search for them, though, it'd take hours, maybe days. Try to get back to town before the X-apoc horde hit, squeeze a few more folks for leads. They might make it in time, but the diner guy must've warned all his fellow X-apoc before he left. Wren's reception was going to be frosty, and that in the midst of a snowstorm.

Beyond that, he was out of ideas. The Apex had been here five years back, he knew that for sure. Somebody had to know something, but he didn't know how to shake that information loose in less than an hour. DNA tests on the bones, maybe, but that would take days. A satellite rewind on all movements over the First Corinthians church dating back five years, but nothing doing without his hackers.

No way forward.

"I apologize for disturbing your morning," he found himself saying. "We broke your door. Someone will come take care of it."

The words spilled out with hardly any meaning. Rogers went down the stairs ahead of him. A dead end. The guy followed them saying equally meaningless words, the kind of things you said when you didn't really understand, were trying to paper things over, were trying to make yourself safe, until-

Wren stopped.

The guy actually bumped into him. Pulled back fast, apologized, took another few steps up, clearly terrified he'd just made a lethal mistake when they were on the home straight.

Wren turned. The woman with the baby was out of the room now, bobbing it up and down gently in her arms.

"What did you just say?" Wren asked.

The guy paled. "Um, I guess, just, don't worry about the door? I'm a carpenter really. It's, um, no problem."

"Before that."

The guy gulped. "Before that? Uh, I think, was it about cornflakes?"

"After, then."

The guy looked lost. Flailing.

"I think he means about the old guy," the woman spoke up. More of a Southern accent, comfortable spinning a tale.

Wren focused on her like a targeting laser. She had curlers in her brown hair, one side at least. The baby chewed on the belt of her cotton dressing gown. She had a swell on her belly, looked like she was already pregnant again. "Exactly. Yes. What old guy?"

The guy hurried back up the stairs, took the baby off his wife and she took a step toward them, more of a waddle. "The old guy, I figure that's why you're here. He came with the property. We put in some complaints with Medicine Lodge sheriffs way back when we first rolled up, and they ignored it. Here I'm figuring you two were a big escalation. He's not here, though."

Wren's mouth went dry.

"Why'd you complain? And how old? And where is he?"

She screwed up her face briefly. Clearly handling the pressure better than her husband. "Seventies, I guess. And we complained because he is one wild sumbitch, excuse my French. I don't know if he's drunk or high, but he tears around that weird pitch of his on his tractor like a punch-drunk gator. Playing his crazy religious music, knocking down our fence posts. Couple times this last season he was out racing through the sorghum, says he was writing God's word on the land."

Wren's heart skipped a beat. "God's word?"

"Willy here sent up a drone on a whim, he's a hobbyist,

take a look at what all God was writing." She looked back at her husband. "Nothing but a big old triangle, wasn't it hon?"

Willy nodded.

The stairs opened up under Wren. Vertigo coming faster than before.

"Where's his 'pitch'?"

"He the one you want, then?" she asked, sing-song Southern intonation. "It ain't hardly accessible by road. Up past our place, you gotta cut through fields for almost a mile. Seems we only got the contract on this place because of him, 'cos nobody else wanted it. He was grandfathered in, you heard that expression?"

Wren nodded mutely.

"Well, he been here on this land for generations, they say, and he ain't gonna sell that pitch of his. I can't tell why, nothing but some old graffitied cabins, them trailers, a bust-up water tower and a dried-up well. The water table's for crap around here, you know?"

Wren tried to speak but struggled.

"We're going to need a bearing," Rogers took over smoothly. "Something more concrete than 'across the fields', especially in this storm."

The woman waved a hand. "Can do you one better. Willy programs the tractor with GPS, so I got the exact coordinates, where we have to avoid, so's we don't crush him in his sleep while the tractor's out. Many times I've thought of doing just that, Lord help me." She took a long-suffering breath. "So, how'll that do you?"

Wren found his tongue. "As fast as you can, ma'am. This is a life and death matter."

"Life and death, huh? That explains all this hullabaloo then. Well come on, coordinates are downstairs."

36

PITCH

Rogers took the Ford out from behind the barn, rolling slow through the driving snow.

"It's a good thing we got coordinates," she said, watching her phone screen, steering toward the pin dropped on the old guy's 'pitch'. "There's no chance we could navigate by landmarks."

Wren grunted agreement, already thinking ahead to who the old guy was and what that meant. He studied the map. There was only a low-resolution satellite image of the surrounding fields, hardly a prime coverage area out this far from civilization. There looked to be one homestead and what could be a water tower.

"And Willy?" Rogers went on, clearly not done. "Cat really got his tongue." She looked over at Wren, eyes dancing. "Always ask the woman first, Boss."

"Noted."

"You count how many times he said 'uh' or 'um'? No, thank you. Give me a good loquacious Southern belle any day, and-"

"Got it, Rogers. Girl power."

She laughed.

The Ford hit something low, had to be the edge of the trail she'd warned them about. On the right track.

"What you make of all this?" she asked. "The guy with the triangle."

"He's gotta be the guy. Seventies doesn't sound like my father, though. Nor riding around on a tractor. So maybe it's X."

"You think X killed the girl at First Corinthians?"

"Could be." He paused a second. "That burial, inverted pyramid underneath a church? It's so on the nose. It feels like an outlier."

Rogers laughed. "You can say that again. Stacking bones? So passé."

Wren ignored the teasing. "The Apex has always been a more metaphorical kind of man. The suffering was the point, not the tableaux. Pits, vats, cages, he liked them for what they did, not for how they looked. The ceremony was the thing, not the trappings or the remnant." He thought for a second. "When Pyramid members died, he didn't do anything special with the bones at all. Just half-assed burials in the desert, where they lay for the coyotes to chew on." He paused a moment more. "That's how Maggie got started in Little Phoenix, actually. Collecting bones, consecrating them."

"Huh. Yeah. I like that broad."

Wren cracked a tight smile at the notion of Maggie being called a 'broad'. "Well, she hates you."

Rogers laughed. They rolled on.

"Those two back there," Rogers said. "Strange time to bring up a baby."

Wren just grunted.

"Where are your kids? Are they safe?"

Wren looked at her. That was a sore point, ever since she'd hidden them from him in witness protection.

"Come on, Boss. I know you've been watching them. We already lost my dad to X. I don't want that for your kids."

He stared out into the static snow. "Gone to Little Phoenix." Keeping it as monosyllabic as he could.

"Good. They'll be safe there. Maybe I should send my mom."

"She'd be welcome." A pause. "We can try to arrange a pickup."

Thirty seconds of silence.

"That'd be good."

Wren nodded, brought up his phone and sent the request through to Teddy.

Five minutes more passed, and their icon of a car approached the coordinates on the screen. A slight incline, like they were climbing a low hill, then Rogers stopped.

"We're here."

There was nothing to see but whipping snow.

"House is that way," Wren said, pointing left. "I'll check the water tower."

"Agreed."

Out the door, the snow was already a foot deep. Rogers headed left and disappeared in the snow in seconds. Wren headed straight to the right. The cold bit through his thin jacket, ice crept in through his trooper's boots. After thirty seconds the tower appeared through the storm like some 1930's vision of an alien invader. Long spindly legs rising some hundred feet high, an egg-shaped tank hidden in white, something large dangling beneath it like a giant pendulum.

Wren ran his flashlight beam up and down, picking out a thick chain tethered to the hanging object; as big as a baby grand piano, panel-beaten metal with stark rivets, shaped like a chunky missile pointing down. It reminded him of something, but he couldn't quite place it.

He strode closer. Beneath the legs of the tower, taking up

the whole of the footprint at maybe ten feet on a side, there was a large twin-doored wooden cover. This had to be the well she'd mentioned, but it was bigger than any well Wren had seen before.

The doors were secured with a thick padlock and heavy chain. Far more than was needed for a dried-up well in the middle of nowhere. Wren pulled his pry bar out, slotted it beside one of the hinges and worked it like a water pump. The hinge's screw tops popped off their threads like daisy heads.

He popped the second hinge, heart in his mouth, and tipped the outsized door open.

Blackness yawned inside, too deep to see the bottom. Definitely not a well. Could be a forerunner to the Apex's desert pits, or maybe the entrance to some forgotten mine? But how much mining was there on arable land in the Great Plains?

He leaned over and looked down. The walls were stone-lined, and fitted together beautifully, stretching down with impeccable craftsmanship. His flashlight beam barely put a dent in the shadows.

"Now you jump in," came a voice from behind.

37

WELL

Wren's body froze but his mind raced ahead.

An old man's voice, sounded like a guttering gatepost, only a couple of good swings left in it. Not like his father's firebrand bass in the X videos, more like an old-timer gold panner declaiming from his rocking chair outside the saloon.

Standing near, too. Just from the volume of that shaky voice, no way he could be more than three yards back. Three yards meant he wasn't shoving distance, so he had to be armed. Doubtless holding a gun, maybe a shotgun. No other way he'd risk taking on a much bigger, younger man.

A second flat, maybe, to think that through and pick a route forward.

"You'll miss," Wren said.

Another flat second passed. "Miss what? My good old momma and daddy? I don't think so, boy, not from this range."

"You packing birdshot?" Wren countered. "Only way you'll lay a slug on me in this storm. But birdshot won't put a dent in III+ Kevlar wrap body armor, reinforced with ceramic plate, ballistic IIIa helmet. I'll ring like a bell, then you'll be the one tumbling down the pit."

A few wheezy riffs of the guy's laughter carried through the storm. "Nice dream, son. What about your legs? They don't look too wrapped up in e-numbers to me. I put a slug across your knees, they going to make a nice high chime?"

"I'm coming, Boss," came Rogers' voice in his ear.

"Who's to say you'll even hit my legs?" Wren asked. "Your hands are getting pretty cold right about now, I figure. Starting to shake. An old-timer like you, you're not built for these conditions."

"Try me. I've been picking off mole crickets at a hundred yards since I was a boy, come rain or shine."

"So it's a rifle? I take a fast step to the right now, you think you can track that? Better off we get a look at each other first, seeing as you're an Apex man."

A few seconds passed after that, then the guy's tone shifted. "What do you know about that name?"

Confirmation. Wren turned.

The guy was tall and emaciated, with a steel-wool beard and a deep-pitted face like a cord of sundried wood, in his late seventies if he was a day. On his head stood a tall navy hat, and in his hands was a beat-up Remington Model 700 rifle, shaking despite the shabby olive surplus German army jacket he wore, smeared with the stains of many years. Oil, blood, human waste. Wren could almost smell him on the freezing air.

What mattered though was his eyes. So dark they looked like holes boring through the storm. Wren focused on the light that went on in their depths, maybe a hint of recognition that showed him a new path forward.

"You recognize me?" Wren asked.

The old man said nothing. Seemed like revelations were

happening in his head. No way this could be X, though. So who was he?

"Got his six," Rogers said. Wren just about saw her stalking through the snow some ten yards off. "Get the bead off you and I'll take him."

"Your bitch talking in your ear?" the old guy said.

Wren inclined his head.

"I seen her. Don't care who or what you are. If she stays back there, I'm shooting."

"Then we got ourselves a stand-off, because she's not coming around front. But that's fine, I've got a good reason to be here. Take a look in my eyes, tell me what you see."

The guy hawked, spat. The shaking was getting worse. "Some kin of the man himself. Apex, you call him. You one of his sons?"

That was interesting. "I am his son." Wren considered his next move. Out here in the depths of Kansas, what did this guy know about the wider world? "He sent me here to check on things."

The guy didn't drop the rifle, but there was a change in his demeanor, like maybe the anger was melting to something else.

"For what? I'm not due."

That was interesting, too. Due what? "Doesn't matter. There's new threats in the air." Wren tasted what was to come next, an unexpected gambit at best, but let it roll. "One of the Pequeños. The sons? My half-brother. He's causing all kinds of trouble. Christopher Wren, his name is. You heard of him?"

The guy looked blank.

"Apex says he might come out here, start digging. We need to harden this place."

The guy snorted, but the cold made his voice catch. "It's p-plenty hard."

"So hard I turfed your pit on the first try, got the jump on you in back, got you out here minutes away from hypothermia?" Wren let that sink in. "That's why he sent me. You need backup. What you're doing here matters too much."

Flattery. Whatever role this guy was playing, it wasn't essential. Not with him acting out in front of the neighbors. The Apex would never let something important slide so far.

"What's your name?" the guy asked.

"Aden," Wren answered smoothly. "Of-The-Saints. Now let's go inside. We'll talk. Have a coffee. Yeah?"

The guy didn't move.

"Alternative is my partner shoots out your brains right now, we bury you in this pit, take up your duties ourselves. How's that sound?"

The guy's crevassed face wrinkled, almost in humor. "Like something one of his sons would say." He let the muzzle of the Remington drop. "So let's go inside. I got c-coffee, but it tastes like filth."

"As long as it's black, hot and caffeinated, who cares about the taste?"

The guy grunted and strode away. Rogers gestured a question at Wren through the snow, barely seven yards distant, and he shrugged back, started following the guy deeper into the storm.

38

AIRSTREAM

They trudged in single file along the old guy's footsteps.

"What's his deal?" Rogers asked from behind.

"He recognized I'm one of the Apex's sons," Wren answered. "You heard that?"

"Pieces of it. The signal's spotty in all this."

"So now I'm passing for one of my brothers. Call me Aden if it comes up."

"Aden." A second passed. "The one you killed in Acapulco?"

Wren was impressed. Her information was solid. "That's right. Maybe he'll spill something, if he thinks we're friendlies come to help."

Rogers managed a frigid laugh.

"I know, it's a stretch."

Five minutes they walked east, into what ought to be sorghum fields, until a low oblong structure took shape through the blizzard, looked like a mobile home. Each step closer brought more details. Tarnished silver sides, rounded corners, mounted on two-foot-high support struts. Looked like an old Airstream trailer, but that wasn't all. Attached at the head and tail were more trailers, different makes, looked to be spot-welded and stretching away like the carriages of a freight train.

"This thing's big," Rogers said.

Now the old guy was at the entrance. Three steps up he went, opened the door, stepped inside.

And closed it.

Rogers cursed.

"Left now," Wren said, and broke right just as a metal slot opened in the Airstream's door. A second later automatic rifle fire roared out, muzzle flashes ripping yellow sparks through the storm where they'd been standing. Wren took four strides and flung himself down against the trailer's side, started burrowing through snow to get under the struts.

"I don't think he bought it," came Rogers' voice in his ear.

"I'm getting that impression. Find a way in."

There was little snow in the dank gloom under the Airstream, and Wren looked both ways. Brown dirt continued into the storm's darkness. He chose right and crawled maybe twenty fast yards over soil, rocks and shale. Still no end in sight. At least the firing had stopped.

"Nothing yet," Rogers said.

Wren rolled out on the other side of the trailer, back into the storm, and stood. Now the Airstream was off to his right and he was looking at the brown siding of a long RV, picking out windows and a door.

"Find a door, blow out the lock in three. We'll come at him from both sides."

"Roger that," came her answer, crackling now with static. Seconds passed. "Got one."

"Three," Wren said, pulled his Mossberg from its sheath, "two," levelled it close to the lock plate on an angle, "one," and fired.

Buckshot ripped through the thin metal, metal slugs

sparked and ricocheted to hiss into the snow, and the sound of Rogers' second blast reached him. He leaned in, touched the hot metal door frame, and cursed.

Plate metal was welded beneath the trailer's thin skin. Reinforced and impenetrable. Not a door at all.

"Run!" he shouted again, just as a slot clanked open nearby and a fresh burst of automatic fire kicked. He hunkered low and ran back toward the Airstream, tipping his thermal monocular into place and scanning the walls as he went.

Nothing. Must have been heatproofed. The guy wasn't as crazy as he'd thought.

"He's near your end," Rogers said. "I have no access here."

"Nothing on thermal," Wren answered, mind racing. They needed something explosive. "Tape two grenades to a door. I'll do the same here. That ought to do it."

"On your signal, Boss."

He stopped in the snow, listened for a second. The automatic fire had stopped. He imagined the old guy lurching along the inside of his trailer-fort, peeking through lookout slits and ready to let rip with the rifle. He thought he caught a glimpse of movement high in the nearby wall, and sprinted low and away.

Bullets puffed through the snow where he'd been standing. "He's following me!" he shouted, arcing back in toward the trailer wall. He pulled two rectangular grenades from their strip as he ran, fumbled in the wheeling snow to peel the adhesive tabs, then slapped them to the shredded lock plate.

"Go," he shouted, pulled the pins then ran, dived and rolled under the structure.

The grenades blew with a massive cough, spraying wreckage and smoke in a bubble that the falling snow quickly erased. Wren was already up and moving side-on to the blast. The exterior walls were blackened, and a fissure had been torn through a weld-line in the interior plates, maybe a yard wide. He pulled two flashbangs and pinged them through the gap like fastballs.

They hit metal, clattered to the floor and burst. The effect inside that contained space would be catastrophic, a pressure wave of 170 decibel sound and a seven megacandela flash bouncing along the trailers. Enough to cause temporary deafness, blindness, send the fluid in the ear canals into nauseating shock.

Wren hauled himself inside, Glock 19 up. Smoke was everywhere. "I'm in," he shouted.

A second rank of explosions rang out from far away. "Coming," Rogers answered.

Wren saw workbenches with pieces of equipment scattered from the blast, various scorched plans tacked to the walls, a large world map scrawled over with dozens of triangles.

Triangles were everywhere. Pyramids too. Molded in plastic on the workbenches, sketched in marker pen on scraps of paper, carved into the wood of the benches. Upright. Inverted. They were pained in a rainbow of colors, and everywhere they surrounded by a swirl of algebraic calculations. The profusion made Wren dizzy. A riot of numbers and symbols and triangles had been etched into the metal walls, the floor, the ceiling like a roaming musical score.

He shook himself and sped on, swept through the smoke and only saw the guy levelling his rifle a second too late. Bullets poured out and ripped a stripe up the wall and ceiling.

Missed. That save was on the flashbang. The guy was fifteen yards away now, leaning against a sheet-metal wall, looked like the welded transition space between two trailers. Swapping out a magazine.

It was an easy shot for Wren, but he couldn't risk killing this guy. No time to run up on him either. He chose a third option, pulled back his Glock and flung it. Another fastball that spun across the distance in a second, cracked the guy square on the hand holding the rifle muzzle. Not what Wren was aiming for, but good enough. The barrel dropped, the guy cried out, then Wren was on him.

No punches. No need. The old guy fell easy and Wren straddled him, pulled the rifle away and forced his arms crossed over his chest, so all he could do was grab handfuls of his own shoulders.

"Clear," he shouted.

The guy laughed. Chewed something in his mouth, went to swallow and Wren slapped him hard. Whatever it was, suicide pill or wad of gum, it went tapping out over the metal flooring.

The guy rolled his face back up to Wren, black eyes darkening further. Snow blew in and landed on his cheeks. Wren gave him a small shake.

"Now how about that coffee?"

39

BULLET

T hey put the guy in a bolted-down chair, duct-taped his hands to the chair arms, his shoulders to the back and leaned in.

"Where's the Apex?"

The old guy only stared with those black-hole eyes. Reeling now from the flashbangs, maybe, but Wren didn't have the time.

"First Corinthians," he said. "The girl buried underneath the church in a triangle shape, that was you, right? Hardly my father's style. He set it up, maybe, some kind of payment so you'll stay on guard duty here? But what's here? What's the pit for under the water tower?"

Nothing came back. Time to get the guy's attention.

"First thing I'll do is break all these joints." He pointed at the guy's arms and legs. "Getting them ready, you know? So when I make them into a triangle, they're ready to go. Dig out your rotten pelvis, hack off your chest, stack you tall in that pit with your skull on top, facing down forever. Like the girl. How does that sound?"

There was a flash of something new in the guy's eyes now. Fear, maybe.

"Start somewhere," Wren said, took hold of the guy's elbow. With his hand and shoulder strapped tight to the chair, all Wren had to do was pull to break the joint. "Name."

The guy gritted his teeth. Wren pulled, putting tension on. A few more pounds of pressure and tendons would start to pop.

"Name!"

"Menaen the Builder," the guy gasped.

Wren frowned. "Menaen, huh? Sounds like a Pyramid name to me. But we're pretty far from Pyramid territory here."

Menaen laughed.

"I say something funny?"

"You claim you're his son? Aden? I knew that was horseshit the second I saw you. You're too clean. The filth of it disgusts me."

Wren raised an eyebrow. "Someone got talkative. 'Filth is clean', that definitely sounds like Apex nonsense. So let's keep that rolling, but unless you want to stare down into the flames of hell for eternity, I suggest you cut the sass and start giving me something real. Where's the Apex?"

Nothing.

"OK, we'll start easier. Menaen the Builder, what did you build?"

"It's all around you."

Wren pulled the elbow. "I know you're not talking about this welded trailer-park fantasy we're in right now. Give me something real, and I want it all, or you're going in the ground looking down."

Menaen gritted his yellowed teeth. "You don't even know what it means. That threat."

"What threat, to 'triangle' you?" Wren almost smiled at the expression, but held it back. "Maybe not. I'll still do it. So why don't you tell me what it means?"

Menaen resisted for a second, but the fear spurred him on. "It's total. Soul-deep. You bury someone like that, they become part of your chattel."

That was interesting. "Go on."

"In the pyramid of souls? Serving you forever in death. As a slave."

Wren grunted. The pharaoh stuff. He looked over at Rogers, who looked back at him with a nod that seemed to say, 'Sure, that checks out.'

"So I bury you like that, you belong to me."

Menaen spat.

"Like that girl belongs to you."

He spat again.

"OK with the spitting, Lars Ulrich. So now we know what it means. I'll do it and you'll be serving me for eternity, if you don't start talking right now."

Menaen stared at him with those dark eyes, his whole body tensing against the duct tape but finding no give. Probably wishing he had another suicide pill. Ligaments pulled taut in his neck, down the wiry cords of his arms, pale face turning red. Maybe trying to give himself a heart attack. It didn't work. After some thirty seconds the tension gave out.

"You through?" Wren prompted. "Or shall I set out and start digging the hole?"

The guy gulped. Making his decision. "One condition."

"Name it."

"You burn me when we're done. Down to the bone, pound what's left to dust. No skull. Nothing left to bury."

Wren thought on that for a second. Figured it had to be an Apex standing threat. "So he can't own you? I thought you'd welcome that. You're loyal, right?"

"Of course I'm loyal! I'd happily serve him another thousand years, dead or alive, if that's what it meant, but it doesn't." Menaen shuddered. "It's worse if he does it himself."

"How so?"

Now fear filled his black eyes, sweat popped in beads on his cheeks. "If he buries me like that, it's pain forever. I mean, forever. Constant, never-ending agony. So you swear now or I go silent to the grave."

Wren held up his hands. "I swear. Cross my heart, hope to die. We'll burn you down, pound the bones, not a stick left to rub against another." He held Menaen's gaze. "Now talk."

Menaen let loose a trembling breath. "OK." Took a moment longer, then looked up. "You want to know about this place. First things, let's be clear. You're Christopher Wren, aren't you? The ungrateful son. Not Aden."

"The one and only."

"Then you have a right to know. You're family." Another heavy breath, eyes now boring into Wren. "Fact is, your father was once my son."

Wren hadn't expected that.

"Not biological," Menaen went on. "Adopted, though not formally. After his real father died. It all happened here."

Wren blinked. That was a lot to take on board. Fascinating, really. But they were here for a reason, and that came first. "Where is he now? When did you see him last?"

"I don't know where he is. Last time I saw him was five years back."

"Seriously?"

"I never joke."

Wren grunted. "So she was payment, then. The woman. For you to stay here."

Menaen looked away. "Yes. A down payment for my chattel. She died with my name on her lips. She belongs to me."

Wren nodded. That all sounded about right. "We dug her up. I'm thinking her soul's free now."

Menaen laughed and looked back. "Her soul's never free. You don't know how it works at all."

Wren pulled on his elbow, drawing a sharp cry. "So tell me, before I get that hankering to dig again. I'm here because the Apex drew a massive inverted triangle across the country, son. Medicine Lodge is the center, and here I find you, a man much-enamored of triangles. I thought I'd find him here, or X, but obviously not, so start telling me something I can use."

· Menaen licked his lips. Opened his mouth. "You want to hear about the Icon?"

"What?"

"The inverted triangle. I can tell you about that. After all, I helped him design it."

Wren leaned in, didn't blink. "So talk. What on Earth happened here, Menaen?"

Menaen smiled. "What in hell, you should say. We came within a stinkbug's balls of shooting the devil right between his goddamn eyes."

Wren had nothing for that.

The smile became a grin. "Your Apex's real father, your grandfather, I guess, he had him some theories." Menaen settled into his chair, even as his voice settled into a new tone, recounting the glory days. "Davis Thackerton, was his name. You ever heard of him?" Wren shook his head. "Had your eyes, I guess. This was back in '71. He fought in Vietnam, came back filled up with all these new theories, just bursting out at the seams." Menaen leaned closer, spoke lower. "That the devil was behind it all; the war, the killing, everything." He sucked in a breath. "He'd had plenty of time to think about it all, back in 'Nam. A six-year tour, and he'd been a Tunnel Rat to boot, volunteered for it, pumped up on the red, white and blue." He paused, eyeing Wren with those black eyes. "You know what a Tunnel Rat did?"

Wren shook his head again.

"Pray you never learn firsthand. See, the Viet Cong, they made all these tunnels under the Vietnam jungle. Called them the Cu Chi. Miles and miles of them, a whole dark world underground, even they had hospitals, barracks, headquarters, training areas." Menaen grimaced, like he was recalling dark memories. "Hell, he called it. Down with the insects and worms, the rot, the damp, the filth and disease, enough to make the strongest man sick for the rest of his life. Your grandpappy used to preach about those tunnels all the time." He took a breath. "How they filled them with traps, like sharp punji sticks dipped in shit for the infection, mines that capsized whole tunnels and took a squad with them, live snakes and tarantulas in pits. Now, the Viet Cong would stay down there for months at a time, wait for US forces to overpass, pop up behind them and blow the rearguard to bits." Another wheezy breath. "Uncle Sam asked for volunteers to crawl down into those tunnels. Tight, insane places, dug out for malnourished men who were barely five feet tall. Davis believed in the cause, so he volunteered, and they set him to killing men underground. Sometimes he did it with his gun, sometimes with napalm, sometimes a knife, sometimes his bare hands. Again and again." Menaen's black eyes grew wide. "I heard they call that feeling, trapped in the dark with an army of little men trying to bite out your throat, the 'Black Echo'."

Wren took a breath.

"Then Davis got himself captured. POW, tortured, lived in those tunnels for months right along with the Viet Cong. Never seeing the sky. He lost all his fingernails, patches of skin, part of his humanity, maybe. A hostage swap deal finally brought him back home. His fingernails grew back, but his mind? He was a different man, so they say. PTSD, they call it now. He came back here, family land, tried to farm, but he couldn't do it. The black echo haunted him, so he swore. He couldn't sleep. He had to do something about the war."

Menaen smacked his lips. Looked at Wren expectantly.

"You saying you want coffee?"

"I'm not puckering for a fat kiss. Last request for a dying man."

Wren turned to Rogers. She gave him a look. He gave her a look back.

"I'll find the coffee," she said, glowering, and set off.

Menaen looked pleased.

"What was he going to do about the war?" Wren pressed.

Menaen snorted. He looked older than ever, in the wan light cast through the high slit windows. "That's where I come in. He started a group. A commune, right here. It was the tail end of the sixties, people flowing across the country like blood on an abattoir floor. Screwing everywhere, protesting the war, hating on politics. I was a conscientious objector myself, on the lam from the draft. I saw Davis' people disrupting a 'triumphant' parade for heroes over in Wichita, got myself involved. Came out here and never looked back. See, your grandfather had some big ideas in that messed-up head of his."

"You already said that."

"Worth saying twice," Menaen countered.

"The big idea being that the devil himself was behind the war?"

"Exactly that. But not only that. He was building a weapon, too."

Wren frowned. "What weapon?"

"A hole in the ground. Where we met."

"The well?"

"It's not a well."

"So what is it?"

Menaen licked his lips. "A bullet casing. Dig it deep enough, fill it with an armor-piercing slug, fire it with the same kind of blast material he used back in 'Nam, and maybe he could kill the devil forever." Menaen smiled, like he was remembering a pleasant memory. "Stop the war, and any other wars before they could begin."

Wren felt strings beginning to pull in his chest. Connections to himself, his father, the Apex's mixed-up ideology.

"You're saying the well's a bullet?"

"A bullet casing. To fire down. To kill the devil and save us all."

"Right. So what's the bullet?"

"You're feeling it, aren't you?" Menaen asked, those dark eyes drinking Wren in. "I seen men roll with the spirit all my life. You're on board."

"What's the bullet?" Wren repeated.

"We used napalm for the blast material, of course," Menaen said, ignoring him. Wren's vertigo started to swirl. "Like he'd used in the tunnels. A Tunnel Rat burning all those other rats alive."

Wren could imagine it. The war, the jungle, men digging their way down deeper into clay, into jungle muck so dark and foul you couldn't breathe. Clearing the traps, bypassing the dead bodies and the spikes and the stinking pits of human waste, rooting for enemies buried like maggots in the deep.

Then pouring in napalm. Lighting the trail. Not even hearing their cries. Smoke pouring up and filtering through the jungle leaves, rising toward the same sun that shone down on Kansas, on the United States, all complicit under the arc of heaven.

"You're not well, boy," Menaen said, eyeing him

curiously.

"I'm fine."

"I don't think so. What Davis had, I think you've got a taste of it too. Your father. Maybe it runs in the blood."

"I'm fine," Wren said more firmly, looked down along the passageway. "Rogers, where's that coffee?"

Only crackling static came back on his earpiece.

"Kitchen's a good distance away," Menaen said. "She'll be minutes more yet, if'n you didn't already blow it up."

Wren refocused on the old man. It was hard to look at his pitted face, nausea swirling the details, trying to grasp the scope of what he was saying. So his grandfather had run a cult too. Tried to kill the devil.

"What was the bullet?" he asked. Coming back to the key question. "At the bottom of the well. The pit."

"The bullet casing," Menaen corrected.

"Whatever you want to call it. What was the damn bullet!?"

Those dark eyes peered through him. "I think you know."

Wren felt sick. Of course he knew. "Say it."

"His people," Menaen said cheerfully. "We laid them out like gut-shot Tunnel Rats. Sacrifices, sure, but to kill the devil you need psychic energy, you know? It makes sense."

Wren let a stray, wild gulp of laughter out.

"There you go," Menaen said. "You're chasing the dragon now, boy."

"How many?"

"How many people? Well. He had me in charge of all the calculations. I was an engineer back then, you know? Knew something about ordinance, despite being a real peacenik. How many black powder grains you put into a casing. How many people you had to stuff into a well to make it fire deep and true."

"How many?" Wren barked.

"Fifty-five. Not just any types, either. I did all the math. Anyone could contribute to the workings, of course, you seen their numbers all over the walls here, I'm sure. I keep it all just the way it was back then, divinely inspired. But truth is, it was mostly me who crunched the real data. The right proportions of men, women, boys, girls, just like you mix napalm in the right ratio. Lay them flat, all alive of course, all willing, tamp them down like ball bearings in birdshot. Then you pack your blast material next." He paused a moment, lost in the memory. "I loved the precision."

Wren was barely thinking. Seeing the vision of it, just like the Apex's pits. People descending below the earth for faith in him. Into the well as human ammo. Trying to prove something, trying to earn his favor, believing him when he said this was going to transform the world for a greater purpose. Hot in the dark, hand-in-hand, whispered words of comfort as the napalm vat descended…

Suddenly he knew why he recognized the shape of the hanging pendulum beneath the water tower. It only knocked him sicker.

"See, Davis grew up after the first atom bomb over Hiroshima," Menaen said, pushing Wren deeper into the past. "Before my time, but he'd seen those images and they sunk in deep. Maybe it made him want to go to war more, avoid that outcome? Trying to be a good man, you know." He paused a second. "You ever hear of the Trinity atomic bomb tests?"

Wren blinked. Trinity. That number again, three.

"First atomic test ever conducted. Out in the Jornado del Muerto desert. That means 'Dead Man's Journey', you know? It's a good name. In New Mexico, 1945. Your grandpappy, he made sure we knew all about it. He'd preach for hours about the logistics, how those scientists unleashed the most destructive force ever known to man. Some of them feared they were going to blow up the planet." He paused a moment, seemed to be happily chewing on that thought. "The tests started with a metal tower, one hundred feet tall. They rigged the trial atom bomb to a chain and pulley, hoisted it up, even stacked mattresses below it, you know, in case it dropped." Menaen smiled wider, lost in the memory. "They wanted to simulate an airburst detonation. So Davis liked that too. He wanted us to do the same thing here."

Wren swallowed. "The water tower."

Menaen shrugged. "It's a disguise, looking like that. For while we were building out the fifty-five black powder grains. The casing you saw hanging there? That held the napalm."

Wren almost gagged, just held it back. The pendulum missile shape swinging on a chain. "It's the same one?"

"As sure as night follows day. I swap out parts sometimes. It's an important point of untapped psychic power, now. The bones of the fifty-five rest beneath it, where they burned."

Wren gagged again, barely held it in this time.

"Don't puke on me, boy," Menaen warned. "I'm not going into the afterlife soaked in some other man's vomit."

"The bones are still there? In the well?"

"Sure they are. Your grandpappy amongst them."

"What?"

"Oh yeah. I said he died, right? It's probably why the blast never worked, why the devil never got killed, why the wars kept right on. Fifty-five was the right number. Not fifty-six. But I guess he knew that, when he shoved Davis in."

Wren's jaw dropped. Trying to make sense of any of this. It was all crazy, but it felt so familiar. There were shades of the Apex's melting-pot ideology everywhere, and he almost knew what was coming next. Mouth dry, throat tight. "Who shoved him in?"

Menaen smiled. "His son, of course. Your daddy. He must have been all of twelve years old at the time."

40

LOVE AND LIES

Wren felt himself falling.

Twelve years old, the same age he'd been when the Pyramid burned and his father left, leaving Pequeño 3 as sole survivor, wandering through the smoke of the fake town alone.

"Hey," Menaen said, and Wren tried to focus.

It didn't work. The world was turning upside down. He pushed himself to his feet, trying just to keep from tipping over.

Twelve years old. He lurched back down the blasted trailer, hands slapping on workbenches, banging against the walls, legs going weak. Ahead snow blew in through the gap in the wall, and he poured himself out into the storm.

The cold helped. Putting ice on the wound. He stripped his helmet and tossed it, found all kinds of straps crossing his chest, ripped them off and kept moving forward. The wind whipped snow into his eyes, crystalizing his thoughts before they could form.

This was why his father had spared him.

At twelve years old, with every other person little Pequeño 3 had ever known dead, the Apex had left him alive.

It was a moment twenty-five years in the past, something he rarely thought about, but now…

He struggled to grasp the scale of it, felt like he was turning inside out, trying to process something that made no sense. As a twelve-year-old the Apex had killed his father. As a father, he'd let his twelve-year-old son live.

Wren fell to his knees in the buffeting wind, gloved hands plunged into the snow. He remembered how it had felt to be in one of the Apex's faith pits, digging a way out beneath the fake town, with little Grace-In-Our-Times by his side. He'd thought he'd tricked the Apex, outsmarted him at his own game, but maybe he never had.

Maybe the Apex had stood above that pit for three days, knowing Pequeño 3 wasn't inside. Letting it happen. That sent Wren reeling into his own black echo, like his grandfather through the dirt of Vietnam, digging deep for men to kill.

There'd been so many theories over the years about why he'd been left alive. That it was a punishment. That Wren was some kind of messenger, heralding the Apex's future return. But never this.

That maybe the Apex had seen something of himself in the boy.

That maybe this was some twisted kind of love.

Wren didn't know what to do with that. The Apex was a monster. A madman. Then there was this.

A voice called his name. He imagined closing his hands around the Apex's throat, choking the life out of him like Aden had died in his arms. What would he see in those crystal blue eyes in his final moments? Hatred? Acceptance?

Love?

Hands came on his back. Words came in his ear, hard to process. "Boss, you're freezing! What are you doing out here, what happened?"

He looked up and saw Rogers' face, but didn't know how to explain.

"You'll die out here like this, come on, let's get inside."

She pulled him up, like she had before. He glimpsed flashes of the firestorm in her eyes.

"That's it, come on," she encouraged, pulling him to his feet. "This way, Boss."

He followed her back into the trailer. Maybe the cold had helped. The vertigo was falling away. Rogers set him in a chair opposite Menaen, came up with a blanket which she wrapped around him. He was shaking hard. She wrapped his hands around a steaming mug of coffee. "Drink it," she commanded.

He drank. Black. Hot. Acrid as filth. He glugged a small gulp, a bigger one, letting the heat fill him up. Like napalm dropped down a well. Started coming back to himself fast. Rogers rubbed his shoulders vigorously, working some heat back into his system.

"That was dramatic," Menaen said. "Was it something I said?"

Wren swigged the last of the coffee. Set the cup down. Dealing with it, now.

"What happened, Chris?" Rogers asked.

He looked at her and smiled. Felt shaky inside, but the edges of this new wound were already sealing up. He'd always been a fast healer.

"I've been getting the lowdown on my dad. Apparently he killed my grandfather."

Rogers made a face. "I'd say I was surprised, but that sounds about right."

"He did it when he was twelve. Same age I was when he left me in the fake town."

Rogers laughed briefly, then clamped it back. "Yeah. Sorry. That checks out."

Wren thought about it for a second, then laughed too. It did. It didn't really change anything. Good to know, maybe. Something he could use.

He put his mug down. Refocused on Menaen.

"So my father shoved Davis Thackerton into the pit. What happened next?"

Menaen stared back but said nothing.

"What? Cat got your tongue?"

"I said I'd tell you about this place," Menaen said. "How it began. I've done that. The rest, it didn't happen here."

"So where did it happen?"

Menaen said nothing.

"Are you really shutting down now? Even after you told me everything?"

"I ain't told you nothing. Not about him. About his father, sure, about this place. About the man himself, though? Nope."

Wren considered. Projected his father's track forward, from a twelve-year-old boy to the leader of the Pyramid. There had to have been in-between stages, where he grew up, learned his craft, really *became* the Apex. "First Corinthians."

Menaen only stared.

"What about our deal?"

"I kept my terms."

Wren thought back to Menaen's precise words, something about 'this place'. That was true.

"Then why you want us to pound your bones, if you've not said anything? It's no betrayal."

"Getting caught's the betrayal. If I could pound my own bones, I would."

Wren grunted. The age-old problem. "Then you're out of luck. There's no way I'm keeping my side of the deal, you don't give me something more."

Menaen shrugged. "Then I suffer forever. I can make my

peace with that."

Make his peace. Wren leaned back in the chair. The guy was a real basket-case. He gazed into those black eyes and glimpsed all the layers of the Apex's lies. Lies upon lies, welded into place over fifty years like steel plate reinforcing tissue-thin trailer walls.

No way to dig them all out, now. He'd been lucky to get as much as he had, as easily as he had. Breaking the shackles of a cult leader could take years, if it ever happened. The walls weren't going to come down now just because he asked nicely.

He was going to need something explosive.

"What's your name?" Wren asked.

The guy's eyes narrowed. "You simple? We been through this. It's Menaen the Builder."

"Bullshit. Both of us know that's a Pyramid name, one hundred percent. It's totally my father's style."

Menaen's jaw tightened.

Wren leaned closer, spoke slow and calm, like he was sharing a secret. "Here's the thing. We already know you're weak, 'Menaen'. You bent for my father, and if anyone's got my father's gift, it's me. You said it yourself, I've got him in me. So you should be afraid of what I'm going to say. How I might bend you back. Because no matter how hard you tried, I'm betting you never could get his nonsense to make sense, am I right?"

Menaen made no move to answer, but that was fine, he had ears like everyone else.

"Fact is, you used to be an engineer," Wren went on, thinking through the play as he spoke. "A man of science, but guided by ideals. You protested a grotesque war, and that took courage. It may be fifty years you've been doubling down on my father's BS, but you know there's no killing the devil with a bullet made out of dead people. You've always known, but you played along because Davis Thackerton made you feel important, like you were key to stopping the war." Wren leaned in, sounding reasonable. "Trouble is, you're starting the war now. We're hours away from mass anarchy across the country, a mass body count that'll dwarf the dead in Vietnam. Maybe it's already started, citizens killing each other in the streets, and do you honestly think it'll be any more effective than the psychic bullet of the fifty-six who died in that pit?"

Menaen's pupils flickered left to right rapidly, looking between Wren's eyes.

"No need to answer," Wren said. "Just let it slip in alongside all his bullshit brainwashing. Fifty years is a lot to go against, and I'm sure it seems too late to turn back." Wren raised an eyebrow. "But you're not an idiot. You know in your un-pounded bones that there's no calculation to transmute dead bodies into a bullet. You know the whole thing's a show." Wren tapped the man's head, feverish and hot. "Just a sham. We both know it, Menaen. He certainly knows it. We're all just enjoying the dance."

Menaen gulped in a breath. "You're lying."

Wren almost laughed. "Am I? They're just simple questions, Menaen. Who changed your name, is one. That's cult indoctrination 101, right there, destroy the past and rebrand the future. Who killed Davis Thackerton? Make followers party to an atrocity for a greater good, that's indoctrination 102. Cherry on top, who locked you up in these trailers?" Wren gestured around them. "103. Imprisonment. I heard you've been mowing your way onto other people's fields. What is that, but your brain still resisting the lies?" Wren's eyes drilled into Menaen's. "You did that yourself. You couldn't help it. Tell me, when's the last time you even spoke to anyone who wasn't already mad?"

Menaen shifted in his seat, eyes roving for a way out. Wren didn't give him one.

"Right now my father's talking about jailers all the time, spewing his poison that half the country need to burn to set the slaves free, but doesn't that sound like the pot calling the kettle black to you?" Wren sucked a fast breath. "Just look at what he's done to you. Lock your brain in lies you can't get out of. Lock your body here for fifty years. Lock everyone into his pyramid, bury innocents face-down in the dirt so they'll serve him forever, like that poor girl at First Corinthians. The worst thing is, you're locked in right there with her, even if you can't see it. He took everything from you, and you still want to protect him. If anyone's the jailer here, it's him."

Menaen was sweating now, his whole body humming. Wren kept boring in like a Tunnel Rat, seeking out targets in the deep past. Countdown to an explosion, like the Trinity tests in '45.

"But it all started with you wanting to stop a war," Wren said softly, bringing things back around. "You were a good man to want it. But he twisted that motivation, and he kept twisting until you thought stopping one war meant starting another. But you tell me, is setting the world on fire any kind of way to save it? Is it any more likely than trying to kill the devil with a bullet of fifty-five, sorry, fifty-six souls shot into hell?"

Menaen laughed. It was involuntary and panic-ridden, but it was real.

"You're right, that is ridiculous. It always has been. So help me stop his war. Tell me your real name."

Menaen's mouth opened. He went to speak. Wren craned for the blast to come, words he mustn't have said for fifty plus years.

"Say it!"

"Jonathon," Menaen gasped. The sound was throttled, his mind fighting his body for every syllable. "Jonathon Gibson."

41

JONATHON

Menaen shook. Wren held his shoulders as the shudders intensified. A man re-making himself inside, rebuilding who he was from the ground up, though Wren was under no illusions. Wear a mask for fifty years, it was hard to ever take it off. Lies were an addiction. This was a bubble at best. Most likely Jonathon would sink back into the comforting grasp of Menaen soon, the role of a lifetime.

He had to get what he needed now.

"The Apex," Wren prodded, gently. "You said he killed my grandfather. Let's begin there. Why did he do that?"

Jonathon looked up. His eyes were different. Not so black, anymore. Even his voice sounded younger. "He said-"

"I don't care what he said," Wren said, gently but firm. "He was a child then. You were an adult, right? You became his adoptive father, so you tell me. Why did he do that?"

It was hard. Wren could see the effort it took. This old version of Jonathon Gibson trying to separate himself from the Apex's reasoning, from Menaen the Builder, from the steel-plate layers of ideology locking him in place.

"I, uh-"

"Jonathon."

His dark eyes flashed. "I think he was jealous."

"Of his father?"

"Of the attention. Of the direction Davis was taking things."

"At twelve?"

Jonathon blinked, and a tear broke down his pitted cheek. "You said it yourself. He was no normal child."

Wren nodded along, adding that to the pile. "He grew up hearing his father preach. The people came and listened. All about Vietnam, shooting the devil in the heart?"

"Everything," Jonathon gulped. "Davis had his son up sometimes to speak in tongues, talk about whatever was in his head. And your father, he always had a thing for pyramids." He winced, like he'd been stabbed in the belly. Confession hurt, but he kept on. "All that stuff, the triangles and pyramids, came from your father. Davis just built it in. A kid's book he read about the Egyptians." He paused, looked up at Wren with a new light in his eyes, like a medium channeling a long-departed spirit. "We didn't have a lot of books at the compound. Things about the war, leaflets, but nothing for kids. Maybe that was the only one. A picture book of Egyptian mythology."

Wren stared. Lots of questions. Only one that would serve as the key to them all. "What's my father's name, Jonathon?"

The old guy looked confused. Like he didn't understand what he was being asked.

"I don't-"

"It's not hard," Wren urged. "You remember your own name. I know you remember his. You've just got to say it."

It took long seconds. Wren leaned in. Jonathon tried to frame the sounds, unspoken for so long.

"Noah," he managed. "Noah Thackerton."

Wren sat back. Felt like something significant had shifted.

The Apex had a name. The Apex was human. The shackles could be lifted.

"Noah."

Jonathon looked down at his lap, like he was expecting the fury of God to smite him down.

"So Noah killed his father," Wren summarized. "Now Davis Thackerton is dead along with all his people, burned up at the bottom of the pit. The devil isn't dead, though, the mission was a failure. What happens next? He start things up again, in a new direction?"

Jonathon nodded.

"But it's a new ideology, now," Wren riffed. "First Corinthians, focused around triangles, pyramids?" He got a nod. "An ideology he kept developing. Melting pot. But he leaves the water tower up, the pit, as reminders of the past. Psychic power, you said." He thought for a second. "What was the new goal?"

Gibson looked up. Seemed to be at a loss. His hands wormed in their duct tape restraints. "See, we only had that one book, and…'

"What was the goal?" Wren pressed.

Gibson went stone cold for a second. Stiff, upright, and Wren thought he was about to pass out. Pulling too deep. Maybe finally give himself a heart attack.

Then the word came.

"Resurrection," Gibson said. Stared dead ahead. "Die and come back stronger. As a god. The book said you could do it. Pharaohs did it all the time. Triangles were the key. The pyramid. The apex, the tomb."

Wren blinked. He hadn't once mentioned those words himself, apex or tomb. "But the apex is here," he said fast, feeling the bubble straining against fifty years of dead weight. "The tomb, too. They're both right here! Center of the

248

pyramid over America. If that's what he wants, resurrect himself as a god, then why isn't he here?"

Gibson's eyes spread wide, the bubble right up to the edge, then he burst out sobbing.

"I'm sorry," he said. Began repeating it. Rocking himself forward and backward, tears pouring from his cheeks. For the dead woman, maybe. For the waste of his life.

"Jonathon, why is he not here?!"

But Jonathon Gibson was gone. Wren knew it. Broken. The weight of a lifetime of lies had pulled him apart, and they weren't going to get anything more now.

He took a breath. Looked up at Rogers, who was staring at him with something like awe. Another magic trick.

"Resurrection," she said. "But how did you…"

She trailed off. Staring into his eyes and seeing something different. The reason behind it all, maybe.

"Resurrection," Wren repeated.

42

RESURRECTION

Wren stood up.

"Where are you going?" Rogers called after him.

His head was filled with thoughts too furious and fresh to put into words. "I need to walk."

Rogers stood too. "You're not going outside again. I'm not in the mood to draw any more snow angels with you, Boss."

He barely heard it, turned, started walking. Didn't matter which direction.

"I'm serious," Rogers said. "No more snow angels! Don't go outside."

Connections were already bouncing around his head, heating up like neutrons in an atomic bomb.

"And he's gone," Rogers said in back. "Never a word of thanks. You save a man's life, you make him a nice cup of coffee, you'd think…"

She was cut off as Wren passed through the gale of snow blowing in at the blast hole, like a silencing curtain. After that it was just him and the workbenches with their crafted triangles and calculations, carved into the walls and floor.

Metal plate was everywhere, insulated with padded silver foil and slitted with gaps for shooting out of.

He passed from the workbench trailer to the next, a long narrow room with fat cathode-ray televisions stacked along both sides, all of their screens dead. It didn't mean anything to him. He kept on, passed through a room with four bathtubs in it, each filled with icy water, no idea what they might be for. He passed through a room with a bunkbed, the top bed perfectly neat, the bottom rumpled like it had just been slept in, as if 'Menaen' were waiting for a friend to come sleepover.

He hit a corner where the trailers made a hard left, and stood for a moment at the welded vertice, looking back the way he'd come. The blast of snow was maybe a hundred yards away. He looked the other way, bisected at an angle of around sixty degrees, enough to make a perfectly equilateral triangle, maybe visible from space.

Jonathan Gibson had kept himself busy. Fifty years was a long time to build this thing.

Wren plunged on, through a neat but molding kitchen, ancient fridge humming off a gas-powered generator, kettle still steaming slightly, finally starting to put words to some of the thoughts in his head.

Anastasi Street. He'd thought nothing of it at the time, but it was a word he knew from an extensive study he'd made of names and their roots. A great way to connect with people; tell them what their name meant.

Anastasia, from the Ancient Greek Anastasis.

Resurrection.

He walked faster, the segmented trailers passing by like carriages in a never-ending triangular train, trawling through more symbolic interconnections in his head, trying to pattern-match for the next step forward. The number three was everywhere now, in the sides of a triangle, in the shape of this trailer, in the Trinity nuclear test.

The holy trinity, he thought: Father, Son and Holy Ghost. Jesus rolling back the stone after three days, emerging out into the light. The Apex buried in an airless pit for three nights, coming back to his people alive.

He walked faster, his mind speeding up in sync as triplets buzzed like angry bees. Mind, Body, Spirit. Past, present, future. Life, death, rebirth. Heaven, Hell, Earth. Pyramids embodied the number three, three sides to every face, the strongest shape in construction.

The Apex. X. Christopher Wren.

A pyramid across America. The first letter to Corinthians, dealing with matters of resurrection. A skull buried peering down into hell as a foundation for the Apex to stand on. The Pyramid. The Foundation. An app made up of triangles, a Pyramid of one thousand people burned alive, the apex and the tomb and the...

Wren stopped walking. Tried that one again. The apex and the tomb and the...

Something was missing. He didn't know what it was. He looked around the space he was in and saw walls decorated with faces. Bodies too. Dozens of them. He leaned closer, and by the weak storm light saw an incredible level of detail brushed into the metal. Looked like the work of decades. Filigreed eyes, cheeks, necks, clothing. Shading, stippling, a chisel point hammering again and again with the greatest care, crafting men, women and children.

Something in Wren's heart cracked.

The people of Davis Thackerton's cult. Had to be. Memorialized here forever. Not only as a prison for them, but as something else.

Company for Jonathan Gibson. Menaen the Builder. Friends, even. A man locked in solitary confinement, steadily going mad, needed some kind of human contact, even if it was fake. He must've spent years drawing these. Wren spun.

Maybe Davis Thackerton was here, preserved forever in the carving. His grandfather. Maybe Noah was here too, the Apex captured as an innocent child. So many memories recorded by Gibson. Perhaps waiting for the day Noah came back, saw this and was proud. Maybe transported Jonathan into his pyramid ark and made it all worthwhile.

Wren's vision doubled. He felt so close. Apex and tomb and…

He started striding back. Through the kitchen, around the corner, through the room of bathtubs, the televisions, toward the blast of snow until he reached the workbenches again where he stared at the wall.

Remembered the Apex's mantra, repeated by X, sprayed out a billion times by millions of voices.

Pain is a doorway. Fear is a portal. Walk in the fire.

A scorched map of America seemed to swell and pulse before him. He reached up and traced the 'Icon' triangle from New York southwest down to Acapulco, northwest up to Seattle and back east across to New York. Medicine Lodge in the center. Apex and tomb, but neither was where the resurrection took place.

Nor should it be. Now it seemed so obvious.

Jesus came back to life when he rolled back the stone. Pharaohs only came back as gods when they left their tomb behind, ascended to the apex and from there commanded the world. Resurrection was neither the apex nor the tomb, but an in-between place, the realm between death and life. It didn't happen at the center, it happened at the edges.

In the portal. At the doorway. Where the flames met the air and burned the hottest.

Wren's finger shook as it drifted left across the map like a water diviner's rod, inexorably leading him to the great triangle's edge. The only place to put a doorway.

For maybe a minute he just stared. Disbelieving. Then

starting to believe. It was in the name, after all. All the clues were there. They always had been.

He knew exactly where the Apex was. Maybe where he'd been all along. The oldest trick he ever pulled, repeated on an epic scale.

Little Phoenix.

The fake town. Site where the Pyramid first burned. At the exact midpoint of the great triangle's line between Seattle and Acapulco. A point decided by predestiny, laid out as an 'Icon' on a map maybe fifty years ago as the site for Noah Thackerton's coming resurrection.

The phoenix reborn from the ashes of his country's death. So the Apex would return stronger than ever, ascendant over all.

43

BRIDGE

W ren pushed through the draft of snow pelting through the carriage wall, feet crunching in several inches of settled white, to see a wintry tableau stretching away before him.

Jonathan Gibson in his chair, lap frosted with snow, with the blanket wrapped over his shoulders. Sally Rogers standing a little further on with her phone held high like she was trying to catch a signal. It looked like a carved fresco in the trailer wall, two more souls trapped in amber in this timeless, lost tomb.

Wren blinked and shook it off.

"We have to go," he said. His voice came out guttural and low, like an animal just emerging from hibernation.

Rogers' gaze levelled on him. "You figured it out?"

"I know where he is."

A second passed. Rogers put her phone in her pocket. Took a step toward Wren, then paused, looked at Gibson. "What do we do with him?"

Wren looked. For a second his first thought was 'leave him here'. He'd freeze to death soon enough, with the wall breached. It would even be peaceful, gradually losing sensation in his extremities, feeling the deceptive warmth as hypothermia lulled his mind into the dark. Nothing like the way the fifty-five had died. The fifty-six. A far easier death than they must have given the woman under First Corinthians.

But he didn't say it. Jonathan Gibson was a victim as much as he was a perpetrator. If there was any lesson to be had here, it was that. They were all victims: Davis Thackerton of a brutal, prolonged war; Noah Thackerton of Davis' delusions, and so on down the line to Jonathon Gibson, the X-apoc and Wren himself.

A thought occurred to him. Christopher Thackerton. Maybe Wren Thackerton? It didn't seem to take.

"Boss!" Rogers said. Shouted, even. "Are you OK?"

"I'm fine," he said, realizing she'd called his name several times. Lost in hyper focus. Drifting on the vertigo of fresh revelation. "He comes with us. We'll dump him in custody along the way."

Rogers nodded, produced a knife from her tactical belt and slit the duct tape holding Gibson to the chair. Wren strode forward and lifted him up. The man was almost deadweight, too mentally broken to take charge of his own body. Wren hoisted him in a fireman's lift and walked away from the incoming snow, toward the front door.

"So where are we going?" Rogers asked.

"Back to the start. To Little Phoenix."

Rogers let out a gasp. "You're kidding. Your town? The fake town in Arizona?"

Wren just grunted, pointed at the door up ahead. There were spent ammo shells on the floor here, brass casings scattered where Gibson had fired at them through a slit. Rogers went to the door, rammed back one deadbolt, two, and the plate metal swung open.

"How is that possible?" Rogers asked, holding the door

open as a blast of snow rushed in. "I thought you knew that place like the back of your hand."

"Me too," said Wren, and stepped out into the gale.

They couldn't talk in the storm. If anything it was worse than before, visibility reduced to a yard or two. No track of their previous footprints, just the sense of a bearing. Wren felt it though, like the workings of this place were tattooed on his skin. He'd seen Gibson's calculations. Surveyed all his many sketches. The triangle of trailers. The 'water tower'. All laid out like an arrow pointing west, neat and clean as a death stroke. Even in that, Gibson had given away his unconscious yearning to be free.

Within minutes the tower emerged through the blizzard like a dark portent. At least the cover was open now, the snow could get into the pit and the 'psychic power' of the dead fifty-six could escape.

Gibson mumbled something on Wren's shoulder. Leaving his land for the first time in years. Wren cut a straight line from the tower to the Ford. He dumped Gibson in the frigid back, strapped him in with a seatbelt while Rogers scraped a thick layer of crusted snow off the windshield, then met her at the driver's side.

"You're wired, Boss," she shouted. "Your eyes are crazy. You're not driving in this!"

He didn't let go of the door handle.

"I'm serious," Rogers bellowed. "We're not ending up in some ditch because your concussed brain spaced out for thirty seconds. Chris!"

He looked at her. Couldn't argue. Let go.

Rogers opened the door, dropped in. Wren circled and got in the passenger side.

"I didn't space out," he said, slamming the door and pulling his seatbelt on. "I was reflecting."

Rogers laughed, hand on the ignition. "Right, like you

weren't making snow angels in a blizzard, either. Honestly, it's a miracle you're moving at all, barely a week out from taking a bullet to the head. I got this."

She turned the key, the ignition coughed, the engine turned over once then died.

An awkward moment passed.

"You got this?" Wren asked.

"She just needs to warm up."

She tried again, the engine coughed and died again.

"Girl power," Wren offered.

Rogers shot him a foul look, focused on the ignition and turned the key a third time. This time it caught. Wren spun the AC's dials to full hot, only then realizing how cold he really was. His fingers were blue. Maybe that was hypothermia. Past the cold, into the numb warmth of nothingness.

The Ford jerked forward. Rogers worked the gears. Wren brought up the satellite map on his phone, but it refreshed and went blank.

"We lost GPS," Wren said. "The storm."

"So I drive by feel."

"And compass." Wren tapped through to a compass app, tying it into the portion of the map he'd studied "It's straight west to the road, then south, turn west when we cross the Medicine Lodge River and we should be coming up on Mills Landing Strip. Hellion set us a jet there."

Rogers looked at him. "You memorized that?"

"It's two turns. We may struggle to take off in all this, but…"

Rogers grunted and sped up a little. Nothing to say to that. If the jet wouldn't take off, maybe that was that.

They bumped over the edge of the track. "I'd kill to know what's going on out there."

"You may have to," Wren said.

In five minutes they passed by Willy's house, a shadowy block in the storm, and Rogers turned south. There were no other vehicles on the road, only the downpour of snow as the storm let them have it. Wren barely thought. Surfing the past and the present, lodged in the present.

Little Phoenix. It worked. It synced up. He'd never have seen it coming.

In twenty minutes they reached the Medicine Lodge River, shot out on a low bridge at thirty miles an hour and almost crashed into a truck sprawled sideways across both lanes. Rogers hit the brakes and they hydroplaned on snow, came within inches of collision.

The F-150 rocked back. Wren let out a breath, back in the moment and surveying the scene. The bridge was narrow and impassably tight. His base instinct was to ram the truck, a gray Chevy, but on a bridge with low railings on either side, snow and ice making the physics unpredictable, he didn't like their odds. Fall over the edge into the icy water below, it wouldn't matter what insight he had into the Apex's mind. It was over.

"I'll move it," Wren said, was already opening the door so Rogers couldn't protest.

The wind hit him at once like a body-blow, snow tearing down the superhighway of the river's channel carved out of the flat Great Plains. He could barely see, hardly hear a thing. No sign of the driver. He leaned in, shaded his eyes, advanced, feeling the temporary warmth of the truck tearing away as heat sucked out of his body.

By the Chevy's passenger window he saw an X flag in the window. Barely had a millisecond for that to register before the gunshot rang out, blowing the Chevy's glass out against his chest.

He spun and dropped to one knee, drawing his Glock. Another shot rang out, spidering the Ford's windshield right in front of Rogers' face. No time to check on her. The shots were coming from the other side of the truck, and he bellied down and burrowed like a Tunnel Rat beneath the Chevy. X-apoc forces ordered to secure all roads to and from Medicine Lodge and any surrounding airfields, most likely.

Out the other side he led with only the Glock, head and hand, and cursed silently that he'd tossed his monocular in some fit of madness. He saw nothing now but driving snow. Still he picked out a trajectory, tracking back from the dual shots to the probable spot in the mass of white for a sniper's hide. Must be they had thermal sight too. Elevated on a truck bed, Wren figured, from the angle. In a tent, if they'd been blockading here for the past hour or so. That meant solid visibility head-on, but abysmal from the sides.

No time to think. He backed up, rolled out from under the side of the Chevy, re-holstered his Glock and laid hands on the bridge's side railing. Three horizontal steel bars designed to steer vehicles back central when they veered. Not designed to stop a man slipping between them like a posted letter.

Wren pushed, his body fell over the edge then hooked sharply when his grip caught. Hanging from the side of the bridge over an unknowable drop to the river below, lashed by a gale wind so hard his body swayed, with only static coming through the earpiece.

Was Rogers OK? Maybe dead already, taken on the first shot. If not, she wouldn't last long if they kept firing.

He started sideways as fast as he could, hand-over-hand to the right. Snow on the railing made it slippery and froze his palms. Moving too fast, he almost lost his hold and fell. The result of that was some real vertigo. Ten more, he told himself. Slowed his breathing, calmed his heart, made a conscious effort to clamp every grip as tight as possible, melt the snow with his residual body heat and get a clean hold.

Gunfire popped above, sliding closer with every crab-like

shuffle. His shoulders burned from the weight. Maybe not much left in the tank. Should be enough.

After ten he gave it another five then pulled himself up the railings, got his feet on the bridge and stood, coming almost face-to-face with a guy leaning over the edge, trying to get a better angle on the Ford with a long rifle.

Black bandanna wrapped like a mask across his face, emblazoned with a white X. For a second he only stared at Wren, then started trying to bring the rifle to bear, but that was a mistake. The weapon in your hands wasn't always the best one for the moment. Wren proved that by clamping one hand on the guy's jacket and pulling him into a massive headbutt. Hit the guy's cheekbone, something cracked and he cried out and recoiled. Wren saw stars. Strictly against doctor's orders.

Then he was over the railing. The guy was bent double and staggering back, holding his face, but there was little time for mercy now. Wren drew his Glock and shot the guy in both shoulders. Destroying the bones, likely to leave him dead, but that fell to his choices. The guy sagged to the snow. Two steps on stood another truck, a camouflage tent propped up in the trailer, the spike of a sniper rifle now desperately trying to reorient but snagged on the canvas.

Wren fired three times, approximating center mass. There was a cry then the rifle barrel jerked and tipped slack. He strode forward, unsheathed the Mossberg shotgun and edged past the front of the truck. Another guy darted away around the indicator light. Wren fired through, took out the headlight, indicator, part of the grille and the guy.

He lay in his X gear lay in the snow, bleeding out from multiple lacerations. Wren kicked his weapon away and circled the truck, a Tacoma, breathing hard. Stared into the white but saw no evidence of a fourth man. He climbed into the trailer bed, found one dead sniper and tipped him out.

"Boss!" came a call.

He looked over the edge. Rogers was there, dragging Jonathan Gibson along by her side. He felt a flush of relief. Intact, uninjured, and making the right call. With the Ford's windshield smashed and the road blocked, it was better to switch vehicle.

Strange though that Gibson should get saved again, right after Wren had gunned down three X-apoc. He almost laughed, then helped her lift the old guy into the Tacoma's cab. The engine was on, a power line running from the cigarette lighter dock out the window to a heater in the trailer bed. Unnecessary now, and Wren yanked it.

"He almost got me," Rogers shouted from behind. Wren saw flecked blood on her face.

"You're not hit?"

"Glass shrapnel," she answered.

He shuffled over to the passenger side and Rogers got in after him. They closed the doors, sharply cutting off the gale, and looked each other in the eye over Gibson's slumping body.

"Looks like you had to do the killing," Rogers said. "But we have our answer about the country."

"America's falling," Wren answered. "Let's get on that damn jet."

44

MILLS

The Mills Landing Strip was invisible in the storm. They only knew they'd gone past it when the GPS on Wren's phone came back to life, assisted maybe by a break in the cloud cover or the ping from a nearby cell tower.

It looked like nothing much from above, an empty field plowed flat. No buildings, no parking lot.

"There's a jet here?" Rogers asked, peering as she pulled the Tacoma around. "It looks like cropland."

Wren couldn't argue. "According to Hellion, she put a ride at every airfield within fifty miles of Medicine Lodge. Let's hope she included this place."

In a few minutes they returned to the edge of the field, then the satellite link went out and their blip on the GPS app disappeared. Rogers slowed and they peered out into the storm. There was nothing to see but white.

"Drive it," Wren said. "Start at this end and work a circuit, they won't have parked in the middle."

Rogers pulled the wheel hard over, they dipped into a low trough then rumbled back up onto the landing strip. "It's bumpy for a runway."

"I expect it's for cropdusters and other light propellor aircraft. I bet they don't get a lot of corporate jets."

Rogers chuckled. They circled for two slow minutes, running around the west edge of the landing strip, where fences steered them back in.

"Other end," Wren said.

They crossed the strip. Maybe seven hundred yards. It was smoother right down the middle.

"How long should an air strip be?" Rogers asked.

"At a commercial airport for passenger jets? About three thousand yards."

Rogers laughed.

"Lots of redundancy baked in there. With good acceleration from intensive fuel burn, ambitious use of the flaps and nosecone, you can cut that in quarter."

"To seven hundred yards?"

"In ideal conditions."

Rogers laughed again.

Then they saw it. A yellow light floating like a lighthouse. Rogers hit the brakes, spun the wheel, pulled around to the loading door, clear of the wing. Closer up the craft's silhouette became clear; a fuselage that was impressively short, with a fat-bellied profile Wren recognized, a Beechcraft Premier IA. A real workhorse. Powerful lift.

Wren was first out, dragging Gibson with him, while Rogers leaned on the horn until a shadow split the cockpit light. In seconds all three of them were standing by the craft in the midst of the storm, waiting as the pilot opened the door and let down the stairs.

Wren was first in. The pilot was young, short-cropped brown hair, wearing a prim shirt with badges and epaulettes. His eyes bugged when he saw Wren. "Are you serious?"

"As a government audit," Wren said, helped Rogers in then closed and locked the door behind them.

"I can't believe this," the guy was saying. "Christopher Wren, in my plane? I never thought, I mean. This is amazing. But..." He trailed off, looking from Wren to Rogers to the window and back again. "You don't actually want me to fly in all this, do you?"

"You do it or I will," Wren said. "And if I do, we'll almost certainly crash. So I think it better be you."

The guy gulped. "Ah. But, this model, it's not certified for these conditions. Heck, no plane is! If we wait-"

Wren laid a hand on the guy's shoulder. "There's no waiting. You're a Foundation member?"

The guy nodded eagerly. "Yes, yeah, I-"

"Then we fly or die. Right now. What's it going to be?"

The guy's eyes flared. Looked into Wren's eyes and seemed to draw strength. One of the benefits of Thackerton blood, Wren figured.

"Fly," the guy said.

"Then no time like the present."

The pilot nodded again, getting a hold of himself. "Yes, sir. It'll be my privilege."

He turned smartly and went to the cockpit. Wren brought up his phone. Battery almost dead. He scouted the narrow, squat fuselage while Rogers settled Gibson into a seat and the pilot ran pre-flight checks. Found a charger, plugged in, and found the plane's Wi-Fi. With its more powerful uplink to satellites, it had a signal.

Wren booted up his darknet. It loaded slow, bare kilobytes per second. Not enough signal for video, even images or audio, but enough to read and write text.

Seemed the snowstorm had slowed the civil war in Medicine Lodge. Nobody had found the X-apoc guys in the field yet, and Wren figured nobody would for a while, not as long as the storm kept dumping snow. Hundreds of X-apoc had descended on the little town, looked to be filling out the main street, but with visibility barely a yard ahead, they were struggling to wage their war.

Across the country the X-apoc were mobilizing, but the trigger hadn't been pulled yet. Pretty much every city across the country was in open revolt, but the violence was still sporadic, the pushing and shoving stage of a fight before the real haymakers were thrown.

Wren paged through his darknet boards. The Foundation hadn't hit back yet either, though they stood ready; the only coordinated force preparing to protect life before the firestorm raged out of control.

The storm over Medicine Lodge had bought them a couple of hours.

In front the Beechcraft's engines fired up. The plane began to turn. Wren looked up, caught sight of Rogers on her phone urgently tapping out a message.

"Prepare for take-off," came the pilot's voice through the PA. "It's going to be rough."

Two hours to a landing strip near Little Phoenix, Wren figured. Possibilities raced through his mind. What they were going to find. What he was going to do. How that might finally put a nail in the X's mythos and force the X-apoc to stand down.

The engines surged to fever pitch and the jet jerked forward. Wren strapped his seat belt tight, then sent out a text to his hacker elite and the head of his Foundation, Hellion, B4cksl4cker and Theodore Smithely III, for their eyes only.

AM GOING TO LITTLE PHOENIX. THE APEX IS THERE. TAKE CONTROL OF COMMS. WE STILL HAVE TIME. PULL BACK FOUNDATION FORCES WHERE WE CAN. DELAY OPEN BATTLE FOR AS LONG AS POSSIBLE.

He sent the message, thought a moment longer, then

started tapping a second message. HERE IS WHAT I'M GOING TO NEED:

The Beechcraft rumbled over the lumpy landing strip. Every fitting in the fuselage shook. Wren imagined the yards tearing by beneath them, only seven hundred in total, and prayed the pilot knew exactly what he was doing. Go one yard over and they'd hit the fences around the strip, maybe a trough or a hillock beyond that, maybe enough to tear the jet apart and leave it a flaming smear across the land.

He finished typing and sent his requirements. The front of the jet jerked up, then dropped with a crunch. The engines screamed. The front lifted a second time, held for a second then they were plucked up into the storm as if yanked by the hand of God.

Wren set down his phone as the little jet juddered and wailed and roared up into the storm, finally leaving the Apex's childhood tomb behind. No view out the window but white. Rogers was shouting into her phone. Trying to command FBI forces. It didn't sound like she was making much headway.

Wren's head pounded. He couldn't believe he was so close. The Apex almost in his grasp. Twenty-five years of hunting, and maybe it could all end. He checked the time, just gone noon. The forecast said snow was going to clear over Medicine Lodge in a few hours. After that, all bets were off.

He wouldn't have thought it was possible, but at some point in the middle of the flight, Wren fell asleep.

Adrenaline crash, or another delayed effect of the concussion tumbling in his head, so many balls to keep up in the air, plates to keep spinning, and-

He woke to Rogers shaking him.

"Boss, we're about to put down."

He blinked up from the depths of an old Pyramid memory. His mind working on the problem even asleep. Standing with his father in the desert at dawn, looking down into one of the desert pits. The Apex was alive with excitement, explaining to his little Pequeño 3 how he'd survived three days and three nights entombed under the ground.

There was no special magic to it. Just a tunnel dug out into the desert.

"I think I know where he'll be," he said, rubbing grit from his eyes. "The Apex."

Rogers handed him a cup of something. Harsh black

coffee, looked like, no milk, cream, sugar, just the way he liked it. "Good."

"Please return to your seats and buckle up," came the pilot's voice over the intercom. "This will be a rough landing."

Rogers put a hand on Wren's shoulder then returned to her seat. He looked out of the window as the jet rocked steeply forward, diving sharply over red rocks and sand. The Sonoran Desert spread like a sandbox, his childhood haunt, place of jagged canyons, warbling cactus wrens and hydra-headed ocotillos. He'd returned so many times, and it had never felt like this.

His stomach leaped and spun. He drained the coffee anyway.

Coming home.

The jet wasn't designed for rough sand and dust, didn't have the hardened landing gear, but it had managed to take off in the storm so Wren figured a Main Street landing wouldn't kill them. Maybe strip the wheels then scrape in on their belly, pray that friction wouldn't blow the fuel tanks.

Wren unclicked his seatbelt and got up.

"Boss," Rogers said.

"It's OK," he said and strode the five steps toward the open cockpit.

"Mr. Wren," said the pilot, turning and looking surprised. "You really should-"

"Don't mind me," Wren said, slipped into the co-pilot's seat, strapped in and looked dead ahead.

There it was.

Little Phoenix. The fake town. Bane of his life. Maybe five miles off still, five thousand feet down and laid out like a child's playset. So much of it was still the same as ever: the saloon, the hotel, the general store. It was easy to picture how it would have looked in his childhood. Cages for babies behind the saloon. Vats for boiling in the basement of the hotel.

He could picture every inch. Right there was the dormitory where the Pequeños had slept, where the Apex had marked his own children with the sign of the Blue Fairy. It had been one of the first structures Wren had burned to the ground. It was easy to see the pattern he'd followed from there on, burning ever-outward.

His heart pounded, caffeine and adrenaline pulling a double on him. All his childhood had been spent here, listening to the depraved sermons of his father. Noah Thackerton. Just like little Noah had listened to his own father's ravings, Davis Thackerton. A family of madmen, passing on the family tradition.

And where were the women? The mothers. Buried, he supposed. In unmarked graves in the desert. At the bottom of the well back in Medicine Lodge. Burned up in the fake town on the Pyramid's last day.

He could see them all now, the one thousand laid out and smoking down Main Street. People he'd known and loved. No remembrance wall for them, etched by Jonathan Gibson. Just nothing. Bones ground to mortar for the Apex's inverted pyramid scheme.

They were coming in fast now, dropping a hundred feet per second or faster, maybe thirty seconds out from a final engine burst to convert all that downward momentum to forward thrust, hit the strip and streak off in a rush of sand and smoke.

He cast his eyes over all the new construction Maggie had put up in recent years. New residential blocks, a fitness center with a pool, the school, the hospital, all for the two thousand children he'd rescued from the Blue Fairy. Broad modern structures that thickened the town, adding depth and life to its once-sallow bones.

To the west though, the concrete foundation bases remained. Flat gray squares where fake town buildings had once stood, they stretched like overlarge pitcher's plates for fifty yards, and where they gave out Maggie had taken to placing new tombs, for the re-consecrated bones of the Pyramid members recovered from the sand.

His nausea burned to rage. All this time the Apex had been hidden right here. It was grotesque. Maybe he'd even had the Pyramid themselves build his hideout, so long ago. Wren remembered that first fateful trek out into the desert, the sun at their backs, to the the pit. The first time the Apex had shown off his 'magic'. If there was ever a fitting entrance to his private vision of hell, it would be there.

Twenty seconds. Down in the town they would have seen him by now, heard the jet's engines roaring like a herald from heaven, the avenging 'Saint Justice' come to set the past, present and future right.

Ten seconds, and now he picked out upturned faces and people running from his path, children in windows gawping up in surprise, maybe his own children, maybe his wife too, all wondering what on Earth was about to happen.

Five seconds, then the ground rushed up and hit the jet like a car crash from below. Enough momentum to keep a four-ton chunk of metal and plastic in the air converted instantly into vibration, heat and noise. The seat slammed up into Wren's spine, the flaps shot to hard brake and the engines roared into full reverse.

In seconds they dropped five inches as the solid rubber tires melted and shredded, sending them scraping along on the landing gear until that too sheared away and the jet dropped a final thump to the earth, scraping along on its fat belly. Heat seared up through the flooring, sand and dust clouded up either side and the grinding grew louder as the engines whined, trying to brake their velocity before they skidded off the semi-flat street and hit raw desert.

The pilot strained at the flaps. Wren could only stare in fascination at the sun halfway down in the west, feeling like things were coming full circle. Arriving in style. Here to bring the Pyramid down for the final time.

At last the jet rocked to a stop. It smoked and creaked. Wren unstrapped, patted the pilot on the shoulder, then moved through to the back. Jonathan Gibson had been sick on himself. Rogers was already on her feet.

"Smooth," she said.

"As Tennessee whisky," Wren answered. Spun the lever to open the door and jumped two feet down to the sand.

46

PIT

Within seconds a Jeep pulled up before Wren, the door opened and out stepped Theodore Smithely III, Chairman of the Foundation. Tall and gaunt as ever, all in black like Johnny Cash, holding two large rucksacks.

The hot air swam with dust kicked up by the jet. Wren glanced through the haze, past the Beechcraft's glowing red side and back along a blackened trail burned down the center of the fake town.

Just like old times.

"Your family have been secured," Teddy said, then looked at Rogers. "And your mother."

"Secure them all," Wren said, and took one of the rucksacks, climbed into the Jeep. "You can bet the X app already knows we're here."

He slammed the door. Rogers climbed into the passenger side, no argument this time, and he pulled away at once, heading west. His memory of the first pit was spotty, maybe an hour's walk due west of the town, which made for about three miles.

Rogers took the rucksacks and opened them in turn,

checking through the contents. She handed a fresh earpiece to Wren and he slotted it in. It beeped as it paired with his phone, then Hellion's voice came abrupt and clear, the first time in hours.

"I can confirm, X app ALERT has gone out. Forces will be incoming."

"You couldn't spoof this one?"

"Negative. It has double redundancy, heavy security over Little Phoenix. Not our security, Christopher." That was further confirmation, if he needed any. "We can subvert this but it will take time."

Rogers held up a small plastic wallet. Within sat a familiar nubbin of plastic, barely a-quarter inch wide. A stub.

"And if we plant the stub in X's phone?"

"Access should be immediate. We will have root directory and source code."

"Sounds good," Wren said.

Rogers continued pulling gear from the rucksacks as Wren raced into the desert: full-body tactical outfits for each of them, in tight-weave para-aramid Twaron fiber sewn with aluminum foil. Rogers began changing while Wren scanned the dry red desert ahead, reaching for any landmark to jog his memory. Cacti, boulders, humps and dips in the land itself. Once he'd known them all so well.

"You are certain this is good idea?" Hellion asked. "To livestream everything?"

"It's the only idea," Wren said, as Rogers slotted a bodycam into her new Twaron jacket, activated it. He'd shared the plan on the jet before sleep had snuck over him. "Words won't cut it now, even killing the app's not enough. We have to show the X-apoc their leader getting felled, or they'll never stop. They have to see this with their own eyes."

"And if instead they see you being felled, Christopher? What then?"

"Then we're all screwed," he said, and hit the brakes. The Jeep skidded, Rogers caught herself smoothly on the dash then continued strapping on gear.

"There," Wren said, pointing off to the right. Maybe he couldn't put his finger on it precisely, but there was something about the angle of the land that felt familiar. Maybe a slight mound. Rogers was already out of the Jeep, and Wren followed.

"Boss," she said, handing him his gear. He stripped his bandoliers, his pants and shirt and pulled on the stiff new material. Pants, jacket, boots. Rogers handed him equipment as he was ready for it; holster for the Glock, magazines into the tactical belt, grenade strip, quad-load chest-plate of shotgun ammo, Mossberg into the long sheath. Last she slotted his bodycam in at the front, and he pulled on a compact rucksack.

"Do not forget to drop amplifiers every turn," Hellion said. "Or signal will die. Livestream will fade."

"Like Theseus and Ariadne's thread," Wren said, pocketing a handful of the small black amplifiers. Battery-powered and as big as old-school pagers.

"What is this, Theseus?" Hellion asked.

"Monster movie," B4cksl4cker answered. "Old Hollywood."

Rogers laughed.

"This way," Wren said, and stepped off the rough track into the desert proper. Felt the sand beneath his boots, the heat burning up and sweat already trickling inside his tough new gear.

The mound was faint but just about visible. Only stray creepers of Devil's Fingers grew atop it. A few black stones marked its rough outline. It was the place. Some thirty years ago his people had camped here and waited, dreaming of such grand things.

"This is it," Wren said, and walked out onto the mound. The ground flexed almost imperceptibly. He remembered how they'd pulled the supply skids across the pit, then piled dirt and sand on top of them a foot thick.

He'd done enough digging for one day, though, and they didn't have the time. Instead he stripped a grenade off his belt, kicked a divot into the center of the mound, pulled the pin and set the grenade in.

"Go," he said.

They broke to the side and laid low. The blast shook the earth and sent up a plume of ancient dust, chased by the rending sound of old timber splintering. One hell of a knock on the back door, but nothing the Apex wouldn't already know. What mattered now was speed, and Wren wasted no time striding through raining sand to the pit. Looked like two supply sleds had been driven downward by the explosion, their skids now bristling at the edges.

"That one," Wren pointed, and took hold of one runner. Rogers took the other and they pulled. The first tug was hardest, displacing the residual heaps of sand, but the next became one smooth drag. They ran backward and the sled came with them. They dropped it and moved to the second, which pulled easier, opening the pit wholly to the air.

Around fifteen feet in diameter and ten feet deep, walls lined with flat stones to make digging a way out harder for the victims stuck inside. Just like every other pit the Pyramid had dug. Wren felt like he was staring down into the past.

"You're sure this is a way in, Boss?" Rogers asked. "Looks like no one's been this way in years."

"There must be a regular entrance," he answered, "somewhere in town, but finding it could take hours. This is what we've got right now."

He jumped down into the pit without a second thought, spun around. The last time he'd been in a pit like this, it was with the sleds being pulled overhead, sealing him in the dark with his elder Pyramid brothers and sisters, along with Grace-In-Our-Times, the little girl his father had marked for death just to spite him.

"There," he said, pointing at the east wall leading back toward the town. "If there's a tomb anywhere, it'll be that way."

"Resurrection," Rogers said.

Wren snorted, already ripping flat stones off the wall with his pry bar. For two minutes they attacked the wall together, tearing stones down and stabbing into the hard sand underneath. Wren remembered doing the exact same thing with Grace at eight years old, while his brothers and sisters gasped in the darkness as the air steadily thinned. Down close to the ground, little Pequeño 3 and Grace-In-Our-Times had lasted longer, digging and digging until finally-

The dirt wall made a sound as he stabbed with the pry bar. Not the dull clink of a rock, not the dry rasp of the dirt, but a thud like he'd hit something hollow. Wood. They both descended on the spot and dug in a frenzy, hacking out chunks of compacted sand until a wooden frame emerged. It was around two and a half feet on a side and sealed with boards, like a trapdoor leading sideways into the earth.

"Back entrance," Rogers said. "Sneaky bastard."

"More like exit," Wren guessed. "There must've been a mechanism to safely bring those sleds down from inside. This is his get-out escape route."

"Not anymore."

Wren tapped his earpiece. "You getting all this, Hellion?"

"Hellion is coordinating pending defense of Little Phoenix," came B4cksl4cker's deep voice in her place. "Many forces incoming. But yes, I have all your footage so far. Will you begin livestream?"

"Backdate it from the Jeep. Give us ten minutes lead time, and run this audio over the top."

Keys clacked. "Awaiting audio."

Wren didn't need to think long, staring into Rogers' bodycam.

"Right now millions of you are taking orders from a faceless individual known only as X. You're burning for X. Killing for X. But who is X?" He paused a second. "I promise he is not some godlike figure come to deliver you from slavers in hell. He is not your savior. He is an avatar of the Apex, my father, AKA Noah Thackerton, a conman cult leader since he dug holes for people to die in the desert of Arizona thirty years ago. They died then. He didn't." Another pause, staring intently. "So let's find out how strong his faith is. If your leader truly believes, let him lead by example and walk first in the fire."

Tense seconds passed.

"I have it," B4cksl4cker said. "Looping over top of Jeep footage. Drop an amplifier, Christopher, then on your signal I will begin the stream."

Wren reached into Rogers' rucksack, pulled out an amplifier and dropped it on the ground. "Good?"

"Excellent signal. Yes. Feed is live and pushing to X network. You have ten-minute lead time."

"That's plenty," Wren said, and put a front kick into the hatch. The ancient wooden boards burst inwards, revealing a tunnel ribbed with support beams leading away into darkness, some seven feet below the surface of the desert. Wren got on his knees, shone a light inward and started forward at a crawl.

47

TUNNEL

The tunnel was hot, claustrophobic and pitch black but for the chaotic bounce of their flashlights, barely wide enough to accommodate Wren's broad shoulders or tall enough for him to pick up any speed. His arms brushed the side beams as he pulled himself forward, his rucksack thumping ominously off the slim roof ribs.

"Steady, Boss," Rogers cautioned in back. "You'll bring the tunnel down."

There was no time. The 'livestream' had begun, and Wren focused all his efforts on forward momentum. A three-mile crawl like this would take an hour. Whatever resurrection chamber they found at the end of the tunnel would be long-vacant by the time they reached it.

"Boss!" Rogers called as he hit the roof hard, dropping a shower of sand over them both, but he kept on, pistoning with his legs deeper into the damp air. A cave-in now and he'd have to back-tread all the way. No way to turn around.

Scorpions, mice and spiders scurried into the darkness ahead as he sped on with only a little more care, until his back stopped hitting the ceiling and his shoulders no longer brushed the walls. For a moment he thought he'd just mastered the technique, until Rogers called out.

"The tunnel's widening."

Wren shone his flashlight and confirmed it. Widening out and dropping, maybe three feet tall already. For some twenty yards he gorilla crawled, knees no longer touching the ground, until they hit four feet and he could run bent double.

Rogers' flashlight spun behind him, slashing beams across the blind white roots, cobwebs and desiccated werewolf mice nests burrowed into the dry walls. Her breath came in gasps, the sound echoing off the walls and merging with his own pulse.

His earpiece crackled and he remembered to drop an amplifier. At once a spotty signal came in.

"Christopher, do … hear me?'

'We have you, Hellion, go on," he rasped.

"There is gunfire … fake town. Many … out of nowhere, they are …."

His heart skipped a beat. "Repeat last, Hellion." He was at five feet clearance now and running nearly full speed into the dark. He dropped another amplifier. "Gunfire in the town?"

"Teddy is … but I cannot protect … your family, Christopher, they …"

His blood went cold. He straightened too much and almost knocked himself out on a beam, approaching a dead sprint. Cover three miles in twenty minutes or less, maybe, in peak condition.

"What about my family, Hellion?"

Nothing came back.

"Hellion!"

"Signal's dropped, Chris," Rogers called from in back.

He barely heard. Seeing red now. Teddy had secured them. No one other than his most trusted key players was supposed to know he was coming, so this couldn't be a trap. No way. It couldn't be.

They hit six foot clearance and he hit his stride. Great fast leaps through the darkness beneath the desert, heart firing at a hundred-sixty. Maybe he'd sent his family right into the lion's den. Loralei, Jake, Quinn. Rogers' mother too. The safest place in the country, he'd promised.

The tunnel reached seven feet and he went all out. Feet pounding the dirt. Leaving Rogers in his dust. Racing that ten-minute livestream clock and whatever chaos was breaking out above. The flashlight did next to nothing in the black. He was little Pequeño 3 again, tearing away from the past and toward some better future.

Then it all went away.

The floor dropped with a sickening lurch as his right foot punched straight through the surface, dust and dirt caving down into some kind of pit. Momentum carried him onward and down, his lower body plowing through the tunnel floor like an off-road jet until his chest thumped into the edge of the floor, blowing the wind from his lungs. His legs hit some unrecognizable pain deep below, then he was slipping deeper, dragged down by his own weight and the combined mass of his gear. His hands scrabbled desperately at the tunnel's dirt as he sank into a deeper agony, felt like his calves were plunging into glass.

"Holy crap, Boss!"

Submerged through the floor of the tunnel up to his neck. He flung his arms to full breadth and caught the support ribs, clung on and tried to pull himself up but all he had was a fingertip grip, and each rough jerk brought fresh showers of sand from above, threatening to rip it all down.

His chest slipped further. He realized what this was, what the pain in his legs meant.

Punji sticks. He almost laughed. Sharpened stakes at the

bottom of a concealed pit, just like the Viet Cong had littered their Cu Chi tunnels with. Drop GI Tunnel Rats into the holes, infect them with tips smeared with feces, have them begging for mercy and hobbled for life.

Panic filled his head. Already it felt like his legs were on fire. The tough fabric of his Twaron suit was bullet and stab-proof to a degree, but not against the persistent force of his own body weight. Nothing he could do. Try to pull himself up and he'd bring the tunnel down. Sink any further and the spikes would just plunge deeper.

Nowhere to go. Nothing to do.

"Rogers, I-"

Abruptly an almighty blast rang out, filling the air with dirt and smoke. For a second Wren thought the tunnel was collapsing, triggering his vertigo. His fingers lost their grip and he slipped further, driving the spikes up into-

Rogers was there. She caught him from behind, rested his weight on her shoulder, and another enormous blast rang out. It hammered his inner ears and peppered his legs with shrapnel of some sort, then the support went away beneath him and his feet hit the ground.

"I've got you, Chris," Rogers' voice came in his ear, hands around his chest and holding him steady. "Can you stand?"

He tried. His legs wobbled but held. "Yeah."

"Good, now don't move."

Her arms pulled away, and it was all he could do to keep his balance. The tunnel floor was above eye level now, but still he clung to it with his arms raised like a child at the deep end of the swimming pool, trying to figure out what just happened.

Rogers must've just fired her shotgun into the pit. That had shredded some of the spikes, then she'd jumped in without waiting for the dust to clear to catch him as he fell.

A true leap of faith. Chase that with another blast to fragment the spikes in his legs, and he was in the clear.

"I-" he began, then there was an incredible sharp pain in his left calf. Rogers grunted and Wren let out a cry.

"That's one of them," Rogers said. He looked but couldn't see anything for the dust. "Hold still, just gluing you up, and there's one more big one."

There was a strange cold sensation on his calf, had to be a superglue patch straight to the skin, followed by another sucking pull that felt like it was scooping straight out of his right thigh. So deep it had to be in the muscle, maybe against the bone. He yelled.

"Yeah, that was a big one," Rogers allowed. "Patch job to stop the bleed, then you're good."

He gasped, coughed, rubbed the stinging tears from his eyes. He should have anticipated this. Punji sticks. The traps Davis Thackerton had preached about all through Noah Thackerton's childhood. Of course they were going to be here.

Could he even walk now? Run? How far had they come, and would he be able to cover the rest of the distance?

"All done," Rogers said. "I'll boost you."

Those questions faded in the face of necessity. It didn't matter if he could, because if the Apex had his family, he would keep trying until he bled out. No doubt about it.

"Left leg up, Boss," Rogers called. She pulled and he lifted, got his boot into her latticed hands, then she thrust. His leg almost gave way but he stiffened it in time, rode the deadlift of a lifetime that flung him up and almost fully out of the pit.

He landed across his thighs, and Rogers shoved him the rest of the way. He was out. Rising to his feet. It felt like there was a bad shin splint in his left calf, but it held. He didn't bother to look at the damage. His right leg was worse, hot and tremulous at best. If he had the wind and the time he might have laughed. Galicia had already pin-cushioned his upper body, it was about time his legs took some punishment.

The whole thing in maybe thirty seconds flat.

"I've got some spikes of my own here," Rogers called from the pit. "But I'll deal with them. You need to get there, Chris. Save them, and I'll be along."

He almost stopped to argue, but didn't. Even if he tried to haul her out, drop to a squat and pull, he'd likely only tear the damage worse. His legs might collapse. Sprinting would do enough damage as it was.

She'd taken the hit so he could carry the torch forward.

"Thank you, Rogers," he gasped, "don't be a stranger." Then he turned to run through the pain. Nothing he could do about more traps. Had to hope that was the only one.

48

BLACK ECHO

Wren ran in a daze, thumping off the walls at full speed, counting his heartbeat or the seconds, he wasn't sure which.

Maybe five minutes gone? His 'livestream' would have reached the tunnel entrance by now. If the Apex hadn't known he was coming from below, he knew now. Hopefully he thought he still had ten minutes to get out. Wren had to turn that into a mistake.

His right leg almost gave way. His left shrieked as it took the weight of the stumble, but held him upright. It all ended today. It had to all end today.

Then the tunnel ended and a chamber began.

Wren lurched to a halt five paces in, flashlight spinning across smooth, distant walls and a sloping ceiling that was sparked with glints of color. The space was too big for the flashlight to put much of a dent in the darkness, though he got the sense of it as he turned. Some kind of hall maybe fifty feet square, lined with hundreds of one-foot-wide stone plinths that rose five feet high. He wheeled the flashlight higher, taking in four triangular ceiling surfaces covered in messy colors and shapes, climbing to an golden apex cornerstone some twenty feet high.

An underground pyramid.

The scale of it dizzied him. It was too big. Something like this would require serious engineering to construct. Metal beams in the walls. Drainage. Skilled labor. And how deep was he now? He looked back but the tunnel swallowed the flashlight's beam after a dozen yards. It must have kept on descending to fit all this. How far had he run?

He took a few steps back toward the tunnel, running his flashlight over the ceiling. Now the colorful images resolved into structured paintings. Hundreds of human figures. All life-size. Men, women, children. Crafted with apparent care but in a dizzying range of skill levels, from crude stick figures to elaborately realized likenesses, patterned here and there with gold or silver leaf.

Not the work of any one painter. Surely as many painters as there were figures.

Self-portraits.

With a sickening lurch Wren grasped what he was looking it. A much larger-scale version of Jonathon Gibson's memorial wall. Real souls recorded and offered up to the Apex's golden capstone above. He brought the flashlight beam down and saw what that offering was.

Triangled bones.

Atop each of the many plinths lay an unholy consecration, just like the woman beneath First Corinthians. Arm and leg bones shaped into inverted triangles. Pelvic girdles set in the middle, ribs balanced in the center, skulls poised above and pointing down through the plinth and into the earth, forever.

Hundreds of them. They ran all around the chamber, as far as he could see. More paintings, more plinths. An onslaught of nausea drove him to his knees and the flashlight beam reeled across the details, casting crazy shadows through rib cages and cracked skulls.

It was worse than anything he'd imagined. It gave the lie to everything he'd said to Rogers. That First Corinthians was an outlier. That the Apex cared more about the process than result. This was all result. A horrific tableau, and worse yet, it was hauntingly familiar. Like he'd been here before. Like the gossamer trails of a dream half-remembered three days later.

Wren stalked the chamber seeking out some kind of confirmation, as murky memories of a midnight excursion flashed through the back of his mind. Only twelve years old, blindfolded and brought here half-asleep, the memory flattened by the end of the Pyramid coming only days later, but growing more vivid every second.

The chamber spun around him and the memories gathered steam. It had all looked so different then. A huge, bright room with a sloping roof and the smells of paint and freshly turned earth in the air. The walls filled with scaffolds where people lay on diagonal boards and painted themselves onto the sky. The other Pequeños had all been there too. Chrysogonus drawing himself with outsized muscles. Galicia festooning herself in a sapphire gown.

He searched until he found what he was looking for. Simple and angular on the east wall, the painting of a boy with nut-brown skin, twinkling eyes, tousled black hair and a secret smile.

Pequeño 3.

Recognition came like a hammer in his gut. He'd painted this. He remembered this. There were no bones on the plinth beneath his image, at least not yet. The black wall of unconsciousness roared up at the edges of his vision. Pulse soaring, breath coming in great gasps, turning within the zoetrope of his own black echo.

The entire Pyramid was here. A cry of anguish escaped

his lips. They had always been here, locked in as slaves. He turned and the one thousand turned with him. His family. A dry heave came and he barely swallowed it back.

His earpiece crackled urgently. "X-apoc are here, Chr- … enough Foundation members to … need to finish …."

The signal died into static. Wren tried to shake off the fuzz of shock. Worse things were happening right now. There'd be time later for horror. All he could do now was find the Apex. Bring all this madness to an end. Get vengeance for this atrocity.

He scanned the walls and saw three more tunnel mouths leading away, one for each cardinal direction. North, South, East.

There was no time to guess. He had to know.

His mind kicked back into gear, over-riding the past. This pyramid had to be at the edge of town, probably underneath the flat foundation slabs stretching to the west. Heading east would take him directly under Main Street, but that didn't feel right. Too obvious, maybe. From what he knew of the Egyptians, pyramids were riddled with false trails leading to false tombs to trick grave robbers. Surely that would have been in Noah Thackerton's childhood picture book too.

So, North? Wren turned but saw nothing to distinguish that exit, seven feet tall and three wide, opening into darkness. He racked his mind for what Tandrews had told him. In Egyptian mythology the tomb provided a passageway for the dead to move between life and Tuat, or hell. The sun god Ra crossed through Tuat west to east every night, battling the god of chaos on his way. Wren looked up, saw Ra symbolized by the golden capstone.

It was all here. But he remembered nothing about cardinal directions.

His head boomed like a cannon. Maybe cardinal directions didn't matter? He dredged his memory for grade-school knowledge beyond crocodile-headed gods and hieroglyphs, settled on Aden's hand on his chest, talking about the heart. Apex over tomb, all aligned down the middle. It made sense, but if this was an inverted pyramid, dug into the ground, then that meant...

Wren immediately ran south and entered the tunnel for fifty yards. It plunged on into darkness, but there was no sense of it descending to some lower level. He needed it to drop. He turned and ran into the north route, but that didn't drop either.

"... chaos here," came fragments in his earpiece. "... have to ... now, Christopher!"

He ran East to be sure, but if anything that tunnel began to rise. The wrong direction. He ran back and spun his thoughts faster, looking for the pattern that had to be there. Everything he knew about his father, Noah Thackerton, murderer since he was twelve years old. First Corinthians. Resurrection. He'd want his slaves close. He'd want them perfectly aligned, just like his 'Icon' was aligned, just like Davis Thackerton's bullet into the devil's brain, just like-

Wren's heart skipped a beat. Straight down was the key. There had to be a direct route between his apex chamber below and this tomb above. At the center of the chamber he jabbed his heel into the beaten earth. It had to be here. Sweat poured down his cheeks, breaths came in gasps, but there was nothing. No flex in the ground, no trapdoor and seconds were ticking by.

Then something hit. A glint in the darkness. Resurrection as reincarnation. The role Christopher Wren himself had played all these years. Tandrews had said it himself, a son of the sun, Rah remade every night through his child. He ran to the eastern exit, where his own portrait hung. Pequeño 3. The only child of the Pyramid Noah Thackerton had ever spared. Eyes roving over the rudimentary work, fingers stroking the contours his brush had made so long ago, until he saw it.

Gold leaf sparks in the his eyes, like he was looking directly into infinity. Except Wren had never painted those highlights. He felt sure of it. Enlivened with the blaze of Ra.

He wasted no more time. Maybe there was a secret button somewhere, a recessed lever to crank a secret hatch open, but he wasn't going to find it now. Instead he simply dropped to a squat, clamped his arms around the bare plinth and heaved.

The massive stone column barely jostled in position, maybe three hundred pounds of unwieldy mass, then settled again. But had there been a clinking sound, like a lock catching on the bolt? Wren couldn't be sure. His heart hammered in his ears. Didn't matter. He squatted so deep he felt muscles tearing, locked his hands tight and heaved again with all his strength.

This time there was no mistaking the clank of metal on metal. He didn't let up, kept thrusting upward until metal screeched and the plinth slammed back down with a mighty crunch. Wren staggered, almost fell as silver lights flashed across eyes. There was no time, though, and he doubled down to heave again. Now the plinth ripped upward like a plug, some internal mechanism cracked loose and the final resistance gave way, sending him staggering backward with the full weight in his arms.

He dropped it to the side and refocused through the blur. Beneath the portrait drawn by Pequeño 3 was a channel carved half through the wall, half through the floor. He flung himself in and down.

49

PHARAOH

Within five yards the channel gave way to a metal spiral staircase drilling down into the earth, and Wren took it at a run, feet slapping on the rungs, hands yanking at the railing. So close. Fifteen steps on he slipped and almost fell but caught himself, heard the sound of voices nearby, then saw a crack of golden light below.

Instantly he could hardly breathe, could hardly see for his vision splitting as his pulse crescendoed. The stairwell spun, split, recombined and vertigo's black wall surged over him again.

Too much. Heart approaching aortal flutter. Lungs working like an industrial bellows. There was no point emerging below only to collapse in his father's arms.

He started stripping his gear: the ammo bandoliers for his Glock and the shells for his shotgun hit the stairs, the tactical belt weighed down with explosive munitions followed, then he emptied the amplifiers from his pockets, unlatched the Mossberg sheath and the holster for the Glock. Every strap uncinched and piece of gear dropped helped him breathe.

His earpiece crackled and a sound broke through, maybe Rogers' voice, but he didn't have time to talk.

Last of all he shrugged off his rucksack and grabbed a bottle from within, spun the lid and emptied the contents over his head. The cool liquid splashed over his scalp, ran down his face and neck, bringing relief and instant clarity. He scrubbed the excess from his hair and beard and took a breath.

Glock in his right hand. Legs almost giving way. Now or never.

He ran down the last stretch of stairs into golden light, through an archway seven feet tall and saw it all at once, almost too much to take in.

A brilliant chamber, walls entirely clad in gold and lit by spotlights that bounced liquid amber light up and around the sloping pyramidal roof. Maybe twenty feet across, as intimate and transcendent as a pit. Wren stared for a long second, overwhelmed. He'd never seen anything like it, like being frozen inside a block of amber.

At the center stood a huge black Egyptian-style sarcophagus, raised on a dais five feet high and big enough to encompass a giant. Fit for a pharaoh. The top was expertly carved in the shape of a muscular male lying flat, wearing an ornate death mask inlaid with gold, silver and glistening jewels, with sparkling blue sapphires for eyes.

Nobody there, though. It was silent. No voices, no movement, and Wren swallowed hard. The savage stink of unburned napalm hung in the air. This had to be it. The Apex's resurrection chamber. The tomb of the Pyramid stood directly above. A straight line to the tombstones above, to Little Phoenix, to the inverted triangle across America.

Wren entered with the Glock raised and his heart racing, sighted some misshapen black monster looming from the polished gold and almost fired, but it was just a burnished version of himself reflected in the polished gold walls. Only blackness for his eyes, rippled by markings carved into the gold. Hieroglyphs? No. Inverted triangles circled with swirling trails of calculations. Just like Anastasi Street.

He padded deeper, circling the huge sarcophagus until he saw the chamber's sole inhabitant, standing calmly on the other side. She was dressed in a flowing cream gown waisted with a broad gold-thread belt, a golden stole draped across her shoulders, embroidered at its ends with twin black inverted pyramids. Brown hair hung down her chest in curls, tan skin glowed in the golden air, wise green eyes watching him unsurprised.

Wren couldn't believe it. Could scarcely get a breath out.

"Maggie?"

She only smiled at him. Just like she'd smiled at him in the field in Iowa, encouraging him to get up, to go out, to seek X in the wild. Just like she'd smiled at him so many times before, telling him that the fake town was his home, that he could return at any time.

Maggie. The matriarch of Little Phoenix. The woman he'd left in charge of all the Blue Fairy children.

"Christopher," she said. Her voice was warm and gentle as ever. She made no move toward him. "I'm sure you must be very confused."

He was beyond confused. He felt like a trigger jammed on the safety, unable to pull. This didn't make any sense. "What are you doing here?"

She took a step toward him. "I think you can figure that much out."

"I-" he began, but found nowhere to go as his mind stop-started, trying to parse everything in a search for the truth. Everything she'd ever said to him, from the start to the end. He remembered the way they'd first met in the fake town, when he'd attacked her group thinking it was a Pyramid clone. How they'd walked together in the desert, and she'd explained her goals for this place he'd only been steadily burning to the ground.

She'd promised to rebuild, and he'd called her out for bullshit empathy. "Nobody does that," he'd said, demanding to know why she was there at all, why she cared so much for victims of some cult she'd never even known, so much that she'd dedicate her life to seeking out and re-consecrating their lost bones.

She'd given him a sob story about losing her family members to the Apex. An aunt, maybe, a mother. A father who committed suicide. He'd believed her.

Except he'd never seen the bones. Not once. Not until today. Never even asked what kind of consecration they underwent before they were interred below the fresh tombstone slabs she'd laid out in the desert. On some level, he hadn't wanted to know. The past was too painful.

"This is your home," she'd said. So many times, repeating it like a mantra. "Come home when you're ready. This place belongs to you."

Now here they were.

The room whirled. There were two Maggies, then three. He'd trusted her. He'd thought she was like him, another soul broken on the fires of the Pyramid. Maybe she was. The gold walls filled his head with stifling light. Everything changed.

He raised the Glock to her face.

"That's better," she said. She sounded almost relieved, like a long pretense was finally lifting. "It's good that you're starting to see."

"I-" he began, but stopped, not clear at all what he wanted to say, where he needed to go. About the betrayal. That she'd helped him so many times. Even helped keep him alive. "Why?"

Her smile spread. She looked kind, as ever. She made no

move toward him. No move at all. In those green eyes he'd once thought there were answers. But now…

"For love, Christopher," she said. "You think you understand love. Your wife and your children, perhaps your country. But you don't understand love like this. A love so fierce it burns you alive."

His mouth was dry. His eyes stung. Love. The same bullshit song cult devotees always sang about their leader. The figure who gave their lives purpose. A love that burned you up in their name.

He had so many questions. Always there were, when it came to blind faith. Why, he wanted to ask again. Keep on asking until she finally admitted there was nothing, no reason, no answer, nothing but raw and naked human need, but he knew she never would. Not now. They never did.

So he switched it off. A lever in his mind, pulled. He'd heard it all before. So Maggie had lied. She'd put herself in deep cover for a year or two, an agent manipulating other agents, and he only had himself to blame. He should have seen it coming, recognized her for what she was, but she'd come at him out of the dark. Come at him through the Pyramid itself, offering him something he'd never been able to find for himself.

A kind of peace. A way forward.

Purpose.

Now all that was gone.

The gun steadied in his hand. Only one thing mattered now.

"Where is he?"

Her smile faded slightly. Like she was hurt. Like maybe she'd wanted to play out that moment longer, really dig into her motivations. "Where's who, Christopher?"

He snorted. Imagining what would happen next. He'd only told two people in all of Little Phoenix that he was coming. Teddy Smithely III, and Maggie. She'd had time to prepare. Set another trap. But how much did she really know?

Another scrap of sound came in his earpiece. Maybe Rogers. You had to hope.

"My father," he said. "The Apex. Noah Thackerton. I'll shoot you in the head right now, Maggie. Is he in here?" He shoved the sarcophagus lid with his left hand, but it didn't budge an inch.

"Your father," Maggie said. Took a step toward him. Only five yards between them now. "Noah Thackerton. I see you've done your homework."

Wren took a step to meet her. "I will blow your brains out, girl, if you don't give me some answers."

Now the smile came back. "Answers. There's only one route to the truth, Christopher. You know this. It's always the same way. Every great visionary has walked that path before you." Her green-gold eyes seemed to bloom and spin like Catherine wheels. "Pain."

Sweat stung his eyes. The silence between words was so complete it ached. So predictable.

"You want me to burn? You go first."

"I couldn't claim that honor," Maggie said. "That falls to you."

He took a step closer. "I'll ask one more time, then I put a bullet in your left thigh. Just to get your attention. Where is the Apex?"

Her smile turned sad. "The things we do for love. But love blinds us, don't you agree?"

Wren hammered the sarcophagus with his shoulder. The lid lifted maybe half an inch this time, dropped back down with a resounding slam. "Ten seconds."

"Love keeps us from the truth," Maggie went on, calm and unafraid. "So you ignore the truth standing right before you, because you love the lies this world feeds you every day, through your ears, your eyes, your broken mind."

He rammed the sarcophagus again, earned an inch but no glimpse of what lay within. "Five seconds."

"We only had seconds in that first pit," Maggie said, sounding dream-like now. "The day you risked yourself to save me. Do you remember how that felt, Christopher, to scrabble at the wall together, so desperate to survive?"

He blinked. The count forgotten. "What?"

Her smile swelled to fill the room. "Think about your hot hand in mine, playing games in the stolen days that followed. The happiest days of my life. Making mud pies while all the Pyramid waited around an empty pit."

Wren's breath stopped in his throat. Her eyes were golden whirlpools spinning in green jade. It wasn't possible. It couldn't be, but…

"We worked together so well," Maggie said, voice drifting like a drug. "You played your part and I played mine. It took everything I had not to call your name, as I lay there across the bodies of your brothers and sisters at the bottom of the pit. Only the hope of this moment kept me silent."

Wren just stared, felt like his insides were scooping inside out. "I-"

"All for this. So we could be together again at the end. And it is beautiful, my little Pequeño 3. I'm so glad that you finally see me."

The gun went slack and slippery in his hand. He saw her face as it might have been, thirty years earlier. As the beautiful little girl laughing by his side, eating strawberry mud pies, dead in the pit.

"Grace?" he whispered.

And there it was, understanding spreading like a deep calm across the desert, after a storm had passed.

"Grace," she repeated. "But you can call me X."

50

X

The gun clattered to the floor. Black tiles flecked with gold, Wren noticed. Now he was on his knees. Drooling, nauseated, the world spinning in every direction at once.

"I'm doing this for you," Maggie said. Grace. X. "Not for him. For you. Because this world is cruel, to you and I most of all. Because the pain is too much. He only shows us the way to be free. To break the chain. So I'm here for you." She was on her knees now, holding his hands.

Grace-In-Our-Times. The little girl that had haunted his dreams for thirty years. As a boy, he'd tried to save her. Plunged into the pit after her. Fought Chrysogonus for her, escaped with her, lived and breathed with her for three days and three nights while the Pyramid wailed over their pit, only to see her dead in that same pit when it was all over. Standing alone with the Apex whispering excitedly in his ear at the dawn, crowing out his victory.

"We were wrong, Pequeño 3! You and I know what's real. She was always dead!"

Now she was alive. Her fingers twined in his. Another

victim. A girl he'd tried so hard to save. A woman lost for so very long.

"I love you," she whispered. "I always did. You asked why? That's the reason. Why I've followed him all these years. Lied for him. Killed for him. For this moment, to be with you and help you finally see how we can be together."

You couldn't cry enough tears. The world tumbled and rebuilt in this new shape. Not only Maggie, but Grace. Not only Grace, but X. A true believer. No way back from that.

Still, he looked in her eyes and took one last shot.

"Then help me," he whispered. "I can kill him. I will kill him. All this can end. We *can* be together. Little Phoenix can be exactly what we promised."

She touched his cheek, stroked her fingers down. "Never in this life, little Pequeño. Only in the next." Then she stood. Stepped back, her voice gathering in strength. "I know exactly why you've come. To destroy the Pyramid. To tear down all our work. But I cannot allow that. So here is my offer."

She touched the sarcophagus' side and there was a click, a hiss of releasing air, then the lid lifted. Inside it was black and empty. No Apex. Nobody at all.

"This will be the true reason you came." Her face loomed, her eyes warping to fill his vision. "Your own willing sacrifice. You will be the Pyramid's final lens, Christopher. Its lasting purification. Through you the lies of the world will be made clean. Its power will pour into him, and he will rise up stronger than ever to remake us all!"

Wren weaved. Hardly thinking but in half-thoughts and stray words, too numb to reason clearly. Resurrection. Destruction. The same old song of the apocalypse cult.

Believe in me.

Something was in Maggie's hands now. Black and sinuous, bulbous in the middle and narrowing to a point at either end, with two sleek handles at the head. An ancient Egyptian amphora. He heard the sloshing of liquid within, smelled the bitter release of familiar fumes.

"First you must be anointed. By your own hand. This is the only way." She held the amphora before him. More of the same. A new voice, a new person, but always the same. "This is the reason you came."

He looked at her face, her eyes, trying to chart the differences. It wasn't a betrayal you could express in words. Barely in emotions. It was too complete. This woman he'd trusted. This little girl he'd loved. This madwoman he'd chased across the country.

"X," he said.

"X," she repeated.

A crackle came in his ear. Maybe half a word, nothing intelligible, but a reminder the world was still out there.

"I never will."

Now her smile turned sad. "You haven't heard the terms of the deal."

She set the jug down, reached into a fold of her flowing robe and brought up a black tablet screen, held it out for him to see. It showed bright blues, oranges and slow movement. His stinging eyes took long seconds to focus, then he went for his Glock, snatched it up off the tiles and held it again to Maggie's face.

"That won't help," she said.

The details resolved. A video feed of Main Street above. The sun glaring in a hot blue sky, his smoldering jet strewn on the orange sand, spewing black smoke in a column. In the middle of the frame, his family.

Loralei wore jeans and a red check shirt. Jake had on dinosaur pajamas and was red-eyed with crying. Quinn's face was hidden by her hands, but her shoulders wracked with sobs. Beside them stood Rogers' mother, gray-haired and afraid, and beside her was the gaunt figure of Teddy, and beside him were others. Children from the Blue Fairy. Foundation members. Maybe Mason, Alli, others. They stretched back in a line as far as he could see, and they all glistened in the bright sunlight. Their clothes clung to their skin. Their hair hung slick to their foreheads like a rainstorm had just struck, though there wasn't a cloud in the sky.

"This is your choice, Pequeño," Maggie whispered, hot and close. "The choice you refused all those years ago. The choice he gave you one thousand times, to reject the lies of your own eyes and accept his truth as your own."

Too much. He couldn't do anything, only play for time, but she didn't give him the chance.

"Do you remember that choice? Before every one of the Pyramid burned, he gave you the power. Time after time. Again and again. Would you take their place." She paused a long moment. "And do you know what you said?"

He didn't remember. Maybe he did. He didn't want to.

"You said no," Maggie said. "A thousand times, no. So the thousand burned. It was your decision then. It's your decision now."

He sucked air. Already felt like he was drowning. All his worst nightmares coming home to roost.

"I know this hurts, Pequeño. Your pride. Your sense of self. I know you despise it more than anything in the world, so don't do it for him." Eyes so wide like that little girl in the pit, gazing up at him for help. "Do it for me. Walk in the fire, for me."

There was no answer he could give. The future stretched out in horrifying shades of violence. If he did as she asked, the image of him burning would topple the Foundation and trigger the X-apoc like nothing else. Confirmation of all their beliefs, as Christopher Wren himself finally accepted their truth.

America would implode.

The alternative was simple. Refuse, and watch his family burn in his place. All of the fake town.

Again.

He made his decision. On some level he'd always known. He finally found his voice. "They live."

Maggie smiled. "Of course."

"They all live. Swear it, Maggie. On his life. Noah Thackerton. The Apex. The second I walk in the fire, you let them go."

Maggie gazed at him. "If that's what it takes, my Pequeño, I swear."

He lifted one leg under him, feeling like he was moving with the weight of destiny now. So the Apex had written all this. Prepared the way. Chrysogonus first, Galicia, Aden, and now it was his turn to step onto the stage. Let America see the truth.

He got the other foot under him and stood. Maggie let out a little gasp. Her eyes were wide. Enraptured. She lifted the amphora and held it out to him. Brought up the tablet and tapped to record.

"Say the words," she whispered, barely audible now, like she couldn't trust herself to speak.

Wren just gazed at her. Trying to see if there was any scrap of the little girl she'd once been. Grace. The only real friend from his childhood. Brainwashed for all her life.

"Say the words, or they burn."

"Fear is a portal," Wren said, and raised the amphora over his head, tipped it. The napalm splashed out in a single slick pour, atop his head, flooding down his cheeks, his neck, his chest and back. He poured until he could scarcely see for the oily burn in his eyes, then he set the amphora gently down.

Maggie's eyes and mouth were wide. Bliss, that looked like. Maybe she'd never been happier. Bending the ungrateful son to her will, where so many had failed. She nodded, a prompt for the words to come, and he knew his lines.

But he waited.

Waited for a sound in his earpiece, maybe. For a sign.

"Last chance," Maggie said.

Was that it? Had it come? It was hard to hear anything over the drumming of his heart, the heave of his lungs. It would have to be.

"Pain is a doorway," he said.

She held something out. Filming with one hand, leaning in with the other. A black metal square.

Wren took it. Felt the contours with his fingers. A flint and metal lighter. It was strange, holding it in his own hand, like an artifact from some ancient civilization. Feeling the same things all those poor women had felt in the firestorm, in the seconds before they died. Hope. Faith. Steven Gruber had been here before him. The one thousand had been here before him. People died all the time.

He was no one special. He took a deep breath.

"Walk in the fire," he said, then held the lighter to his throat and struck a spark.

51

WALK IN THE FIRE

F lames engulfed him.

Wren snapped his eyes shut at once, dropped the lighter and brought his hands up to cover his face and pinch his nostrils closed.

That would earn him seconds only. The sound of the napalm blaze was an instant roar, far louder than he'd ever imagined possible, as the fire lashed up his temples and into his hair, swallowing his ears, rippling over the backs of his hands, racing down his battered chest legs and tracing the spill across the floor.

Consuming him from without, burning down to the nerves.

In the blazing heat behind his eyelids he glimpsed his brother again, arms spread on the D.C. stage, striding to the edge and throwing himself over to ignite the masses...

She'd sworn.

She'd promised.

That would have to be enough. It was all he had as the pain receptors in his skin finally began to scream like never before under the two thousand degree inferno. That stage would be brief, at least. Napalm burned out the nerves fast, left you a mindless blazing candle fuming carbon monoxide within seconds.

At least there were no munitions strapped to his chest to set him off like a firework. The Glock was on the floor. The heat seared like the fires of hell, and Maggie was right there. He could almost see her through the black shadow of his hands as the fire beat him down.

She'd sworn.

He moved.

Left juddering leg forward. Trusting everything to his memory and his training. Where she was standing. Where the tablet was in the air. His right leg shot up like a trebuchet arm, too fast for her to react, already stunned by the flames. He heard her cry come muted through the flames, then maybe an impact.

There was no real sense of impact as his foot struck her wrist. Every nerve in his body was overloaded with the heat. It was more some deep shift in his inner equilibrium. His body belonged to the flames now, but the feel traveled up his core and into his chest.

Her wrist maybe broken. The tablet flung through the air.

X's tablet. X's level of access.

Then there was just screaming. Maybe it was his? Maybe hers. Five seconds gone, could that be right? He couldn't think. The earpiece crackled and died in his ear. Three seconds. Three hours.

He was in the Beechcraft again by Rogers' side, soaring west toward Little Phoenix, long before any of this had happened.

"High weave count," B4cksl4cker was saying, "many threads is dense, this helps."

"Dense threads," Wren repeated. "What fabric?"

"Lots of possibilities," Hellion answered, taking five

minutes from her efforts to manage the war with X. "Polyester."

"Polyester?" B4cksl4cker laughed. "This is organic material, makes very fashionable clothing, but hardly effective even if high density. Much better is tantalum carbide."

Now it was Hellion's turn to laugh. "This is solid state material, useful for painting on spacecraft!"

"Could be plates."

"What good are plates against liquid?" Hellion asked.

"Polybenzimidazole," Wren said, ending the bickering. "PBI. That's what I want."

"This is mouthful," B4cksl4cker said. "What is it?"

"Sewn through with aluminum fibers. It's a polymer. Commercially available. You can get it there in time. Contact Teddy."

"Only Teddy, yes?"

"Only Teddy for this."

"And this is enough?" B4cksl4cker asked. "What about face, hands?"

"Super-absorbent polymer gel," Wren said. He'd done his research. "Mixed into a slurry, it'll look clear, if gelatinous. Like sweat. I can apply it at the last minute."

Silent seconds passed.

"Like makeup?" Hellion asked.

"Like a bottle I dunk on my head."

"Ah. How will it work?"

"The polymer contains billions of water bubblets trapping air. They burn incredibly slowly. Hollywood uses them for stunts, but you can get them online. I'm sure you can source this in time too."

Keys clacked. "Super-absorbent polymer gel," Hellion repeated. "I am finding this for you, Christopher. Yes." More keys flew. "Bubblets."

B4cksl4cker laughed.

"Bubblets absorb all thermal energy, yes, this is correct," Hellion read. "Very hot flames, this will be OK. Requires even coating of slurry. One millimeter layer gives thermal protection for one minute, perhaps. Less, if fire is very hot. Like napalm."

"So we'll need a back-up," Wren said. "Maybe Rogers can-"

Back in the flames, wearing his PBI firefighter tactical suit sewn with aluminum and slathered with stunt-grade super-absorbent polymer gel, Wren felt the sudden rush of powder jetting over his body. There was no sound through the flames, no sensation and nothing to see, only the gentle hosing of siliconized monoammonium phosphate from the type A powder extinguisher she'd brought with her.

Rogers.

He'd bought enough time. She'd made it.

"Will this be enough?" Hellion had asked. "One extinguisher. Napalm re-ignites, yes?"

"She'll need more than one. Get rucksacks, different types of extinguisher. A fire blanket will help. She can pat out any extra flames."

B4cksl4cker grunted. "We saw this with Steven Gruber. Napalm may re-light minutes later, Christopher. Need complete oxygen-free environment for sustained period."

"We'll have to improvise."

"And hold breath," B4cksl4cker added. "Chemical extinguisher is toxic. Do not breathe this in. Can you hold breath very long?"

Wren laughed. "Let's hope long enough."

"How likely is this outcome, Christopher?" Hellion asked. "Walking in fire?"

Rogers answered before Wren could. Leaning over the seat, listening in. "This is the Apex, remember. He loves to burn everything that moves. And his ungrateful son, in the depths of his seat of power?" She laughed. "He'd never miss the chance."

"Yes," B4cksl4cker said. "He is fire fetishist, this is true."

Wren laughed.

Now he felt another rush spraying over him. The texture was different, more liquid, maybe the foam extinguisher. He didn't dare take a breath or lift his hands from his face, though. Then he felt Rogers pushing him. He staggered off-balance, his thigh thumped against what had to be the sarcophagus, but she kept on pushing, maybe shouting something now but he couldn't hear well.

Then he grasped it.

Improvise.

He let his upper body tip, let Rogers push him the rest of the way, and rolled into the black interior of the huge stone coffin, catching the tail-end of what she was yelling.

"… do, don't breathe!"

He would have laughed. A fresh spray of powder hit him in the chest, then the sarcophagus lid slammed down on all sides, sealing him in with the toxic dust.

An oxygen-free environment. Buried alive. Another of the Apex's pits of faith, where he would either asphyxiate or emerge reborn, resurrected by the flames.

52

CAVE

Wren's lungs burned and heaved. He'd lost count of the time somewhere in the midst of burning alive. Maybe two minutes already. Heading toward three? He figured he was safe and pulled his hands away from his face, instantly catching the acrid tang of napalm.

With his eyes screwed tightly shut in the dark of the sarcophagus, he patted himself down, felt the dry and grainy extinguisher powder embedded in a sticky layer coating his clothing and skin. Had to be the remnants of the bubblet gel mixing with unburned napalm. There were sore patches too, parts of his hands and head felt painful and raw. Maybe poor coverage of the gel, too-thin areas where the fire had bitten through. The PBI firefighting outfit seemed to have done its job well around his core though.

Silver blots swam behind his eyes. Coming up on four minutes? Too long. But thinking about the re-activation time for napalm. It could burn underwater, in the right conditions. It could burn without oxygen at all, if the solid-state fuel provided enough. It could-

His body jerked, his lungs convulsed, and that was the

final warning. He was out of time. As the silver clots clamored to open his throat, he pounded on the sarcophagus lid with both fists.

It cracked open in seconds. Air hissed in along with soft angelic light across his eyelids, and Wren opened his eyes to see Rogers haloed in gold.

He laughed. Couldn't help it, then regretted it as he gulped in foul-tasting toxic dust. Rogers dragged him coughing and spluttering out of the sarcophagus.

"Are you all right, Boss?" she shouted. He barely heard her, mostly read her moving lips as she thumped his back and checked his airways, looking into his eyes. He couldn't hear. Maybe the fire had destroyed his ears? He didn't want to reach up and find out. He hadn't paid the best attention to applying the gel in the stairwell coming down. Too hot, too rushed, too ready for the fight.

"Fine," he croaked, lurching away from the cloud of powder spilling from the coffin, sucking in air that tasted of spent napalm. Each breath bent him further over.

"Here," she said, and now cool liquid ran over his head, down his back and chest. Not polymer gel this time, but water. He caught some in his hand, rubbed it in his face, wetted his lips, swallowed some powder and coughed again.

"Drink," Rogers said, and pressed the bottle into his hands. For a second he worried he was about to swig bubblet gel, but Rogers would never do that to him. He tipped his head back and swallowed cool, clear water. It felt good.

He straightened up. Felt like he'd been put through some severe industrial process; wrung out, baked, steamed and deloused, and he still wasn't done yet.

"Where is she?" he asked, voice coming out a croak.

Rogers pointed.

Maggie lay flat out down the side of the chamber,

drenched with extinguisher foam, hands zip-tied behind her back and unconscious.

"You set her on fire," Rogers said, the words coming tinnily now, as though underwater. "Mostly her hand where you kicked her. I put her out as best I could, then knocked her out when she started screaming." She whistled low. "Maggie, though. That's a blow, Boss."

It was a blow. Wren struggled to get his brain working again. Minutes ago, Maggie had held all the cards. Burning alive had flipped that, and also played havoc with his thought processes. He remembered the kick, and the tablet, and-

"Did you get it?" he asked urgently, scanning the black and gold floor.

Rogers patted his shoulder, pulling focus. She holding Maggie's tablet. The screen was cracked but operational, now showing the familiar inner screen of the X app, ALERT button flashing. Wren blinked, took the tablet and turned it.

The stub was in position.

"They're in," Rogers confirmed. "Hellion and B4cksl4cker are hacking the X network right now. I'm guessing your earpiece is busted, or you'd hear them whooping like animals."

Wren grunted. That was as good as he could've hoped for. "Tell them to get ready. He's close by. Maggie was talking to someone."

Rogers' eyes flared and she spun. Wren looked at the sarcophagus. Getting all his ducks in a row. Perfectly aligned, so to speak.

"A dollar takes ten he's right here. Beneath us."

He reached up and took hold of the open lid, hung out at a forty-five-degree angle, the edge at around head height. Hopefully on a firm hinge. The sarcophagus had to weigh a ton, it hadn't budged when he'd rammed it before, but with two of them and a lever to increase torque?

"You're on, Boss," Rogers said, and took hold of the lid too.

He counted three, then pulled, sinking everything he had down through his arms. The hinge creaked but held, and the sarcophagus shifted slightly. Rogers said something that he couldn't hear for the rushing in his ears, then counted three herself and they pulled again.

This time the whole thing lifted. Wren saw silvery spots, and the sarcophagus quadrupled like a kaleidoscope. Pretty. He saw himself reflected in the gold walls again, a blackened, smoking corpse on its feet, but overlaid with other versions of himself too: the mischievous Pequeño 3 making mud pies in the sunbaked desert; the uncertain young man he'd become in the forest of Maine; the angry DELTA Corporal he'd grown into, earning the nickname 'Saint Justice' for unfailingly following his own moral compass.

These versions of himself revolved and overlaid, then Rogers hit three again and he pulled. The sarcophagus teetered on its edge. He bellowed and pushed down with everything, and now it tipped. His legs gave out as the immense weight shifted and bore down. About to be crushed. Then something hit him in the middle, a shoulder-tackle that drove him against the golden wall.

The crash as the sarcophagus hit the marble floor rang like the Liberty Bell's last chime, smashing cracks through the stone. Wren gasped, Rogers straightened, and there in the center of the room lay an opening. Stairs leading down.

"Here," Rogers said, holding out his Glock.

"Don't need it," he said, struggling to catch his breath and find his feet. He pulled away from Rogers, took three shaky steps and scooped two items off the floor. The black square of the lighter. The amphora still sloshing with residual napalm dregs.

She gave him a look. He started shakily down the steps.

There was raw industrial lighting pinned to the walls. Fifteen steps down, smoke still rising off his fireproof outfit, twenty, hardly daring to hope. At the base a circling tunnel ran back around, no doubt heading to a final chamber directly beneath the sarcophagus.

Ducks in a row.

This was it. No more escape routes now. No way out.

"Chris," Rogers said.

He turned to her, above him on the steps. Had forgotten she was even there. She looked beautiful, in her own way. Powerful. Trustworthy. And there was something in her tone now. Something imploring, maybe? Trying to steer him. He knew why. What she wanted to say.

"It's OK, Sally," he said. "Trust me."

She stared at him like she could read his heart through his eyes. Maybe she could. "You do this, they'll never stop hunting you."

"You don't know what I'm going to do." He smiled. "That's a strength."

She laughed. A small thing. A strange thing, in that place, but Wren appreciated it. That maybe he wasn't lost, and so she wasn't either. "I'd rather have strength as my strength," she said. "Or invisibility."

"Be prepared," Wren countered. "And unpredictable. That's my motto. Now go. Little Phoenix needs you."

A second more she looked. No need to say they needed him too. Right now the past needed him more. Right here, buried in the dirt, with the rats and spiders and long-buried cicadas, waiting to taste the summer air again.

His father.

"Thank you," he said. "I'll see you real soon."

He didn't wait for her to go. Started walking around the circle, right leg limping, face burning, hands steaming. Ten strides maybe, and no sound she was following, no sound at all, until he reached another open doorway. Within was a tall three-walled space, triangular in cross-section, like a tall column of structural space left over in some mezzanine skyscraper floor, so the building could flex in the wind.

A nothing space. A cave. Black walls. A black chair in the center surrounded by three large screens, one on each wall. One showed Wren's family dispersing through the fake town. One showed the golden chamber above, Maggie lying by the wall, the sarcophagus rolled aside like a stone. The third was a high angle on this cave-like room itself.

Wren looked up, saw glass panels concealing cameras. A livestream going out, no doubt, to capture every moment of the Apex's resurrection.

And there he was. Almost unbelievable in the flesh after so many years of searching. Sat on the chair, his father.

Noah Thackerton. Apex of the Pyramid, here at the inverted tip of the greatest pyramid yet.

53

APEX

"Pequeño 3," said the Apex.

His voice was gravel. A voice to slaughter millions. He had raw carved cheekbones, short-cropped gray hair matched by a perfect salt-and-pepper stubble on his jutting chin, with those liquid crystal eyes in between. A mass killer. The architect of Wren's entire life.

"Dad," Wren said, held up the amphora. "I brought you something."

The Apex's gaze didn't waver. Neither did Wren's. There would be no give here at the end. Nothing to say. It was all right there. Every moment encapsulated in those mad sapphire eyes.

Son of Davis Thackerton. Creator of the Pyramid. Father of X.

Twin possible paths spun out before Wren. Tip the amphora, and he knew his father wouldn't move. Light the spark. He wouldn't scream. He'd just stare, finally walk in the fire himself, see the hell that lay beyond.

It would be so easy. Justice done. But via the cameras above, he would become a martyr to his X-apoc. The greatest trigger to send them over the edge, and in the old man's eyes

Wren saw that understanding. Luring him in. Defiance and a death wish to make it happen in his final moments.

Do my will this one last time. Be my slave.

Or he could take the Apex in. By the book, right and proper. Put on the cuffs, frog-march him up to the surface, hand him over to the government for a years' long trial that would doubtless be the most-watched global television event in history. Watch along as he rallied his X-apoc from the dock, bringing on fresh insurrections every day. Fresh rage, fresh intolerance.

That didn't seem so good either.

"What to do with me," the Apex said. Perfectly mirroring Wren's thoughts. Like he knew everything, like he always had. Always one step ahead, setting traps for his Pequeño 3 to fall into.

"Is this how you saw it ending?" Wren asked.

The Apex's eyes shone. The same eyes that had watched over the pits, and the vats, and the cages. Not just sadism. Purpose. A vision, no matter how demented. Something others would flock to. Something Wren had tried so hard to believe in as a child, but simply couldn't, because it wasn't real.

"It isn't over yet," the Apex said.

Wren took a step in. Wait too long, listen too much and it might never happen. The Thackertons had that power, Wren included. He raised the amphora and tipped the remnants over his father's head. The Apex didn't move. The dregs of napalm dripped, dripped, dripped down through his thick hair, down his cheeks like tears, rivulets running to his lap.

"It'll be over soon," Wren said, and held up the lighter. "So tell me something, Noah. Anything, really, to save your life."

The Apex gazed back. They both knew he'd never beg.

"They'll come for you," he said, nodding to the cameras. "My people. They will tear you and this country apart."

Wren grunted. True. Martyrhood. Fresh X-apoc leaders would rise up within hours to rally the storm, and it would take many years without oxygen to fully quench that fire. By the time it was done, the damage would be all-consuming.

But maybe that was the point.

Maybe it always had been, and the Apex's presence had just blocked it out. He'd never seen the stars for the giant figure in the way, keeping him and all the Pyramid small and scared and alone, but knock the giant down and suddenly the sky was all yours.

Now the giant was falling, and with it the pillars of Wren's old world.

"Your X-apoc kill me, then we'll both be dead," Wren said, mind racing as he finally started to put the pieces together. "An end to the noble Thackerton bloodline. So let's meet in the middle." He leaned in. "Tell me who paid for it all, Noah."

The Apex's eyes narrowed slightly.

"I've seen the scale of it," Wren went on, spinning the past like tumblers in a lock. "First Corinthians? I hear those roaming churches were huge. Right after you killed your father, with you penniless on the Kansas plains? The money came from somewhere."

The Apex only stared. Maybe there was anger there now.

"And then my brother, Chrysogonus? He was no tech entrepreneur. Somebody gave him all that. Somebody backed him with hackers, programmers, influencers, a lifetime's worth of wealth." Wren sped up, really feeling it now. "All these cults, from the Saints to the Ghost, group after group, you must've had backers. It must have cost millions, Noah. Billions, maybe. So who paid for it all?"

The Apex said nothing.

"Your boy Jonathan Gibson sang like a bird," Wren went on. "About your stupid bullshit at Medicine Lodge. And it was stupid. All this nonsense I've had around me since I was born, pyramids and resurrection, does it really all come from some kid's book on the Egyptians?" He peered into his father's eyes, trying to see through the crystal and know if the hits were landing. "Then napalm, just because of Vietnam? Punji sticks in a tunnel, all because Poppa Thackerton had PTSD and wouldn't shut up about it until you shoved him down a well? Doesn't it all strike you as pathetic? You're a full-grown man playing out a childhood revenge fantasy that doesn't even make sense. You've executed that insane vision with incredible competence, I can't argue with that, but ultimately it's deranged. The only possible reason anyone would back it is for the damage it would do to this country." And there it was. "So who paid, Noah?"

The Apex's gaze sharpened. He clearly saw what Wren was trying to do. Belittle him in his own livestream. Make him ridiculous. Destroy the hold he had over the X-apoc.

"My people will string you up, Pequeño 3," he boomed in that firebrand bass. "You will pay for this in ways you cannot even imagine."

"What ways? I already walked in the fire once today, and look at me now." Wren spread his arms. "What else have you got?"

"You never saw the zoos in operation, little wren. The things my people will teach you in the darkness and cold will-"

"Enough! Do you really think I'm in your trap now? Or are you in mine?"

That shut him up for a moment. The exact hit Wren was looking for.

"You controlled my whole life with your lies. Controlled the Pyramid to their deaths. Now it's the X-apoc, half the whole country, but lies are a double-edged sword, Noah. Anyone can wield it. Last chance. Tell me who paid."

The Apex's eyes burned. Wren unzipped a pocket in his fireproof jacket, pulled out a phone and scrolled through screens until he reached the video B4cksl4cker had prepared hours earlier. He held it out for his father to see and hit play.

The Apex watched. Confident at first. But that changed. His eyes widened slightly. His knuckles whitened on the chair grips. Cords stood out in his neck. Beginning to see.

It showed the Apex sitting in a dark triangular chamber. Not this one, but very similar. A guess Wren had made and landed. It showed Christopher Wren standing before the Apex and putting on the handcuffs. In this video there was no amphora. No napalm or lighter. The Foundation had mocked it all up on a green screen within hours, using actors as stand-ins. The Apex's own MO. They'd learned plenty about producing real-time deepfakes after seeing his human zoos.

"By now my hackers will own your app," Wren said. "They'll own the X digital avatar, and the eyes of the X-apoc, and your livestream too." Wren pointed up at the concealed cameras. As if on cue, the video from Wren's phone appeared on the large screen on the middle wall, and his smile widened. Hellion and B4cksl4cker listening in and playing along, boosting him to 'god mode'. "They own the second skin on the Internet, after all, and nobody hides from them for long. So this is what we're transmitting live across the X network. This is what your people are seeing, right now. Not your feed. Ours."

The Apex glared up at him. Blue eyes churning. "They'll never believe it."

"Keep watching. It's not over yet."

Now the Apex was weeping in the video. On his knees. Begging Wren for forgiveness.

Not real. The real Apex was turning white as a winter sky. Winding up to say something.

"We'll spin forward," Wren said helpfully. "Get to the highlights."

The screen responded, rolling forward to the next video. Now the Apex was in a suit, head bowed, sitting in the middle of a grand jury federal trial. It looked real. Noah Thackerton was silent and shame-faced as an array of his victims passed through the witness stand, giving testimony. Highlights showed him weeping, apologizing for the harms he'd done.

Pleading guilty.

The real Apex's eyes blazed. He looked from the screen to his son. His own MO turned against him. If Wren could bottle that moment he would.

Justice done.

He gave a signal that killed the feed, then just looked at his father. "You and I know what's real, though, don't we? Noah. It's up to you, how much of this video I show. Your legacy, let's call it. So tell me, who paid?"

The transformation began small but accelerated fast, coming over the Apex like a fresh fall of snow. The fury in his crystal eyes calmed. The lines in his brow smoothed out, his hands released their tight grip, and Wren knew what it meant. He'd seen it countless times before, in cult leaders with their backs to the wall. A last surrender to madness, the Apex reincarnating himself from conman to the con itself.

Finally believing his own lies.

"I'll see you in hell, Pequeño 3."

He went for his pocket, maybe a gun, a lighter, a dead man's switch, but Wren was faster. He sparked the lighter's wheel and tossed it.

The flame arced toward the Apex.

The lighter struck.

Caught.

"Walk in the fire, father," Wren said, and flames rushed over Noah Thackerton like a second skin.

He didn't make a sound, didn't budge an inch, only stared at Wren as the licking tongues of orange, red and yellow climbed taller and spewed a stinking black smoke. He stared until his eyes and his face were gone, and his muscles thinned out, and then he collapsed, and then he just burned.

Wren stayed despite the foul smoke, watching every second because he had to be sure. That those crystal blue eyes had forever shut. That his poisoned tongue was finally still. He watched until the fire became a flicker and the air turned black, until the flames dwindled and the Apex was nothing but smoldering charcoal in an airless cave.

Then he turned away and never looked back again.

54

RESURRECTION

Hellion and B4cksl4cker had an iron dome over Little Phoenix by the time Wren emerged into the light. Nothing in and nothing out that they didn't control.

The air was painfully fresh. The sunlight harsh in his stinging, smoke-burned eyes. Not the Wren from the deepfake video, but the real Wren.

Burned. Bleeding. Limping. Barely alive.

The exit from underground had been through the north archway from the Pyramid's tomb. Rogers had helpfully marked it out with a series of glowsticks like Ariadne's thread, leading up into one of the new buildings Maggie had built, the gymnasium.

A mirror popped open, and Wren found himself in a sunny space filled with weights, machines, black mats and mirrors.

His reflection looked terrible. Skin singed, blackened, ruptured. He still had ears, which was good news. Burn marks on his neck, in his scalp, half his hair gone. Almost like he'd just survived burning alive. He smiled and it hurt his raw cheeks.

This is what a resurrection really looked like, he figured, phoenix dragging itself from the flames.

He hobbled out onto the street. People were moving everywhere. The doors to the hospital were thrown open, doctors and nurses were running back and forth with stretchers, medical equipment, towels and gauze.

Looked like Rogers and Teddy were leading the clear-up. The deepfake video of the Apex's unconditional surrender must have done the job, because there were many X-apoc figures with their heads down, letting themselves be herded by much smaller Foundation forces. Some were openly weeping.

When the scales fell from their eyes, and their god crumbled into dust. Hopefully the same thing was happening all across the country.

Wren kept walking. His right leg twinged, tried to give out, but he wouldn't let it. Ahead lay the Beechcraft, smoking still. Only one thing mattered now. People saw him and pointed. Children, survivors of the Blue Fairy. Members of the Foundation he'd sent here for safety.

They came toward him. They gathered in a kind of tunnel either side as he moved forward. They pressed themselves to his sides and supported his weight, helping him walk. Unafraid, though he looked like the devil. Calling his name until it became a chant, until the entire fake town rang with the name of a long-dead architect he'd liked as a child, from a book he'd read about great feats of renaissance engineering.

Christopher Wren.

Not so different from his father, then. He smiled, though it barely felt like his name anymore. Certainly not a celebration of him or what he'd done, but of them all. He wasn't the apex of any pyramid, and didn't want to be. He was just another member of the Foundation, serving so others could climb on high.

Then they were there before him.

Attended by medical personnel. Towels wiping away the napalm slick from their faces. Children crying. Jake. Quinn. Loralei. He saw them and they saw him.

A hush fell across the crowd. Spreading back and back, his name forgotten, every eye on them. Wren lurched closer in dead silence. Barely the sound of wind or cicadas humming in the desert. He knew he looked monstrous. He knew how terrifying that could be.

Still they came. Jake and Quinn ran. Arms outstretched. He dropped to his knees and pulled them in. So long he'd been away. Their small shaking arms wrapped around his back and he squeezed them tight. Told them he loved them. Too long. Told them he'd missed them. Would never be away again.

Beyond, Loralei's eyes filled with tears. Nothing else mattered, in that moment. Not the people who'd funded the Apex. Not the trails of danger leading away across the world, to whatever eyes were watching in anger, feeling the temporary sting of defeat.

All that mattered was his family. This embrace. He kissed their heads. The chant began again.

He was finally home.

THE NEXT CHRIS WREN THRILLER

BACKLASH

They downed his jet. Let the backlash begin.
A passenger plane forced down over Texas air space. A state
on the edge of secession, taking orders through unseen back-
channels. One man on board may have something to say
about that.
Christopher Wren.
What begins as the backlash to a year of chaos soon becomes
Wren's personal odyssey for vengeance. They ripped his
country into pieces. They forced those pieces to the brink of
self-destruction. Now they're looking to warp what remains,
and corrupt America forever.
The backlash is only just beginning.

AVAILABLE IN EBOOK, PAPERBACK & AUDIO

JOIN THE FOUNDATION!

Join the Mike Grist newsletter, and be first to hear when the next Chris Wren thriller is coming.

Also get exclusive stories, updates, learn more about the Foundation's coin system and see Wren's top-secret psych CIA profile - featuring a few hidden secrets about his 'Saint Justice' persona.

www.subscribepage.com/christopher-wren

ACKNOWLEDGEMENTS

Thanks to Julian White, Monte Montana, Barb Stoner & Sue Martin.

   - Mike